The
Disintegration

By

Tony Drury

City Fiction

ISBN: 978-1-910040-42-3

ALSO BY TONY DRURY

The DCI Sarah Rudd series
Megan's Game
The Deal
Cholesterol
A Flash of Lightning
The Lady Who Turned
I Will Find You

The early career of Sarah Rudd
On Scene and Dealing
Journey to the Crown

The Novella Nostalgia series
Lunch with Harry
Twelve Troubled Jurors
Forever on Thursdays
The Man Who Hated
A Search for the Truth

PART ONE

SPRING

Yeah, I miss the kiss of treachery
The shameless kiss of vanity
The soft and the black and the velvety
Up tight against the side of me
And mouth and eyes and heart all bleed
And run in thickening streams of greed
As bit by bit, it starts the need
To just let go, my party piece

('Disintegration': The Cure Album: 1989)

CHAPTER ONE

Damian Hannon knew that he faced a wait after the completion of the first part of his appointment and found himself watching the news channel on the wall screen. It had been two years ago that the pandemic arrived from Wuhan in China and the world was turned upside down. Finally, the vaccines began to have an impact and slowly, painfully slowly, life began to return to normal and the turmoil of the Brexit settlement filtered through to re-energise British industry. The news presenter was explaining that another deal had been negotiated by the Government's trade officials. Damian's attention was, however, diverted because he was being called back in by the dental nurse.

He trailed after her from the waiting area and noticed her slightly tantalising shape. She was wearing green overalls and her face was covered by a mask overlaid with a plastic visor. He hung his jacket on a hook to which her outstretched finger was pointing. He was aware of another person in the room but his attention was focused entirely on her. She had told him her name but had already forgotten it possibly because he hadn't heard her words. The moving digit was now indicating that he should lie down on the chair described by its supplier as 'unsurpassed ergonomic access to oral cavity'.

Damian dreaded the annual check-up with his dentist and was even more demoralised on hearing the diagnosis that a back tooth required root canal treatment. That meant possibly three hours out of a working day and, as he sat in the waiting area, the receptionist had come over and handed him what transpired to be a quotation for the coming dental treatment. His budgeting brain exploded as he read the details. Seven hundred and forty pounds together with today's costs of fifty-five pounds with Mr Choudhary, who owned the practice, and now forty-six pounds for the unpleasant experience of the coming hygienist's cleaning of his teeth. The total of eight hundred and forty-one pounds was nought point eight per cent of his annual disposable income.

The anonymous assistant came in from his left and placed protective glasses over his eyes. He tried to relax and stretched out his legs as the benefits of his self-imposed keto diet, and the loss of sixteen pounds in weight, gave him plenty of self-confidence. From his right-hand side, the hygienist loomed over him and they reached an unspoken agreement. As he spotted that she was holding an evil looking scaler he opened his mouth in passive surrender. She needed no second bidding and, within seconds, was scraping away the plaque which had accumulated between his teeth. It went on and on, tooth by tooth, as she seemed determined to rise to the challenge that Damian's lack of commitment to vigorous brushing, presented.

He never ceased to chuckle to himself that the reason he visited the hygienist was because his life was full, twenty-four seven, and whilst he did clean his teeth, morning and evening and use a mouthwash, he solved his lack of dental expertise by paying a sum of money, twice a year, to go through this unpleasant twenty-minutes experience, one third of a chargeable working hour, of pain. Boudica, as he had named her, was now leaning even closer over him and cleaning a back molar. He could smell her perfume and it was pleasant, particularly as her left hand was resting on his arm. He imagined she was squeezing his flesh, but then he had always been a fantasist.

She drew back and he attempted to stand up but was politely informed that she needed to clean and polish his teeth. He groaned although he was relieved to see the scaler disappear to be replaced by the peppermint taste provided by the dental floss she was using and then by the whirring of the brush she had attached to an ominous-looking drill.

She stepped back, the protective glasses were removed and he stood up from the chair. She asked him if he had ever considered using an electric toothbrush commenting that he was threatening the health of his gums and the teeth they held in place, unless he took his oral hygiene more seriously. In fact, he had done just that, following his last visit to the hygienist when a perhaps older lady had not minced her words. On that occasion he'd gone on to the internet and sourced the best-reviewed product described as being 'triple bristle sonic' equipment. He then read that it cost ninety-six pounds and went back to his toothbrush.

As he prepared to leave he promised Boudica that he would take matters more seriously and on reaching the door he glanced back: she was watching him. He exited, reached reception where he proffered his American Express credit card in settlement of the final bill, pocketed the payment receipt, booked his appointment for the root canal treatment, called in to use the toilets and then stepped out into the Spring sunshine. He gasped with relief that it was all over and moved towards his car when he heard a voice coming from behind him.

"Mr Hannon, please."

He turned and there she was in her green outfit but minus the mask and visor: he thought that her skin was glowing. He said that he had paid his bill, thanked her for looking after him so professionally, was puzzled that she glanced over her shoulder but stood there as she turned back to face him.

"I've never done this before, but I would like to see you again," she stuttered.

Damian Hannon confirmed that he'd make another appointment in six months' time.

"I don't mean that," she said.

He was now eying her up and down.

"What do you mean?" he asked.

"Socially," she said.

"I'm married," he said.

"Yes, I know you are. Mrs Hannon came in for an appointment several weeks ago," she said, again looking behind her.

"Do you realise what you are suggesting?"

"Yes. I must go back in."

He looked across the car park, pointed to a break in the wall where the road out of the town was visible and told her that he'd pick her up at seven o'clock that evening. He turned round to see her disappear back into the building, reached his vehicle, sat back into the driver's seat, shook his head in bafflement and began to realise the ludicrous nature of his response. He did not know her name, her age, her phone number, nothing about her and he had, three years earlier, before the pandemic restricted foreign travel, spent a holiday in South Africa with his wife Cathy to celebrate twenty years of marriage.

4

What he did know was circulating round in his head. She was perhaps in her late-thirties, was maybe five foot, six inches tall, weighed around one hundred and forty-seven pounds, wore her fair hair cut short, was attractive, did not wear a wedding ring and possessed a mesmeric smile, which he had seen once. And he had smelt her fragrance.

He used the twenty-two minutes car drive to his office to reach a decision: it was nonsensical and the whole matter had to be dismissed. He arrived back at the premises of Hannon, Shannon and Smith, Chartered Accountants, waved his hand at the receptionist, entered his office, closed the door, sat down in his senior partner's chair, took out his phone and read the 'missed-calls' and text messages. Mrs Hannon was going to be late home because she had called back a patient, his son wanted money, two clients needed urgent calls, the text he least wanted to read confirmed that a letter was in the post to him and he should take the matter seriously and there was one more:

I'm serious/genuine. Your hygienist.

He groaned as his internal phone rang. He dealt with the matter and then replied to her message:

I need to think. DH

He was surprised to receive an immediate reply:

Understand.

He skipped lunch spending an hour with his two partners discussing the latest auditing guidance notes from their Institute which left him totally demoralised. He was not sure he could continue as an accountant where the wishes of his clients were being submerged by the tsunami of regulatory dictates from Her Majesty's Revenue and Customs. That had been the thinking behind the decision to use his personal assets to back the property development venture his friend had introduced. He thought back to the text message he had received and, again, beat himself up for not reading the documentation more carefully.

He spoke to his son Arthur who assured him that the four hundred pounds he needed would be the last time he used the bank of Mum and Dad. Damian told him to ask his mother in future and then discussed the final results of the rugby season. He left the office around six o'clock and arrived home to find Cathy's car in the driveway. They exchanged pleasantries and he told her about the call from their son. He explained that he had to go out to see a client which was well received because it would allow her to watch the final three episodes of the latest Netflix drama. He went into his study, pondered on his decision to meet the hygienist, realised the irrationality of his actions and the fact he was deceiving Cathy but decided to keep to their arrangement. He sent her a message:

Is seven o'clock meet still on? DH

Her response was immediate:

Oh yes.

As he neared the dental practice, he spotted that she was sitting on the wall so he drew up alongside her and she bounced up and opened the passenger door. She slid in beside him allowing her flowery skirt to ride up and reveal her suntanned legs resulting in a gasp from Damian which caused her to smile and explain that she had recently spent a two-week holiday in Egypt. When he suggested that it was an expensive way to acquire a suntan, she said that she had gone with a friend to study the Great Pyramids. He wanted to ask about the gender of her friend but concentrated on driving away, round the traffic island and out towards the countryside: he explained that he was well known in the town and they needed some anonymity to allow them to talk.

She suggested they went back to her house which she described as being fairly secluded and backing on to the canal and in reply to his next question, she explained that she had walked to meet him and her car was at home. They arrived at the address she gave him, pointed to the side where he was able to park in relative privacy and moments later, they were through a back door and into a well-equipped modern kitchen.

She pulled up a stool and, as he sat down, she opened a bottle of wine which she placed with a single glass on the marble work top. He explained that he didn't drink alcohol to which she responded by saying that she'd read that in his medical questionnaire, went to the refrigerator and pulled out a jug of freshly prepared fruit juice which she placed in front of him.

"Seducing strange men into your lair is clearly a well-practised pastime," he suggested.

"You're not strange: I know a lot about you," she said as she drank some of the white wine. "I've never done this before," she revealed. "I've survived a marriage break-up and five months ago I was forced to throw out the man I thought I was going to be with for the rest of my life and I've been alone ever since."

"But you must get offers," he said and then beat himself up for his pathetic comment.

"Ever the patronising male," she smiled.

"You asked me," he suggested.

"Yes, I did."

The unopened envelope on the surface of the island

unit gave him her name.

"So, Rosemary, what are we doing here?"

"It's Marie," she said. "The letter is from my mother." She drank some more wine. "The answer to your question is that I wanted to meet you, socially."

"Despite the fact I am married," he smiled.

"You can always leave if your conscience gets the better of you." She laughed with a sound that was intriguing. "Enjoy your fruit juice, I'm going up to change."

He found himself looking round at the array of greenery in which there was a single pendant light and swirls of pink marble. He lifted his eyes towards the cobalt blue loft railing. On the one wall were a series of photographs in which Marie appeared with perhaps her father, a boy, a teenager, several men and a woman who was standing in front of a colossal pyramid. He stood up and stared out of the window to a stretch of lawn at the bottom of which was a water inlet and a moored boat.

She re-appeared wearing a light green jogger suit and suggested they move into the lounge where they talked about themselves, their work and people they both knew. Marie suddenly stood up.

"You're nervous, aren't you, Damian?" she suggested.

"I'm not quite sure why I'm here," he replied.

"I've a suggestion to make," she said. "We both know why we are together but it's a bit of a jump, so to speak. Go home and think about things and if, after a period of reflection, you want to continue our contact, come back tomorrow night."

He drove home utterly confused and spent a restless night thinking about a woman in a jogger outfit.

The tension was manifest in the kitchen from the start of the day as Cathy made her annoyance clear by pushing past Damian. He was absorbed with the making of his breakfast following a recipe which guided the culinary preparation of Keto pancakes. He poured a half cup of almond flour into the blender followed by three eggs, half a teaspoon of cinnamon, a tablespoon of butter and half a cup of cream cheese. The noise of the blender irritated her even further. He poured a little oil into the frying pan, added two tablespoons of pancake mixture and cooked each side for three minutes. He placed his pancake on a plate, added more cinnamon, strode over to the table, sat down, turned over a copy of 'The Times' to the back page, looked at the crossword, sipped a cup of green tea, pondered the first clue, filled in the eight-letter solution and looked at his wife.

"Busy day ahead?" he asked.

"If you ate properly, we could have breakfast like a normal couple," she snapped as she began eating her scrambled eggs on toast topped with sliced tomatoes. Damian decided against pointing out that they were having breakfast together because he suspected that an eruption was about to take place.

"You are on a diet that is dangerous, Damian. I'm a nurse and I have been trained to help our patients adopt healthy lifestyles." She slurped her cup of coffee. "I looked up ketosis and I've discussed it with one of our partners." She took out a piece of paper and started reading:

Ketosis is a state of being where your body has a therapeutic level of ketones circulating in your bloodstream. It is a natural occurrence that happens when you don't feed your body carbohydrates and it exhausts its store of glucose. Where does the body look for its energy? It looks for fats either using your stored body fat or fat that you eat which it can convert into ketone bodies to use for energy.

"It's plain madness, Damian. You are rejecting carbohydrates and proteins and just eating fats and just look at you. How much weight have you lost? Your body is emaciated."

He wanted to tell her that it was possible someone else had different thoughts but recognised that the admonishment had further to run.

"I see patients daily who are trying hard to change their way of living and adopt a healthy lifestyle. I witness their pain and suffering. We had a visitor last week from the university medical team who explained to us the value of holistic dietary regimes."

"What's a holistic diet?" he asked.

"If you'll stop interrupting me, I'll explain it to you. It's a recognition that the psychology of dieting is as important as the physical considerations. A person starts a diet, fails and then their self-respect collapses, they become concerned about body image, and comfort eat. That is why the work I do is important because fad diets like yours are dangerous."

"Can we agree that there are a lot of people carrying too much weight and so can't you see that any method that helps weight-loss should be taken seriously?"

Cathy Hannon stood up and glared at her husband.

"Does your bloody keto diet help you make good investment decisions?" she asked. "Where are our savings, please, Damian?"

He spent the day with half his attention on client

matters and the other part trying to decide what to do. When it reached mid-afternoon, he sent a text message, as perhaps he always knew he would, confirming he'd see Marie at her house at seven o'clock. After arriving home and sensing a continuation of the morning's tensions, he made an excuse for another evening out, not that Cathy was really listening to him.

He reached Marie's home, noticed that the rear door was open, parked his car and went straight in to find a jug of fruit juice awaiting his arrival. She welcomed him with a peck on his cheek, sat down on a stool, smiled and said that she was pleased he'd come back.

"I'm not sure there was too much doubt," he admitted.

They talked for some time and then Marie said that she was going up to her room. He read his mobile messages and reached the decision he knew that he was going to make. He followed her by climbing up the stairs and moving along a passageway towards an open door and towards the sound of piano music. He entered into a spacious room: she was lying on a bed and, as she watched him arrive, she propped herself on her elbow.

"Are you going to join me?" she asked

He stood still for a few moments and then followed her suggestion. The hard work he had put in during the last few months reflected in his athletic forty-nine-year-old body. As he paid a silent tribute to the keto diet, he undressed, moved towards her and climbed on top of the bed.

*

11

They lay back and he stared at the ceiling.

"Can I assume you now have what you wanted?" he asked.

"Yes, you can," she laughed, "but even more than you think."

In the short time he had known Marie she surprised him more than once and now she was suggesting that their time together exceeded her expectations which coincided with his own emotions: he was in seventh heaven. She lifted herself up and leaned over him.

"The sex was lovely, Damian, but you have given me something else." She placed her finger over his lips. "You reached climax perfectly and the bang, bang, moan, groan, "how was it for you" was great."

He raised himself on his elbows, looked into her eyes and felt her hand over his mouth.

"Just before the end, you did something wonderful." She chided him as he struggled to speak. "You stopped and gave me a fantastic body squeeze and then you kissed me." She smiled her special smile. "That's what I wanted: in fact, I have dreamed of it. I needed to belong to somebody: for two to become one." She removed her hand and kissed him. "I spent twenty minutes leaning over you yesterday morning and, in that time, I learned so much – your body, condition, odour – it was breath-taking, so I decided to see if you would take me to bed."

Marie climbed off the bed and put on a white shirt which resulted in Damian wondering whether a second round was on the cards. He looked at the bedside clock which featured Mickey Mouse and laughed.

"Are you saying that you think you now belong to me?" he asked. "You said "for two to become one," which is frightening."

"I'm not frightened," she said.

"What happens if I leave and we never meet again?"

"I'll be left with a memory which will sustain me in the weeks ahead and are you going home?"

"I must," he said.

"That's not a good idea," she cautioned. "The moment you walk into your house your wife will know you have been with another woman."

"What do you suggest I do?" he asked.

She came round and pulled on his arm. They reached the bathroom in which there was a separate power shower: she selected a plastic bottle containing an azure blue liquid from a shelf. She explained that the body wash was similar to the fragrance she had detected on him and then she turned on the water. As her shirt became wet and she soaped his body, he experienced an overwhelming sense of closeness and then she whispered into his ear. He sat on the side of the bath: she dried his hair and did not stop him putting his hands on her legs.

As they returned to the kitchen, he explained that he wanted to talk to her. They sat down, and she gazed at him as she suggested that he should go home.

"When do I ask my questions?" he enquired.

"Go home, Damian. I'm going back to my bed to relive that squeeze you gave me."

As he drove away, he reflected on her final embrace and on what she had whispered in his ear during their shower together. His emotions were shredded as the battle began between the elation of being seduced, the sex, her enjoyment and his first-ever betrayal during his, until recently, generally fulfilling marriage. He slammed his hand down on the steering wheel as he once again angered over Cathy's accusatory attitude towards their investment: they were not going to lose their home.

He parked the Mercedes in the driveway and could not be bothered to open the garage doors and secure the vehicle during the night. He walked to the front door with her words resonating around in his head.

"There's nothing we can't achieve together," she had whispered.

There was again an atmosphere at breakfast which was cut short as Cathy said she wanted to go into work early, waving at him and hurried out.

Her day did not start well as she arrived at the surgery to find that someone had parked in her space and she was forced to leave her car on the road. The first hour was taken up with administration following the fundamental changes to General Practice forced on the NHS by the coronavirus pandemic. Her first patients arrived for their weigh-ins. They were part of the control programmes designed to help overweight and obese patients based on dietary changes and regular exercise. Some were benefitting from the special classes now established in conjunction with the council, but, in truth, far too few. At eleven-fifteen Cathy hit a problem.

"I'm taking off all my clothes," the patient exclaimed.

"There really is no need," pacified Cathy. "Mrs Reynolds, I usually allow three pounds for clothing which I deduct from the reading when you stand on the scales."

"But the doctor says I must lose twelve pounds by the end of June. You can only find that out if I am weighed naked."

"How about if you undress to your underwear?" suggested nurse Hannon.

The situation was solved by Linda Reynolds, single parent of three children, removing all her clothes. She stalked over to the scales and stood on the platform. A rather oriental sounding voice announced that 'Your weight is one hundred and sixty-one point three pounds' whereupon Mrs Reynolds screamed.

The talking scales had been an initiative introduced by Cathy because she became exasperated by the arguments with patients over the exact digital readings shown by the previous equipment: she seemed to spend her time defending the extra half pound being denied by the patient.

"No fucking Chinese bitch is telling me I'm eleven and a half stones," an increasingly desperate Linda shouted. The door of the weight-loss clinic opened and in came Dr Wellings. Cathy explained the situation and the GP suggested the three of them sit down: he poured them all cups of water.

"I'm trying to lose weight," he said.

"You haven't got three hungry kids to feed," said Linda. "Do you think Mediterranean seafood salad is going to fill their stomachs? They want chips with everything, burgers and Knickerbocker explosions. I'm trying my best to be a good Mum but I just can't stop eating myself. I know the nurse is trying to help me and I'm sorry I made a fuss about the weighing. I have to buy my clothes from Oxfam." She broke down in tears and Cathy nodded to Dr Wellings in thanks and said that she'd handle matters. He put his hand on her shoulder as he left the room.

Cathy changed tack. So often the real problem was more financial rather than pure diet. She knew that

Linda Reynolds was a survivor and her more immediate need was paying the bills. She discussed with her patient the possible additional benefits that might be available and on which she had put in some research. Mrs Reynolds appeared to brighten and stood up.

"Sorry nurse, I'm grateful to you. I'll try to lose a pound next time."

"Linda, that would be fantastic," responded Cathy and gave her a hug.

As she left the room she turned back.

"I'm dependent on the foodbank," she said.

Cathy left work and returned home by early afternoon. For some unaccountable reason she disliked using a phone. Much of her communicative activity was by email and text and she disliked Zoom intensely. She had developed a schedule whereby she allocated an afternoon and made all the built-up calls in one session.

First on the list was her mother. They followed their usual topic: she was fine and her split shin was healing, Father was on antibiotics for his chest, the weather on the south coast was warming up and she thought the Prime Minister was wonderful. Then came the bomb-shell.

"Darling, we are comforted by the knowledge that our grandchildren are forging their way in life, Arthur phoned us the other night, and you are well placed. You are so fortunate that Damian is successful and now the children are away from home I can imagine that the bank balance is healthy." She paused, sneezed and continued. "Your father and I are moving into an upmarket retirement home."

"You're selling your house!?" exclaimed Cathy.

"We've sold it and we were amazed at the price it

fetched. We move into our new home in six weeks' time. Have you got a pencil to hand: I'll give you their website? We've taken a double bedroomed apartment on the first floor and darling, the views from the balcony. They provide full medical care and all our meals and your father has worked out the finances very carefully. We can pay our way for eight years."

"Mother, I'm your only child. Why didn't you discuss this with me? Do father's costings include any operations you might need?"

"No, we'll have to use our savings in that event but we are both in good health."

"What happens after eight years?" asked Cathy.

"Ha, we won't be here, Darling. If one of us is left perhaps you and Damian can look after us." There followed a pause. "You are pleased, aren't you Catherine? Your father and I wanted not to be a burden to you." She hesitated. "My dream is to have a great grandchild."

Cathy finished the call, put her hands around her face, came to an abrupt halt as she remembered what her mother had said, redialled the number and waited for a response as she feared the call was going to answerphone.

"Hello."

"Mother, you said that Arthur phoned you?"

"Yes, Catherine, such a polite young man: he chatted with your father for some time: you must be proud of him?"

"Mother, did he ask for money?"

"Your father and Arthur discussed the change of manager at Harlequins: such a surprise so Harry tells me."

"Mother, did he ask for money?"

"We were surprised he seemed to have plenty of spare time in the middle of the afternoon but he assured us things are going well for him and he spoke in glowing terms about Damian."

"Did he ask for money?"

"He's our only grandson and he makes us laugh."

"Mother!"

"Just a little, yes, and I know that we promised we'd not give him any more but he's acquired a new girlfriend and he wants to take her away for a weekend. They are flying to the Costa del Sol."

"How much money did you give him?" angered Cathy.

"We've sold the house, darling: we've plenty of money."

"Please tell me it was not more than a hundred pounds."

"Don't be silly darling, that's not going to buy them a decent weekend in Spain. He gave us the website of their hotel while he was on the phone and your father and I think they'll have a lovely time. Four stars and the reviews are excellent."

"How much did you give him?"

"Five hundred pounds. Goodbye, Catherine."

Cathy went over to the side of the kitchen and poured herself a vodka and tonic. She then went into action, contacted the practice manager, agreed that she'd complete her list tomorrow morning and then be back on the following Monday. She booked a crossing on the Isle of Wight ferry for six o'clock the following evening, texted her mother to say she'd be arriving around eight in the evening and she did not want a meal. She cancelled a meeting of the charity committee, went to the supermarket, on to the petrol station, back home where she did the outstanding washing and then ate a salad together with a half-bottle of wine. She then came to a shuddering halt. Without realising, she'd been drink driving but reasoned that perhaps one vodka is not the most heinous of crimes. She spent an hour on the computer before retiring to the lounge to watch the evening news and await the arrival home of her husband.

Damian seemed a little thoughtful as he joined her in the lounge. He had sneaked past her to reach the bedroom and the chance to change his clothes.

"We need to talk," said Cathy.

He stared at his wife as the alarm bells began to ring.

"My mother and father have sold their house and are moving into a home. They've given Arthur five hundred pounds. I'm catching the six o'clock ferry tomorrow evening and I'll stay two nights."

Damian thought back to the text message he had received from Marie suggesting she would be at home from seven tomorrow evening. He realised that his wife had more to say.

"The house sale is already up on the website and I've studied the residential terms of the retirement home: it's in Ventnor. My mother says they'll have enough money for eight years." She handed him a piece of paper. "These are my calculations and the figures do not include any hospital costs in the future."

He scanned the details and nodded in acknowledgement of Cathy's meticulous analysis.

"Your father has agreed to leave Luccombe?" he exclaimed. "He's spent the last ten years walking on the sands in the bay."

"Mother told me a little time ago that he could no longer descend the landslip down to the chine. He's on antibiotics at the moment for his chest. I thank the Lord they did not catch Covid-19."

"What are you hoping to achieve by visiting them?" asked Damian.

"I wish I knew because they're on their way, there's nothing I can do about that and we'll have another row about Arthur." She paused and looked at her husband. "Damian, I have to go." She paused. "Mother has booked for me to visit the home."

"Yes, I know you do," he said.

"Is my analysis accurate?" Cathy asked.

"It's well done if not frightening," he said. "Even with their pensions they could run out of money within six years and if there are further medical costs, Christ!"

"My Mother knows that."

"They're relying on us, aren't they?"

"Yes". She referred to how successful you are. "Will you please answer me a question?"

Damian gave an affirmative nod of his head as he anticipated the coming interrogation.

"The money you have lost, eighty thousand pounds, why did we have so little saved?"

Which was exactly the same conundrum that he had wrestled with a week ago. He spent a Saturday morning in the office completing a reconciliation of their twenty-three years of marriage, income, expenditure, capital spending and pension contributions. They had two children early on in their marriage but the two items which stood out were the costs of the accountancy partnership break-up when he and Glen Shannon broke away from their current arrangement amidst rancour and downright hatred, and Arthur. He tried to summarise this for Cathy but she already knew the answer: she was point scoring.

"I've given Arthur four hundred pounds," he said.

Cathy stood up, cleared the room, went to her bedroom and closed the door.

CHAPTER TWO

"I hear that there is another man in your life, Marie?"

They were lying back on the bed listening to the background music. Damian had received the message he wanted in that Cathy had arrived safely in Luccombe and was with her parents. He had been with his hygienist no more than half an hour before they were in bed and she was receiving a special squeeze. It was a mild Spring evening and there was no need for bed covers. The piano music filled her room with magical orchestral support.

"Mr Rachmaninov," she chuckled as his piano concerto no 2 in C minor provided a thrilling musical background.

"He only wrote four works for piano and orchestra," announced Damian.

"Five."

He hoisted himself onto his elbows and leaned over her at the same time smacking her leg.

"I'm never wrong about statistics, understand?" He kissed her. "He composed four piano concertos, got it!?"

"And the Rhapsody on a theme of Paganini," she laughed. She placed her hand around his neck and pulled him towards her. "Would you like me to play it for you?"

She jumped off the bed, put on her white shirt, grabbed his hand and led him downstairs and into another room, off the kitchen, where there was a grand piano. She sat down and patted the end of the stool, an invitation he immediately accepted.

"I've changed my mind," she said. "I'm going to play you Chopin." Her hands floated over the keyboard as the Nocturne in F-Sharp Major came alive. The three movements flashed by as she came to the end when she stood up and danced around the room.

"My father paid for me to train up to concert standard and, at one time, I thought music would be my life. It wasn't to be but I love the classics."

"And that is what you love playing the most?" asked Damian.

Marie returned to the piano, sat down on the stool and played and sang Jamie Cullum's 'Don't Give Up On Me'.

Damian examined the wood on the grand piano and read the name: 'Yamaha'.

"This must have cost around fifty thousand pounds," he said.

"Add a few dollars and you're spot on," she responded.

"On a hygienist's salary?"

"Fifty per cent of the house came from my ex-husband and an inheritance paid for the piano." She smiled at him. "Shall we have a quick walk along the towpath before you shower and have to go home?"

On hearing that he could stay the night leaving at five in the morning, Marie threw herself into a much longer walk alongside the canal which was filled with moored barges: there was birdsong and springtime flora.

"I have a question for you," announced Damian as they ducked under a leaning oak tree.

"Is this the first of the thousand questions you've

threatened?" smiled Marie.

"You spent twenty minutes leaning over me, a complete stranger who you knew virtually nothing about, rush outside, ask me out and lead me into your bed saying you have never done that before."

They moved aside to allow a couple with an ugly mongrel dog to pass by them.

"We can argue about your passive role in all that a bit later," said Marie, "But it's a fair summary."

"And it's wholly accurate, is it?" asked Damian.

"Almost."

The daylight had virtually gone and they turned back towards her home never letting go of each other's hand.

"Can we examine your use of the word 'almost'?"

Marie tripped over a hidden stone and used Damian's immediate clutching gesture to haul herself back up.

"When you followed me into the clinic, I had never thought of asking you out but I did know something about you and I'm going to breach patient confidentiality but let's live dangerously. Every Friday, late afternoon, Mr and Mrs Choudhary, who own the practice and who both work as dentists, invite us all back to their palatial home. There's a lot of money in dentistry, Damian," she laughed. "I go about one week in three and always enjoy the time. Their daughters prepare genuine Indian dishes: their modaks, that's rice, flour, coconut and spices pressed into steam dumplings, are delicious. The talk is mostly about patients, of course, especially as the wine flows. Mr and Mrs Choudhary don't drink alcohol but they are generous hosts. Two weeks ago, Mrs Choudhary told us about this patient who came in with raging toothache and there was absolutely nothing wrong with her mouth. She was X-rayed and Mrs Choudhary said that at one point she thought of getting a second opinion, the patient was so disturbed."

They were now reaching the last few yards of their walk, rounded the inlet and climbed over the stile into her garden. He lifted her up and their faces came together whereupon she hugged him with a surprising ferocity. They entered the kitchen, she made him a cup of green tea and poured herself a glass of wine.

"Mrs Choudhary suggested the woman sit on a chair and asked her if she was in any way stressed. It's well understood that the gums can be a repository for tension: grinding your teeth at night and all that. The patient burst into tears and spent the next few minutes unburdening herself. Her husband had lost all their savings in a speculative investment and she thought they might lose their home."

Damian stood up and was looking through the window.

"Cathy," he said.

"Yes. Mrs Hannon. I was looking at my list on the morning of your appointment and I connected the names. When I was working over you, something happened, it was totally seductive and I wanted more than anything to go to bed with you. You said "yes." Marie stood up, went over to her partner and looked into his face. "Is that it, Damian, is it all over between us?"

Cathy Hannon was feeling the effects of her long drive to the south coast although she loved the ferry trip over to the island. She suggested that her mother go to bed and felt a kiss on her cheek. Her father poured them both a liqueur, sat down and began to talk about their coming move, their health, the cost of running a home, Arthur and Scarlett, a name for his granddaughter that he had never liked as it reminded him of the Catholic church, the Conservative Party, illegal immigrants and his distrust of the French.

"The Brexit agreement is a joke, Caths, they're stealing all our bloody fish."

"I never thought that you'd leave Luccombe Bay, father," said Cathy. "I need to know that you are completely happy with the move to the home.

Harry (Henry on his birth certificate) wiped his brow, stood up, fetched the bottle, refilled his daughter's glass and then his own. His head was covered by a few strands of wispy white hair, there was a mole on the side of his face, he had lost several more teeth and his hands were shaking.

"The covid thing made us all more aware of our mortality, Caths, and our bodies are deteriorating. You know, your Mother and I are usually in bed by nine in the evening and we invariably sleep in the afternoon. I don't read the newspapers anymore and we often ignore the TV." He smiled. "But we are together, and we talk a great deal about our sixty odd years marriage, and we talk about you, Damian and Arthur." He sipped his drink. "I gather we're in the doghouse again. All we did was agree to pay for a weekend trip to Spain."

"Do you talk about Scarlett, father?" asked Cathy.

"She came to see us in February, unannounced, there was a knock at the door and there she was. She stayed several days and went for long walks."

Harry explained that she was never away from her mobile phone and used her laptop much of the time. Scarlett seemed troubled but finally admitted, out of the hearing of her grandmother, that she was thinking of leaving University. She begged her grandfather not to mention it to her parents.

"What's happening to her, Caths?" he asked.

She finished her drink. "I've not heard from her for some weeks. We had a disagreement because she said I was interfering too much in her life and we agreed to communicate only from her side."

"Meaning what?"

"She asked me to leave her alone. It was settled that I would not make any form of contact for three months although I sent her a birthday card." She spotted that her father was falling asleep and then he opened his eyes.

"There's just one thing I'm going to miss, Caths, and that's my walks in the bay. I haven't been able to get down there for some time. I just wish I could have one final walk on the beach and imagine the smugglers using the chine to hide their contraband." He wiped some spittle off his mouth. "Bedtime," he said.

The next morning, following a holiday breakfast including two sausages and black pudding, Cathy announced that all three of them were going into Ventnor and ordered her father to pack his wellingtons. They arrived at the harbour about an hour later as the sun was warming the coastal area: there were no winds. Cathy's mother disappeared towards the shops and she made a dash to a bank cash dispenser before speaking to several fishermen. There appeared to be an agreement and some cash was handed over. Cathy guided her father to a sleek vessel whereupon several deckhands lifted Harry over the rail and onto the boat. Cathy helped him put on the wellingtons. They were soon on their way out to sea before turning to port and reaching Luccombe Bay.

Harry was elated and never stopped talking as the skipper edged the boat towards the shore before dropping the anchor. The two lads leaped into the seawater and waited for Harry to be handed over to them. They reached the beach, checked Harry over and confirmed that they'd be back in two hours: Cathy took a picture and sent it to her mother. They walked back and forth and Cathy, who was relishing the sun on her legs, established that a chine was a gorge created by the sea. At times Harry was lost in his thoughts and finally they found themselves walking together.

"We said lots last night, Caths,"

"It was a wonderful chat, father," said Cathy, "and everything is just between us."

"We do realise what we have done, you must understand that."

"What do you mean?" she asked.

"The move to the home and the costs. We are spending your inheritance and there's a possibility there'll be nothing left. We've put some money into trusts for Arthur and Scarlett for when they are twenty-five." He struggled to bend over and pick up a pebble which he threw into the sea. "We argued a bit about it but, in the end, I have to do what's right for your mother and anyway, you and Damian are well placed, aren't you, Caths?"

She stopped, wrapped her arms around her father and kissed him.

"You've done absolutely the right thing, father, and please don't worry about the inheritance, Damian and I are fine."

Harry was now staring at the sandstone cliffs and did not see her wipe the stress away from her eyes.

Damian thought, in a completely professional way, that Rachel Smith was gorgeous. Glen Shannon and he had offered her a partnership a little over a year ago and Hannon, Shannon and Smith LLP, Chartered Accountants, was created. Over and above her ability to generate revenues, she was liked throughout the office but the pluses did not stop there. Rachel was married to a premiership rugby player, four years younger than her, who was edging towards the England squad. He occasionally secured hospitality tickets for Damian and Arthur who proved adept at mixing with the players in the after-match bar.

They were at the board room table surrounded by files, laptops, calculators and half-drunk cups of coffee, in Rachel's case. Their mission was for her to secure Damian's sign-off on the accounts of an importer of luxury goods from Italy. The two brothers had been trading for eleven years and always increased turnover and profits whilst never requiring any financial assistance from the bank.

"This is an unusual situation, Rachel," said Damian. "Your team have prepared the accounts, your audit files are immaculate, my tests are all satisfactory and I'm happy to sign the certificate. So why are you hesitating?"

"Smell," said Rachel.

"A fishy smell?" asked Damian.

"Perhaps."

Damian went into action. There are seven well known frauds that can appear in company accounts and few accountants go through their careers without being taken in at least once: it is a horrible experience for the individual. Damian was shouting out for information as he pored over his calculator, turnover year by year for the last five years, gross profits, creditors, debtors, lists of expenses, rates of inflation, exchange rates for the pound and the euro, on and on. Finally, he sat back.

"They are clean, Rachel. Absolutely no doubt, so what's the problem?"

"I don't like the brothers," she said.

Damian stared at his protégé. He asked her how much she didn't like the clients but she seemed unable to explain her answer very much further.

"Forgive me, Rachel, but I have to ask you. Has there been anything unpleasant, suggestive comments, hands on legs, that sort of thing?"

"With my husband looming!" she laughed. "No man would dare touch me." She paused. "Their handshakes are limp and the atmosphere in the offices feels, oh, I don't know, not right."

Damian started to collect everything together and went over to the side table where he poured his partner a glass of wine which he handed to her.

"Are we finished, Damian?" she asked.

"We'll sign these accounts off and we'll resign the account once the filings are completed."

"But Damian, it's eight thousand pounds a year, Glen will be furious."

"Have they ever questioned our fees?"

"Never, they always pay our invoices within thirty days, usually by return and they settle their corporation tax on time."

"And we don't act for them on personal tax matters?"

"No, I try each year but it's a brick wall with them."

Damian stood up and went over to collect the bottle of wine.

"That, Mrs Smith, is the eighth sign. If it's too good to be true, it's too good to be true. I sensed that tonight's meeting might head in this direction and so I checked their payments record and mentioned to Glen what might happen. He's fine about it."

"I'll go and see them tomorrow," informed Rachel.

"You'll do no such thing. I'll write them a formal letter as senior partner." He hesitated as she put her hand over the top of her glass. "Right, you're driving."

"No, Matt's collecting me. He's bringing a shirt for Arthur."

She stood up and went over to the window where she watched her husband park their BMW Convertible.

"He's here Damian but there's something I need to tell you."

She walked over and faced her boss.

"I'm pregnant."

For Damian the thrill of Rachel's news was soon overtaken by her next announcement. She had now turned thirty and had previously suffered a miscarriage. She proposed working up until the end of the summer and then she would be taking her full fifty-two-week maternity leave. She went to the entrance, let in Matt who handed over the gift for his son and was soon talking rugby with Damian. Finally, he waved them off and stood inside the building watching an animated couple walk to their car.

"Fuck," he said.

The kitchen island was lit by scented candles: Marie was wearing a flowery dress. Damian sat down and relaxed following a phone call giving him the reassurance that Cathy was enjoying her time on the Isle of Wight, would be home by late tomorrow afternoon and wanted to talk. He looked at the glass placed in front of him.

"It's a keto smoothie," announced Marie. "Almond milk, banana, mango, pumpkin seeds and vanilla protein powder." She did a twirl. "And in about ten minutes I shall be taking out of the oven the Marie Special Keto Lasagne, made with ground beef, sliced zucchini, shredded mozzarella and Italian seasoning."

A few minutes later they were sitting on their stools eating their supper and fighting to talk as there was an explosion of questions and answers and a gap during which Marie served second helpings. The focus shifted towards her first and only marriage, the early joys and the decision to move out of London into this house which was derelict and which they rebuilt, brick by brick, room by room, the construction of their inlet off the canal and the purchase of a boat. That was until he discovered that he was unable to father children, the collapse of his self-confidence, the increasing moods, the intervention of the medics and his disappearance until he turned up in South America. He transferred the house into Marie's sole ownership and signed the divorce papers. She took out a mortgage, paid him half the value and set about paying off the borrowings supplementing her salary as a hygienist by giving piano lessons to the children of ambitious parents. She had left music school after graduating, trained to be a nurse, changed direction into dental work and found another partner until he hit her.

"What happened to nurse Marie?" asked Damian.

"I couldn't cope," she said. "I seemed to be on a downwards spiral because so many of my patients never recovered. Finally, six months on a paediatric ward shredded me and I started to drink to excess:

watching children die of meningitis, cancer and biking accidents was too much for me." She refilled their glasses and carried on. "With dentistry we are bringing pain relief all the time and I accept that little boys like you dislike the hygienist but, be fair, you like the results of our labours."

"You said that your father committed suicide," said Damian.

"That's not on the agenda."

Marie told Damian that she was going to play him some of the greatest music ever composed. He sat down and listened for around twenty minutes as she played, without sheet music, the whole of Bernstein's West Side Story. As she reached the last few songs, she slowly began to sing:

There's a place for us,
Somewhere a place for us
Peace and quiet and open air,
Wait for us somewhere.

Then they went to bed.

At around three in the morning, he became aware that she was shaking him. He tried hard to focus helped by her pinching of his ear.

"Damian, wake up, I want to know."

"Know what?" he slumbered.

"What are you doing about getting Mrs Hannon's eighty thousand pounds back?"

Cathy used the hours of motorway driving to reflect and re-evaluate her life: her choice of background music was sombre. She was satisfied by the visit to meet with her patents who, she felt, had made a decision which took away the constant worry of their wellbeing. She would miss the annual visit to Luccombe as she and the children loved staying in the house. But that was in the past and Arthur and Scarlett were gone. She enjoyed her work as a surgery nurse and her focus on weight loss although she knew that she was actually helping few of the patients but NHS targets had to be respected! She wanted to hold on to the independence that her salary afforded.

Her main concern was her husband. Their wedding anniversary celebrations had been spectacular but there followed a series of issues. Six months ago, Damian came across the keto diet and became obsessed, losing perhaps a stone in weight and cooking all his own food: he had never drunk alcohol. Their domestic routine changed almost overnight and before too long they were in separate bedrooms. He said that the demands of being the senior partner at Hannon, Shannon and Smith, were considerable and she understood that. She knew that Rachel Smith was attractive but she dismissed any thought of infidelity.

Now, in the last few weeks, she had become aware that Damian had invested their savings in a speculative investment which promised mouth-watering returns. He never discussed the original decision with her and it was only after she had opened a letter marked 'personal' and his volcanic reaction, that the truth slowly emerged. But she wanted to know exactly what were the facts and she also needed to discuss the situation with their son.

Arthur was in a London apartment after walking out of his university degree in economics from Birmingham. He had talked about a career playing rugby but quickly became disillusioned as his lack of speed mitigated against his other skills. They had subsidised his efforts but there came a day of reckoning and his decision to get work in London. But still the requests for money kept coming in.

Cathy understood why Scarlett and her father had a distant relationship: perhaps only she did. Their daughter was bright and was, she had thought, until her conversation with her mother in Luccombe, sailing through the academic demands of Oxford University. She had become distant and then the three month's agreement was reached.

She called in at the services and treated herself to muffins, being one of those lucky people who could eat all she wanted without putting on weight. She was finishing her coffee and reflecting on a call she had taken from her next-door mate, Alice, she of the daily disasters, who was worried that Damian had not gone home last night. Cathy made an excuse for him, added that to the questionnaire and knew that she would be home in one hour for their Friday night conversation. She was pleasantly surprised to find, on arriving back, that her husband was already home and had bought her a cake.

Marie had agreed with Damian that they call a halt to their contact until the following week: she wanted to walk the hills and think about two important matters. He had showered, changed into sweater and jeans and Cathy reflected on how fit and well he seemed: they assumed their usual positions in the lounge. She had already slipped in the question about last night and Damian immediately said that their neighbour had it wrong and he was home all the time.

Cathy reported on the visit to the Isle of Wight and

avoided mention of the inheritance simply saying that she thought it unlikely her parents would live another five years and the likely outcome would be that they would go together. Damian listened carefully and thought that his wife had handled matters well but asked about the grandparent's generosity towards Arthur and nodded as he heard the grandfather's usual riposte. She told him about the visit from Scarlett but it raised little interest.

After making a coffee for herself and a green tea for Damian, Cathy heard about Rachel Smith's news and beamed without realising the impact on the partnership. Whereupon they reached the financial agenda which Damian had carefully prepared for by providing Cathy with an analysis of their position, making clear that her money entirely belonged to her. His annual disposable income was around ninety thousand pounds depending in the performance of the business. The mortgage, which had been increased to cover the demands on the bank of Mum and Dad, had ten years to run and there was an equity of around three hundred thousand pounds in the house. His pension was fully paid and, at the age of sixty-five, he would be drawing around four thousand pounds a month together with their Government pensions and she, of course, would receive a small pension from the NHS.

Damian said that he'd been introduced to an investment scheme by a client with whom he had a good relationship and had invested their savings: he admitted they might lose it all. He proposed that they committed one thousand pounds a month into a savings scheme which, over ten years, should yield them one hundred and twenty-five thousand pounds.

Cathy listened carefully and found herself relaxing;

it was much better than she dared to imagine but she had failed to see through the gossamer of half-truths: she had her one secret but she could think of no reason why it would ever come to light.

"I forgot to ask you, how did your visit to the dentist go?"

"Expensive," grimaced Damian. "I'm booked in for some root canal treatment."

"Did you see the hygienist?"

"Probably, can't really remember."

Cathy was puzzled by what she thought was a strange reply, but she wanted to go to bed and waved her hand in the air as Damian said that he'd be leaving early for the office in the morning.

The following day there were three members of staff in the offices of Hannon, Shannon and Smith but Damian was able to shut himself away armed with a bottle of tap water. He sorted the problem into separate paper piles: the first was the original investment contract wherein he invested one hundred thousand pounds into a property development involving the conversion of a disused shopping centre in the Midlands into luxury apartments overlooking the canal: it made perfect sense with the changing face of retail shopping. He had the option of an annual return of eight per cent and five per cent of the profits from each of the sales of the eighteen units or forgoing the interest but receiving seven per cent of profits. The units were due to be sold at an average price of six hundred thousand pounds and the costs were estimated at four hundred thousand. This would generate returns of two hundred and fifty-two thousand pounds or forty per cent on his original investment which would be repaid at the end of the two-year development. In the post-Brexit settlement atmosphere of optimism, it could not go wrong especially as his contact knew the sponsors of the investment personally.

There had been a series of challenges at the outset during a period of intense activity at the partnership. Damian had seventy thousand pounds in savings and borrowed twenty thousand pounds from his bank, topping up the balance of ten thousand pounds from his credit cards. At the same time, and as a result of Covid-19 restrictions, the partners agreed to reduce their drawings by thirty per cent and so Damian stopped his pension contributions. The equity on their house was nearer two hundred thousand pounds because he had re-mortgaged for a higher amount than he had told Cathy who had signed the forms without reading them.

He remained positive: he and Glen Shannon had a committed working friendship as partners and they both then had high hopes for Rachel Smith although her news was now a setback. Moreover, it was a spectacular investment which is why he allowed his contact to hurry the signing of the contract which he failed to read fully and, in particular, clause 23(f). This said that the developers could, at any time, and by giving one month's written notice, require the further investment of an amount of up to eighty per cent of the original investment. Clause 23(g) contained the dynamite. If the investor failed to provide the additional funds, if requested, the developers could seize his personal assets, including his house and pension.

Five weeks ago, a 'Personal and Strictly

Confidential' letter had arrived at his office asking for seventy thousand pounds as required under clause 23(f) and suggesting the recipient re-reads clause 23(g).

Scarlett Hannon stared again at the letter which she had received in a plain white envelope. It was made up of letters cut out from newspapers: its message was clear:

Damian Hannon is not your father

She had travelled to Luccombe to discuss it with her grandfather but was shocked by the decline in his health and decided against it. There remained the conundrum in that her father, so attractive and flirty, seemed unable to relate to her and took little interest in her progress through the adolescent years despite her academic prowess. Her mother never stopped asking her questions. Scarlett had a close friend, Joshua, with whom she had agreed a non-tactile relationship and she confided in him. A bottle of red wine and loud music gave them a background to an evening spent compiling the key questions:

+ Is it true?
+ Who wrote the letter and why?
+ Who is her father?
+ Does her mother know (99% yes)
+ Does Damian Hannon know?
+ Does her real father know, care, follow her progress?
+ What happens next?

Scarlett knew that the one person who could solve

the mystery was her mother but she realised the possible consequences of showing her the letter. An event then took place which accelerated her next move: a second letter arrived:

I'll tell D Hannon (not your father) in the next month

She and Joshua regrouped and discussed involving the police but quickly dismissed the idea. They mulled over about involving Arthur but that idea was soon rejected with Joshua arguing strongly that Scarlett should see her 'father', Damian, and she understood the logic to his thinking in that Damian was going to have become involved at some stage.

As she ran and ran on the treadmill at her health club, where the subscription was paid for by her grandmother, she finally reached a decision.

+ + +

CHAPTER THREE

Mr Arjun Choudhary relaxed in his office on a bright Monday morning as Marie asked for a few moments of his time to which he immediately acceded. He poured them each a cup of coffee.

"I am humbly sorry, Mr Choudhary, but I have acted foolishly and committed an act of stupidity and even perhaps worse." She placed a letter on his desk. "This is my resignation. I will go immediately."

The senior dentist pushed the letter to one side and asked Marie to explain to him what was troubling her. The hygienist sat very upright and delivered the explanation she knew he would require with careful articulation which resulted from several hours of rehearsal while walking the canal towpath. She left no stone unturned as she explained the appointment, the approach, the subsequent events and the circumstances in which she heard of Mrs Choudhary's session with Cathy Hannon. Her employer asked several questions which she answered and then awaited his acceptance of her departure.

"We seem to be dealing with two issues," he said. "First, was your approach to this patient unprofessional and second, was the revealing of Mrs Hannon's consultation with Mrs Choudhary unprofessional or, perhaps, more serious."

"That is exactly my conclusion, Mr Choudhary," said Marie. "I am so sorry."

He picked up his phone and spoke to a receptionist.

A few moments later Mrs Panisi Choudhary entered the office, smiled at Marie and sat down. Their families had come from India in the nineteen-eighties: they met at the City of London Dental School and set up their own business ten years later. They managed to have five children while working ferociously hard to create the efficient and well-respected dental practice they now ran. Their staff turnover was negligible as they focused on their 'family' of dental professionals. Mr Choudhary explained his conversation with Marie and turned back to the hygienist.

"You should know that after the staff gathering at our home I spoke to Mrs Choudhary with great seriousness and chastised her for revealing the details of her consultation with Mrs Hannon."

Mrs Choudhary turned and faced Marie.

"I am sorry, Marie, it was wrong of me."

"Let's try to make some sense of all this," said the senior dentist. "You, Marie, are an important member of our team and you are a fine hygienist." And with that he tore up her letter. "Did you breach confidentiality bearing in mind that Mrs Choudhary committed the main offence and the details were heard by everyone present." He paused for a few moments. "My judgement is as follows: you had no way of knowing whether Mr Hannon already knew about the circumstances. Surely Mrs Hannon, on getting a clear diagnosis from Mrs Choudhary, would go home and tell her husband? Perhaps you strayed across the line but it is the first time and I am fining you a week's earnings which will be donated to a local charity. The other matter took place outside the practice. You spoke to Mr Hannon in the car park which we do not own. It is nothing to do with me, nor with Mrs

Choudhary. Please, Marie, go and see your patients."

They had communicated briefly and agreed to meet on Tuesday evening.

When Damian arrived, he sensed that Marie was keen to talk as she handed him a smoothie and told him about her meeting with Mr Choudhary. He mulled over the matter before responding.

"You were right to tell him, Marie. He sounds like a wise man."

"In the last week I've done things I could never imagine," she said. "I walked for miles over the weekend and thought through the two main issues," she reflected.

"Possibly breaching patient confidentiality was one so what was the other?" asked Damian.

"You."

"Did you reach a conclusion?"

"Yes."

"Has it occurred to you that this is about sex? What did you say to me after the first time? It was the feeling of togetherness, the squeezing of our bodies which gave you total fulfilment."

"I've decided that's a wrong conclusion," suggested Marie. "As you once suggested, I do get offers, my health club is full of lotharios and there are plenty of athletic men to cuddle."

"Therefore, where's this going?" asked Damian.

"The real problem I have, Damian, is that you are an immodest, chauvinistic, male nightmare."

"Not very far, I suspect," he frowned.

"You are also the most handsome, charismatic, funny, interesting man I have ever met: I relish every moment with you in or out of bed. I have made my decision and that is until every possibility has been exhausted, I'll remain locked in the hope that we can be together for evermore."

"That will mean you'll be a husband stealer."

"No, I don't buy that. You could have said "no" when I first asked you but you said "yes". There had to be something wrong with your marriage because you're not the type to go round looking for cheap sex. It is possible, more like probable, that the initial impetus was lust: we just clicked and then in hours, days, something happened. We're not going to bed tonight: will it matter? I'll be frustrated because you're a magical lover but "no" because tonight is the first time that we've had a personal conversation about our feelings and it's getting better and better."

"Where do we go from here?" he asked.

"I wish I knew."

"We could go to Reading, together," he said.

Damian explained that he had a client whose main warehouse was situated on the south side of the Thames Valley town and, as part of the annual audit process, a senior member of staff needed to go and physically inspect the stock held inside. He was intending travelling down there on the following Tuesday. Marie promised him an answer in the morning after she had spoken to Mrs Choudhary. She had several days of untaken leave owing and had enough time to contact the five patients booked in that day and to re-arrange their appointments.

It was around two o'clock on Thursday when Damian's receptionist, Louisa, came into his room and said that he had a visitor waiting in reception asking to see him. He checked his computer which showed a clear day as he had planned because of the need to review the financial performance of the practice for the first three months of the year. He was annoyed by the interruption to his concentration.

"It's Scarlett, Mr Hannon, your daughter."

Within a few minutes, father and daughter were settled into the board room where Louisa had prepared a tray of coffee and a plate of biscuits usually reserved for clients. Scarlett was smartly dressed: she was around five feet eleven inches tall, athletic and with a healthy glow. They played around for fifteen minutes catching up on their individual news and family matters: Damian already knew why she was in his office.

"This is difficult," she said. "It was Joshua who persuaded me to come and see you."

They ascertained that Joshua was a friend who advised Scarlett on 'events'. She opened her bag, took out the first letter and placed it in front of him.

"I want to know if you are my father?" said Scarlett as the tears came into her eyes and began to flow down her face.

Damian opened a file he had placed on the table, took out a sheet of paper and handed it to his daughter. It was a single sentence made up of individual cut-out letters from a newspaper:

I know that you are not Scarlett's father

She read it carefully, compared it to her letter, took out some tissues and wiped her eyes. She repeated her question to Damian who stood up and started to pace round the room.

"I received the letter two weeks ago. Until then I had never questioned the matter and I'm certainly shown on your birth certificate. I must be honest but

45

I've found it difficult to forge a relationship with you but that is probably down to me. You are gifted and an important part of your mother's life." He paused. "This Joshua, have you and he managed to solve the key questions: who sent these letters and why?"

They discussed the matter, the parameters and possible solutions before reaching the logical way forward. Damian called Cathy and said that he'd be home in thirty minutes.

They entered the house through the front door, Scarlett running into the kitchen and there followed cries of joy. The family were soon sitting in the lounge each with a drink as Damian explained the day's events and asked Scarlett to show her mother the letter she had received. He then handed over his version: Cathy sat still and said nothing. She put down her glass, stood up and changed seats so that she was facing the two of them before beginning to speak.

"I think it's possible that Damian is not your biological father, Scarlett," she said. "We can organise a test to find out the truth but, first, I think it best I tell you what happened and then you, Damian, can scream and shout. I am so sorry, Scarlett, that you should have to go through this."

Cathy began her revelations by explaining that, for several years before having children, she and Damian were part of a social circle which became both close and increasingly brazen. They were in their twenties and early thirties, the economy was booming, society was liberating and their weekend parties were becoming excessive. She said that she was watching a neighbour who clearly fancied her husband and spoke to her after one particular evening, although she never doubted his fidelity. There was a two-week period when Arthur was teething and Damian was working late hours as the business expanded. They took to sleeping separately purely because he needed his sleep and this resulted in a temporary loneliness which came to a head at a Valentine's Day Party when Damian was unusually responsive to one of Cathy's friends and she found herself in the kitchen with a local man.

"Even now," said Cathy, "I don't understand how it happened, but we slipped into the garden and had sex: I didn't even enjoy it: he was rough and coarse. To add to my sins, I forgot to take my pill, became pregnant and realised that there was a possibility he was the father so I went to see him: he reacted aggressively and said that if I revealed anything, he would wipe Damian out." She paused and gulped. "That was the phrase he used: he'd wipe Damian out." She finished her glass of wine. "You were born, Scarlett and I adored you from the beginning. As you grew taller, I worried that questions might be asked but until now nothing happened."

"The letters, Mum?" asked Scarlett.

"Yes, I'm coming to those. I know who has sent them: it's him."

She continued by explaining that a few weeks ago at the surgery one of the GPs came into her room with a patient who she wanted introduced to the weight reduction programme. "It was him. I had no option but to do my job. I'd seen him a few times over the years but never to speak to: it was difficult to miss him." She seemed to shudder. "He hadn't changed that much except for being about two stones heavier. I tried to be professional but he leered at me and then I could not stop him undressing. The doctor was right: he had a BMI of thirty-six and was clinically obese. At one point I was writing up my forms and leaning over the desk when he came up behind and goosed me. I was humiliated and hurt and then he said that I needed a proper man, laughed and sneered "but I forget, you've had one!" There were so many things I should have done and I have an alarm button in my room, but I knew that this was about my daughter, and her future, so I said to him, "with your tiny dick you couldn't shag a watermelon."

Damian and Scarlett looked at each other and both burst out laughing.

"If I'd thought of a hundred alternative insults, I could not have landed a more damaging blow: his personal life is a mess with two divorces and his career has hardly been spectacular. He snorted and said he'd get even with me and so now you know who sent those letters."

"Who is he, Cathy?" asked Damian.

"Inspector Paul Marston of the Bedfordshire constabulary."

"You mustn't see him again at the surgery, Mum," said Scarlett.

"His blood tests came in two days after the events I have described. He is in serious problems with type two diabetes and hypertension and is now on extended sick leave. My GP colleague told me that he has been transferred to the special unit at the hospital. He's on the list for bariatric surgery so I doubt he'll be sending any more letters."

"I'm going outside for a walk," said Damian. Cathy and Scarlett went into the kitchen together. They were waiting for Scarlett's father on his return.

"What do we do?" he asked.

"We do nothing," said Scarlett.

Cathy and Damian stared at one another.

"We don't know if there is any real possibility that this Paul Marston could be my father and Mum's maths are so bad, she'd probably have got her dates wrong." Scarlett looked at Damian. "You're my father: end of story and I'm going back to Oxford."

Damian took his daughter to the station and perhaps for the first time shared a genuine hug with her. He drove around the streets before returning home where he found Cathy in the kitchen.

"I thought that you were magnificent today, Cathy," he said.

She turned and faced him.

"I've got a present for you," she said and took out of her pocket a bottle of shampoo which she handed to him.

"Tell your girlfriend that you don't rinse a man's hair with body wash."

*

Six o'clock in the morning of a near perfect Tuesday Spring day with no wind and just fluffy clouds in a blue sky was a good way to begin their journey together. She closed the front entrance and skipped to the open passenger door: she was wearing a matching green Boucle jacket and jeans with sandals on her feet that showed her green painted toenails. They kissed and he started the engine as she sank back into the luxury seat.

"I see it's climate change day," he laughed.

"Jest you might, Mr Hannon, but we must reduce gas emission by seventy-six per cent by 2040 if we are to have any chance of restricting average temperature rises to below two degrees centigrade."

She became absorbed by the music he had selected as he waited for the traffic lights to change to green when he executed a smooth left turn onto the main road.

"We'll join the M1 at junction 11a, leave at junction 6a onto the M25, down to 15 when we turn right on to the M4 and at 10, I'll take the slip road, the A329 and you'll see the warehouse on the hill." The route is sixty-nine point five miles and the journey time is one hour, twenty-five minutes."

"Are you going to serve peanuts with the champagne?" she asked which resulted in a smacking of her leg.

They resumed their banter after sliding into the heavy HGV traffic on Britain's premier motorway which reflected the buoyant state of the economy following the exit from the European Union and the defeat of Covid-19. Marie was enjoying the aftershave the driver had used that morning.

"Good choice of music," she said, as she mentally played along with the Brahm's piano concerto No 2. "It's exciting, isn't it? Will we reach the M4 before the finale is reached?"

Damian had no idea that the total time to play the four movements was fifty minutes because he had grabbed the CD from Cathy's collection as he rushed out of the house, but Marie was not going to let him off lightly.

"The composer was known as one of three Bs of music. You, of course, Mr Hannon, FCA, can name the other two," she laughed.

"What's this FCA business?" he asked.

"Brahms composed the concerto, Bach and Beethoven were the other two members and I've been researching you: Fellow of the Chartered Institute of Accountants in England and Wales. Impressive." She ran her hand through her hair. "I've been reading my book of funny professional jokes," she said. "Would you like to hear one?" She ignored his declining of her suggestion. "How do you describe an actuary?" She smiled at the silence that followed. "An accountant who found the job too exciting."

She was puzzled that they were exiting the M4 towards Windsor and thrown by Damian's explanation that it was clear she was too exciting for him and she would be left at Slough station to find her own way home. She therefore could not understand the reason they were parking in the grounds of a country hotel. Damian turned off the engine, came round to the passenger side and opened her door with the announcement, "breakfast, Madame."

Marie went to the buffet on three separate occasions and rivalled the American guests at the hotel for gross food consumption although she did omit the plate of waffles, honey and cream. As she left the lady's facilities, she found Damian waiting for her, and threw her arms around his neck in an embrace that they held for some long moments, and then, not for the first time, whispered something into his ear.

The traffic west was lighter as Damian asked with whom she went to the Pyramids and why? The answer was in two parts: they went to Egypt because Marie had read the biography of a man who, on hearing that he had around six months to live, drew up a list of twenty challenges he must undertake. She turned to the index, shut her eyes and put her finger on one of the headings which is why she spent two memorable weeks visiting the tombs of the pharaohs. She pre-empted the inevitable question and told Damian that the author had died while trying to complete task number eleven which involved climbing Ben Nevis in the Scottish Grampians.

The answer to the second part was Miss Khristina Babikov. They were now nearing the turning to Reading and Marie was offered the choice of sitting in the car for perhaps an hour or catching the bus into the town centre. She selected the lazier option and dozed for around ninety minutes before Damian re-joined her. They drove north west out of the area and within an hour were parked by the river Thames at Henley. Damian looked around, took off his suit and put on a pair of shorts, sweat shirt and running shoes. Marie protested loudly that he was cheating until she found herself receiving a similar outfit, changed and asked how he knew her shoe size? He said that he had bought three pairs to be on the safe side. The temperature was rising as they ran together for nearly an hour. They stopped and bought drinks and, for her, sandwiches before turning back: half way along they sat down in the long grass on the embankment.

"Miss Kris…?" he asked.

"Miss Khristina Babikov," corrected Marie. "She's my step-sister and lives in London not far from my mother. I was the product of an English lady and a Russian diplomat who divorced and he then married a French woman, she gave birth to Khristina before he disappeared into Russia. Khristina and I met and tried to find out what happened but all we were told was that he had committed suicide. My mother has shown no interest whatsoever and has re-married while Khristina and I have remained friends."

"What is your surname?"

"Guess."

"Tchaikovsky."

Marie laughed and applauded him. "I was born Rosemary Magellan Babikov and became Mrs Robinson. When we divorced, I decided to change my name by deed poll and so the answer is Rosemary Magellan Cameron."

"Not after the prime minister?"

"I thought he was wonderful and what a lovely wife."

"He caused us to leave the European Union!" exclaimed Damian.

"He didn't. It was the back bench Brexiters and Nigel Farage who led to us exiting."

They returned to the car, changed and began the journey home. Marie took out a CD from her bag, ejected Brahms and replaced him with Miles Davis.

Damian was cutting through the Chiltern Hills and heading for Aylesbury when she asked him about the keto diet: he told the story as succinctly as he could manage. He was visiting a client who he noticed seemed to have lost some weight from his previous visit when he spotted on the table a book titled 'The Keto Diet'. His customer needed no second invitation and relished telling his story which was that he and his wife were looking at their holiday photographs one day and did not like the bulges and so they decided on joint action, went speed walking every morning, cut out fats and ate salads. They achieved an initial weight loss and then two problems resulted: the first was that acquaintances were asking if they were ill and he did not like his emaciated appearance. The second was that they became bored with their diet and exhausted by the dedication needed to retain the weight-loss.

His wife capitulated and put back on all the weight she had lost but he had a chance meeting with an associate at a Birmingham conference. He was told about the keto diet about which he had never heard. He researched it and decided to try it on himself: his wife was not interested.

Damian paused because Marie was unusually quiet but she urged him to continue. He explained that ketosis is a natural state the body finds itself in when it is using fat as its main fuel which happens when the individual is following a very low carb ketogenic diet.

"I accept it is difficult, at first, to grasp but, if I can make one point, I also struggled to understand what he was talking about because unlike conventional dieting which is based on reduced food intake of fats and allows for lapses, keto is absolute. You cannot afford to slip up because it is totally dependent on the elimination of carbs and protein. This is why they talk about a state of ketosis which means you have achieved the ideal balance. The actual diet is, in fact, based on an intake of natural fats which make up ninety per cent with ten per cent being selected carbs."

"You eat fats and lose weight," said Marie.

"If only," replied Damian. "I was so impressed by what I'd heard, I researched it and started the process. It takes weeks to get going and there were serious problems at home because I was cooking my own meals. But," he hesitated, "I'm rather single minded" ("Oh yes" Marie said to herself) "and I began to relish the new me. I went to see my doctor who was sceptical until he took my blood pressure readings which were normal and a blood test which showed that my blood was pure. He was fascinated by the Triglyceride level which is the main constituent of body fat and mine was perfect."

They were approaching her home and Damian said he must go to the office. They alighted from the car and hugged.

"I've something to tell you," said Damian.

Marie briefly grimaced.

"Cathy knows," he said.

"Yes, that's to be expected," she said. "I think you should come in."

They sat at the kitchen island. Marie asked how Cathy knew and he told her about the bottle of shampoo. In answer to her question about what happens next, he said that there was a hand-written note awaiting him that morning. Cathy was calling what she called a 'summit meeting' for eleven o'clock next Sunday. He was tempted to write back and ask which of the world's leaders would be attending.

Glen Shannon entered Damian's office, closed the door and asked if the visit to Reading had been useful? He then asked if it was the best use of partner's time undertaking stock valuations? He brushed aside Damian's answer and said that there was a matter which he needed to discuss. He had brought a coffee latte in with him and was carrying a bulky file which he placed on the desk.

He and Damian had worked together for over fifteen years and had united to force the partnership break-up five years earlier that led to the setting up of Hannon and Shannon which became Hannon, Shannon and Smith. The two chartered accountants shared professional values and client priority and that was about it. Glen was married to an effervescent school teacher who was a devoted mother to their three children all of whom seemed thrilled by their surroundings. Glen rode a bike and had a camera on his helmet so that he could report to the police, car drivers who did not respect his right to space on the roads. He was a committed supporter of the Labour party and spent his free evenings listening to American singer-songwriter Bob Dylan. He was ferociously committed to his work and to maximising his earnings.

"I'll get straight to the point, Damian," he began. "We've had an offer for the business from Malkins."

There was an intake of breath as Damian immediately switched into analysis mode. They regularly received approaches from other firms the majority of which offered tantalising sums of money on an earn-out basis. This entailed agreeing the amounts and then, after joining together, generating the earnings from which they would be paid the initial purchase price. He and Glen always rejected out of hand such approaches.

Malkins, however, were a different proposition altogether. They were in the top twenty list of British firms and had recently opened up in Malta, the off-shore financial centre that was prospering in the post-Brexit European expansion. Malkins were also buying firms across England in preparation for floating their shares on the London Stock Market. Glen indicated the file on the desk and said that he had prepared a full report for him but perhaps he could summarise the deal.

Damian was stumped that Malkins had talked to Glen: after all, he was the senior partner.

"In a nutshell, Damian, it's basically a cash offer. Your deal will be four hundred thousand pounds of which three hundred will be paid on the signing of contracts and one hundred will be on an earn-out. You will have to sign a non-competition agreement which will last a year and which means you cannot approach any client. They will indemnify you personally against any future liabilities and they will require a limited due diligence process. In fact, they've unofficially told me it's a done deal."

"Are we talking in the past tense?" asked Damian.

"They want me and Rachel to stay and are quite happy about her taking maternity leave although I think she's decided to reduce it to three months. We will be making three staff redundant on generous terms.

"What about me, Glen?" shouted Damian.

"They don't want you."

"They don't want me," repeated Damian. "I built this firm with my own money. We've one hundred and fifty-three clients of whom I act for what, seventy? Each year we increase profitability by an average of eleven point three per cent."

"Except last year," retorted Glen, "and I accept that Covid-19 caused huge problems but this year we are already down and recently agreed to reduce drawings." He drank his coffee. "Now we find you gallivanting off on ridiculous stock checks that a junior auditor could undertake."

"Did you instigate this approach, Glen," asked Damian who was regretting his trip to Reading.

"You are not the person I've known over the years: you seem distracted. The receptionist is called Louisa."

"Yes, Louisa."

"You call her Lucy."

"We're selling out because I call the receptionist by the wrong name?!"

"Don't be childish, Damian."

Damian reached for the file and then changed his mind.

"Have I any choice, Glen?"

"None whatsoever because Rachel and I have signed a memorandum of understanding: handover is scheduled for the first of June." He opened the file and took out two pieces of paper. "This one is a letter to the staff and this is written to the clients. I'm sure you'll want to alter the wording but it's what the solicitors recommend we say."

"You've instructed solicitors? I think we should call in Rachel," said Damian.

"She's been off for the day," said Glen.

"How convenient," he grimaced. "You've been planning this behind my back?"

Glen Shannon stood up and left the room. Damian moved towards the file he had left but pushed it away. He went over to the cupboard where he stored bottles of wine for his clients, opened one and poured himself a glass. He then realised that he'd not be able to drive home. His head began to spin and he decided that events were becoming rather messy. He closed his office and walked out of the front door hardly noticing the receptionist who wished him a good evening: he could not remember her name.

He walked the two miles home, noticed that someone had been walking over the front garden, opened the door and went in to find Cathy in the kitchen eating an iced cream bun. He poured himself a glass of water and told her about the meeting with Glen Shannon. She appeared to be overtaken by anger and then rage as she went red in the face. She stood up and announced that she was going into the garden.

"We'll add this to the agenda for Sunday," she said.

CHAPTER FOUR

By half-past ten on Sunday morning Damian Hannon had completed a list of the changes he could identify and shook his head in bemusement and perhaps a degree of intrigue. The garden had been partially renovated: he knew he had been slow to repair its appearance after the winter storms and the lawns had been neglected. Both the back and the front were in a better state, the borders in apple-pie order, the fountain had been cleaned out and the drive had been meticulously swept. Cathy's car was shining after a full wash and valeting which in itself was a surprise as she was always reluctant to spend the money. The windows had been cleaned and the rubbish bags taken away out of the garage. The house carpets appeared to have been cleaned and he liked the fresh linen on his bed together with the crisp feel to his shirts. The tiles in the bathroom were sparkling and the tooth brush holder replaced.

At eleven o'clock Cathy appeared in the lounge carrying a file, writing pad and pen. Damian gasped as he absorbed her new hair style and two-piece light blue suit. She rarely wore perfume to any great extent partly because she was blessed with a natural beauty and because she could, and did, eat anything in whatever quantity she wished and never put on the pounds. He recalled that she sailed through childbirth and was back at work within three weeks with both Arthur and Scarlett. She sat down having poured them both glasses of iced water.

"Damian," she began, "there are two conditions, one of which I'll tell you now and the other will come when we have finished our discussion. Then I will have some important news for you. We agree that both of us will tell the absolute truth on every matter and neither of us will use omission to avoid embarrassment. Agreed?"

Damian nodded his head and waited for the guillotine to come crashing down.

"Right. I make no apology for my intemperate use of the English language but this bastard Glen Shannon and his pretty, double-dealing sidekick Rachel Smith, how do we get them?"

"Get them?" exclaimed Damian. He had never heard Cathy speak with such venom.

"They're stealing our business, my livelihood, we've devoted our lives to establishing the practice: you are highly respected in the town and we have a position in society. I suppose they're blaming you for Covid-19 but everybody had a shitty time: we've come through and we're prospering. They cut your drawings while Mrs 'I'm married to a rugby player' Smith gets pregnant and now they are trying to sell out under our noses: it's not going to happen."

"You insisted that we must be honest," said Damian and while Cathy was nodding her head, he explained that he had experienced a sense of relief after the meeting with his partner. The business had lost some of its shine and perhaps it was his fault. He said that, frankly, he wanted out of accountancy and now the opportunity seemed right.

"That's what I was expecting you to say, Damian, so we are in agreement."

"What agreement?" he asked.

"I'll agree to sell the business."

"Er…well, yes. It's a good offer."

"It's nothing of the sort. I telephoned Malkins and spoke to Stuart Oliver who is their commercial partner."

"You did what?!"

"He seemed pleased to talk to me especially as he asked if I could persuade you to change your mind."

"Change my mind over what?"

"Glen Shannon told him that you had said you wanted to give up accountancy."

"I think that Mr Shannon and I need to have a chat," he said.

"Hold your horses, Damian. I had to play it carefully because I didn't want to jeopardise the sale of the business so I told Stuart that you were torn because things are going well and you are expecting an increase in profits of around twenty-two per cent."

"Where did you get that from?"

"The Prime Minister. He keeps telling us about the prospects for post-Brexit Britain and Mr Oliver seemed convinced."

"Did he confirm the deal?"

"Yes and no. Yes, Malkins are buying our business and "no", not at the agreed price. I've negotiated an extra hundred thousand pounds for you. Not quite what I wanted: the cash is now three hundred and fifty thousand pounds and the earn-out will be one hundred and fifty thousand over seven years. Mr Oliver promised me that they'd play fair and, as they are nearing the public offering of their shares on the London Stock Market, we are in a better position because your settlement will be included in what he referred to as the prospectus."

"That's the document produced and approved by the regulators to enable them to sell their shares to the public."

"He was adamant about the non-competition agreement and I told him that I thought the deal will mean you'll walk away from accountancy."

"What happens now?"

"Stuart Oliver will be at your offices tomorrow morning. He wants to move quickly and suggests that you go by the end of the week."

"Holy Moses. There goes a career."

"Don't try the poor little Damian on me because here comes a new beginning." She stood up and brushed herself down. "That completes the first item."

Damian stood up and said he wanted some fresh air: he was told to sit down.

"We have lost our savings on this property development. I need to know the details." She sat expressionless while Damian gave her the information she wanted: the investment of one hundred thousand pounds made up of seventy thousand in savings, a bank loan of twenty thousand and ten thousand on credit cards. He explained the clauses in the agreement which allowed them to demand a further seventy thousand pounds and their claim on the house and his pension. She asked for the full amount due on credit cards and remained impassive on hearing that the total was currently around seventeen thousand pounds. They then discussed the house and the higher amount outstanding because of the re-mortgage, partly because of further amounts given to Arthur: the equity was probably fifty thousand more than recently stated because of the general escalation in house prices. Cathy asked that she be given the property investment file and she'd take over the matter.

"You must be careful about the seventy thousand pounds additional money," chided Damian.

"To hell with that," she said. "I want our original investment back."

They now agreed to take a break and Damian seemed busy with his calculator. When they reconvened ten minutes later, he advised Cathy that he wanted to update her on two matters. On receipt of the payment for the practice he would pay his pension contributions up to-date and by his calculations, in twelve years, he would have the option of drawing a twenty-five per cent lump sum and still have a monthly payment of around four thousand pounds together with their government pensions giving a total of over five thousand pounds and she would have her pension from the NHS. As she absorbed this information, and wrote down notes, he continued by explaining his personal income tax liability resulting from the sale of the business. He said that the tax year had fallen favourably in that the proceeds would be received after 5 April and so he calculated a liability to Her Majesty's Revenue & Customs of nine point eight per cent resulting in a payment of thirty-four thousand, three hundred pounds on the last day of January, 2024. Cathy nodded and smiled.

They reviewed the situation with Cathy's parents and Arthur. It was recognised that they really had no idea what was happening with their son and Damian would go to London and meet up with him. He was puzzled that they were not discussing Scarlett but his wife moved the conversation on.

"That's been satisfactory, Damian. We should have

had this chat ten years ago and I blame myself. In many ways I have let you down. I have become so absorbed in my work as a nurse, which I relish, that I have committed the cardinal sin of taking my husband for granted. The only answer I can offer is that we will focus on going forwards. I said that there is a second condition and then I'll give you the news."

Cathy stood up and he thought that there was a change of mood as she had become somewhat apprehensive.

"You must give up the keto diet. This is non-negotiable. It is wrecking your life and, in fact, is contributing to your self-destruction. As you know, I have talked to one of the doctors at some length who told me that it is controversial although there are some heavyweight backers."

She paused and laughed wherein Damian saw her face light up.

"I think there's a pun in there somewhere but you know what I mean. I want you to go back to a carbohydrate and protein normal diet with some fat and, of course, the odd glass of wine won't hurt." She came over to him. "We can have our meals together again and I can have my kitchen back. Do you agree?"

He nodded his head mainly because he knew what the coming news would be. He wondered which firm of solicitors she would be using. He knew by now that she wanted an amicable divorce and to be able to tell their friends that whilst they are still very much in love and want the best for their children, it was time to explore new opportunities.

"Thanks. I have arranged for you see a doctor tomorrow morning: eleven twenty."

"Why Cathy, I'm not ill?"

"You will be undertaking a serious change of diet and your body has become used to the intake of fats. He wants to check you over and discuss the next few weeks."

Damian had reached the point of no return.

"What's this news you are talking about?"

"It's good news, Damian."

And now he realised what this was all about. Cathy wanted to maximise her payment from the divorce and he'd managed to give her all the ammunition she needed. There was nothing she did not know about their finances and he began to imagine the letter her solicitor would write which would be the opening salvo. He began to mentally wander and could not understand why he did not feel an elation that he was going to be free to live his life with Marie: they had so much to talk about, the canal towpath would be worn down.

He looked across at his companion for the last twenty-seven years including the courtship following a drunken party at the rugby club. He was in a queue for this stunning barmaid who was in great, if not drunken, demand and then she made a play for him and they never looked back. There was nothing to dislike about her: quite the opposite as she exuded warmth and her drive down to the Isle of Wight to see her parents was Cathy at her best. Her dedication as a nurse had reached his ears on numerous occasions and their holiday in South Africa was memorable. Cathy acquired a pair of leather shorts which she wore on their safari walks in the bush and which tested Damian's self-control to breaking point.

He shook his head in bemusement: he was relaxed about the circumstances when he met Marie and believed that the years ahead with her were certain to be fulfilling. Did he want to lose Cathy? Who was this woman who since eleven o'clock had taken control and rationalised several difficult matters? She still cared for him as her obsession with the keto diet demonstrated so had he shot himself in the foot? He stood up and faced her.

"I want to say something, Cathy, before you give me the good news. I never set out to betray you. It was like a whirlwind with the other person: this loss of our savings has hurt me, bearing in mind I have spent my career telling people how to manage their finances, Arthur's constant demand for money and the realisation that I want to chuck being an accountant. I'm making excuses and I deserve everything you are going to throw at me. Let's hear the good news and I'll get out of your life."

"You are Scarlett's father."

Damian's face exploded into a mosaic of expressions.

"What! How? What do you mean? How do you know?"

He sat down as Cathy revealed she had collected the glasses after Scarlett's visit and with the help of a doctor used the practice licence to send them for DNA testing. Their daughter's DNA was fine but his glass revealed nothing and so she collected samples of his hair which proved decisive.

"I'm Scarlett's father?" he said. "No doubt?"

"There's a four per cent chance it's wrong."

"Does Scarlett know?" he asked.

"She broke down in hysterics when I told her and said it was the happiest day of her life." She put her hands on his shoulders. "That was a really pleasing time together." Cathy smiled and released her hold. "Right. We're finished."

"We're finished?" he asked. "No, I mean we're not finished?"

"I am," she laughed. "I'm off to reclaim my kitchen."

"But!"

"But what?"

"Marie."

Cathy immediately changed tack and faced her husband.

"I don't want to know her name and you are never to mention her or anything about her, to me, again."

"Where does this leave things?" he pleaded.

Cathy pulled up a small pouffe and sat in front of her husband.

"I have let you down badly, Damian. It must have been awful listening to me telling Scarlett about having sex with PC Marston in the garden especially as I had watched you resist the clawing of sex-starved women at the party. I have been pig-headed about the keto diet and selfish about my work at the clinic. I have committed the cardinal sin of neglecting the bedroom and I suppose I should have paid more attention to stockings and suspenders." She stood up and turned back.

"You are forty-nine years of age: you have strayed for the first, and I promise you, only time. You are a wonderful human being, a great father, you are the sexiest man I have ever met and I love you to the bottom of my heart. We are going to fight our way into a new beginning and I have a business idea for us." She paused. "Just work out your lust on this Marie and when she chucks you, they always do, my marriage door will re-open."

"Bugger," thought Damian because he had become so libidinous, he was, emotionally, half way up the stairs to her bedroom.

*

Monday was a busy day for both Damian and Cathy Hannon.

The Malkins partner, Stuart Oliver, arrived with two other colleagues and was shown into the boardroom. Damian asked Louisa, who was pleased to hear her name pronounced correctly, to invite Mr Shannon and Mrs Smith to join them. He waited for their arrival and began the agenda not giving them an inch as he detailed the agreement that the three partners would be signing. There was a discussion over the letters to the staff and the clients and when on each occasion Glen Shannon made a point, he was overruled. Damian announced that he would be leaving on Friday, there was to be no party at the office and he and Cathy would be inviting a majority of the staff to their home for a barbecue in two weeks' time. He left the meeting saying that as Glen Shannon would be the face of the partnership in the future, he should work with the Malkins team to ensure that the changes were handled with sensitivity and consideration from everyone's point of view. There was a brief discussion on the members of staff who were to be made redundant and Damian ruled that he would see them all after lunch. He stood up and went back to his office without a glance to his two partners.

Late in the afternoon Rachel Smith knocked on his door and was invited to enter. Damian stood as she faced him.

"I'm not sure if you have been told yet," she said, "about the two brothers and the Italian business. They were raided by the police on Saturday because their lorries have been used for bringing in illegal immigrants: they are claiming they are innocent."

"You should take the file immediately to Mr Shannon and Mr Oliver," instructed Damian. "They will need to put in a report to the regulator."

"I think I owe you a debt of gratitude, Damian," she said. "One of the accountants from Malkins has spent the day on the matter and spoken to his compliance officer in London. Their initial judgement is that the file note I made after our audit meeting and your letter to the brothers resigning the account has saved us from a rather difficult investigation."

In the face of his silence, Rachel said that the signing of the memorandum of understanding behind his back was all Glen Shannon's doing and she had gone along with him because she was thinking about her baby.

"Please understand Damian that you have seemed distracted of late and there are whispers," she said as she moved towards the door.

"Hold on, Rachel," said Damian. "I have something for you."

He went into a cupboard and took out a rugby shirt which he handed to her.

"Neither Arthur nor I want it," he said.

"What's your secret, nurse Hannon" laughed Doctor Martin Armstrong.

"What do you mean?" replied Cathy.

"Whatever you're taking, I want some. You're bouncing around like a teenager. The NHS is collapsing, the surgery is inundated with this sickness bug, I'm stressed to high heaven and you are serenely sailing through the whole chaos!"

He asked her to join him in his room and, once she was seated, explained that he had seen Damian in the morning and they had agreed he could talk to her about his condition. Cathy frowned.

"His condition?"

"His general health is fine and all the vital signs are encouraging. He has lost a lot of weight while on the keto diet and, medically, I can't fault it. But it's against everything I've been taught in medicine. Whenever I'm faced with a perplexing situation, which seems about every other day at the moment, I go back to nature. Did primitive man live on fats alone? Damian tried to argue that there is evidence they did but they grew wheat, bred cows, sheep and pigs and fished." He took a phone call and said he needed another ten minutes. He confirmed that he had suggested that Damian gradually change back to a normal diet and, if he suffers any reaction, he must come back to see him."

Cathy relaxed and thanked her colleague.

"Cathy, I'm talking to you now as a human being, not as a doctor. Bluntly the world is getting fatter. Yes, I know as a doctor I can't say these things. Did you see the article in the papers? There are currently around four hundred people suing the NHS for embarrassing them about their size. One was a lady of huge dimensions who required two paramedics to lift her down the stairs into the ambulance. She's claiming damages because she says the one paramedic laughed at her. In fact, he was grimacing and he was subsequently off with a bad back and he's suing the NHS! The world's going mad, Cathy."

"Martin, the circumstances are aggravating a dire situation. The lockdowns over the last two years resulted in many people putting on weight especially due to the rise in alcohol consumption, the NHS is so far behind with the surgical needs of its patients, the changes to general practice and, in particular, the reduction in face-to-face consultations, and please, I am not criticising doctors, I wouldn't dare because you're all so sensitive, but despite the various initiatives, the simple truth is that people are getting heavier, overweight and obese."

"You're well respected for your work at this surgery, Cathy. What's the answer?"

"Can I write you a paper on the subject?"

"Two conditions: it's confidential to me and it's brutal."

"You have a deal, Martin, and, from the sound of it, a screaming baby to see."

Marie listened attentively as Damian took her through, in detail, the events of his summit meeting with Cathy the previous day. The passing traffic on the canal waters and the evening strollers on the towpath were not distracting either of them as they sat in deckchairs placed at the bottom of her garden. She ran her hand through her hair and asked Damian what were his conclusions?

"Conclusions?" he repeated. "Today has been hectic with the accountancy deal being finalised, the appointment with the doctor and the outstanding issues from yesterday." He paused and swatted at a fly that was annoying him. "It was imperative that I came to see you."

"Why?" asked Marie.

"Why?" exclaimed Damian. "We've been building something special."

"Is that in the past tense?" She uncrossed her legs, stood up and waved back at a group of lads on a passing barge. "Cathy is fighting back and I admire her." She laughed. "It's a really clever move to suggest you carry on with me until I break it off. She's not giving you any room to resent her and the admission that she feels responsible for what has happened is seriously crippling."

"What does that mean, Marie. Crippling?"

"She wants to save her marriage and she's shut all the doors to you finding a basis for blaming her. Her condition that you stop the keto diet and then make an appointment with the doctor to discuss it, is stunning. She nets an extra hundred thousand pounds from the sale of your business: this is one seriously scary woman."

Damian also stood up and walked around. He told Marie that he was puzzled by her reaction to the news of the meeting with his wife. She was praising Cathy and offering generous compliments when there must be a chance that he'd succumb to her entreaties and resume married life.

"And get back into her bed," added Marie. "Cathy knows exactly which strings to pull." She grabbed him by his arm as though she did not want any passer-by hearing her words. "Let's stop the amateur dramatics shall we Damian?" She smiled. "You want me to shed buckets load of tears and beg you to stay with me. That will make it so much easier for you. Well, Mr Hannon, you have a big disappointment ahead because I have no intention of doing anything. Look at me, Damian, I am Marie and you already know what that means. We have found a chemistry between us and the thought of spending my future life with you is riveting. But there is a simple condition. The decision is yours and yours alone." She put her hands on his shirt and pulled him round as she pointed to the back door. "The exit is there. Make your choice and walk through that door. I'll immediately disappear out of your life because I can only commit to a relationship with you if it is your decision. Go home and tell Cathy you want a divorce and you'll treat her fairly or go home and re-build your marriage because you stand a ninety-five per cent chance of it working." Marie appeared to hesitate and rub her neck.

"Before you say anything else, Damian, you said "yes" to me in the car park. This situation is entirely of your making and the solution is one only you can decide." She wiped her eyes. "I have never made any stipulations and I have no intention of starting now but I have a life to live. I'm giving you six days and until you've made your decision you cannot come here. You have until midnight next Sunday, six days, when you will send me a text: it will either say 'Thanks Marie' wherein I shall cry my tears, get up the following morning, see my patients and rebuild my life, or it will read 'There's nothing we cannot achieve together', in which case I'll expect you in the evening, you'll stay the night and, in the morning, we'll begin a new life together."

He started to walk towards the exit but turned back. "Six days?" he said.

Marie remained silent, the sinking sun briefly lighting up her partly uncovered body. There was laughter from the canal and a woman shouted out.

Damian edged away as he wondered if this would

be the last time that he would ever see her.

+ + +

CHAPTER FIVE

The day started with Damian noticing the freshly cut flowers on the breakfast table and smelling the poached eggs which were being prepared. He was careful to protect his dark grey business suit which was offset by a plain red tie. He sat down and scanned the headlines in 'The Times': the government was trying to play down the coastal tensions between English and French fishermen. He turned the paper over, scanned the crossword, looked at the clue for 'One Down', 'Fresh buns, adjust heat to brown (8)' and filled in 'sunbathe'.

He held the freshly made pot of tea, poured out two cups and added semi-skimmed milk to each: it was the first time in many months that he had not used unsweetened almond milk. He looked up at his wife who was humming the words to a folk song knowing that within thirty minutes they would both be driving to their respective places of work. Cathy relished being part of the primary health care team and had ironed her blue Smart Scrub Tunic and ensured that the white trims were pressed correctly. She removed her apron and sat down with her husband whereupon they exchanged small talk.

The text message arrived at approximately eight-twenty and he knew, immediately, it felt wrong. Cathy sensed his angst but trod carefully as she wanted to maintain the dignified start to their day. Damian re-read the short missive and spoke the words to her:

"Damian. Can we please have a private Zoom call at nine-thirty: Stuart Oliver, Malkins." She snapped immediately. "Damian, promise me, there is to be no re-negotiation of the sale price. Are we together on this?" He nodded and pushed his half-eaten plate of eggs away from him.

He arrived at the office, nodded towards the receptionist who wasn't there, entered his room, slammed the door closed, went to his desk and picked up the Malkins file. The staff sensed something afoot and no-one tried to either speak to him or enter his territory. At the agreed time the face of Stuart Oliver appeared on his screen, there were no pleasantries and the Malkins partner, having explained that his two colleagues were individually speaking to Glen Shannon and Rachel Smith, came, without any fuss, to the point: Malkins were withdrawing from the proposed transaction. Damian immediately referred to the signing of the memorandum of understanding but he knew that it had no legal status.

"We were surprised that Hannon, Shannon and Smith were so ready for a deal," he continued, "but, in truth, it was only Mrs Hannon who showed any fight." He coughed. "As yesterday progressed all three of us felt uneasy but in the afternoon, Mr Shannon said that he did not think he was capable of being a senior partner and went rambling on about cyclists not being shown enough respect on the road by motorists."

"And Rachel?" asked Damian.

"A real talent and totally lost: at one point she broke down in tears and said it was the baby, but we knew it wasn't."

"And me?"

"You, Damian, are what provincial accountancy is

77

all about. You are respected by everyone: Hannon, Shannon and Smith LLP is you, the staff feed off you, the atmosphere is about Damian Hannon and there's the rub. It's nonsensical that you're giving up your career: you're in your prime. Frankly I can see no point in going any further."

"One final question, please Stuart," stuttered Damian.

"Of course."

"Everything you are saying is about people. What about the business because what is worrying me is that you found things and you're not telling me?"

"We found nothing. You're a bit behind the times but that can be said about most provincial practices. The incident concerning the brothers and the illegal immigrants: we were dazzled by the way in which you and Rachel Smith acted. The file was immaculate, Rachel's notes were written up correctly and your letter of resignation was a masterpiece. But that was not what really impressed us. Nowhere in the file, apart from one brief comment by Rachel, is there any mention of the loss of the eight thousand pounds audit fee. I can think of many senior partners who would have been crying in their soup. We all applauded that: anything else, Damian?"

There was nothing else and Stuart Oliver's face disappeared from the screen just as Glenn Shannon walked into his office, sat down and stunned his partner.

"The letters have not gone out and I think the three redundant members of staff should go. I never wanted to be a partner and I hate it. It's your show, you run it, Damian, and you are bloody good at what you do." He handed him a scribbled note. "This is my proposal. I resign as a partner and you'll pay me one hundred thousand pounds over five years at a rate of twenty thousand pounds a year starting next January because you can't afford it this year. I have written down my salary but will only take fifty per cent until next year because we're in a hole. I will be retiring in six years and, until then, I'll give you everything I have to offer: just keep me out of office politics. Agreed?"

"The partnership name: it's an expensive and prolonged business to change it," said Damian.

"Is six months ok?"

Glen left the office as he told Damian that Rachel would be coming in which she promptly did, almost brushing past her former partner colleague. She sat and sipped her coffee and was perplexed when Damian asked where was his? When she said that she thought that was not allowed by the keto diet she blinked as she was told that keto was a thing of the past. She placed her carton on the desk, went out and could be heard talking to Louisa, who, minutes later, delivered a latte to her boss.

"Louisa, before you go," said Damian, "I think I might have called you Lucy by mistake once or twice, I do apologise."

"Apology readily accepted, Mr Hannon," she smiled. "You've been calling me Lucy for the last three months."

Rachel sat still and had her head down. When asked if she knew about Glen Shannon's decision, she nodded her head. She remained impassive as Damian suggested it was now just the two of them. She looked up and seemed tired.

"There's been a change in my life," she said.

"The baby?" exclaimed Damian.

"Baby Smith is fine, thanks Damian. It's the other baby that's the problem."

She drank her coffee and began a detailed explanation of her weekend. Husband Matt had been told by his employer that he was unlikely to reach international rugby standard and they had reviewed his position. He would remain a member of the squad but his first team appearances would be limited to when the international players were not available. His salary was to be cut by half; he would be given a three-year contract but he had to hand back his car.

"How do you feel about that, Rachel?" asked Damian.

"Concern, at first, for Matt but he told me that they were right. To me he's massive but at six foot, two inches and sixteen stones, he's being dwarfed by the newer generation. He told me about a game against a northern side who were importing forwards from South Africa. The Springboks are huge and the game became ill-tempered. They had a new lock forward who was six foot ten inches tall: at one point, Matt tried to hit him on his jaw and missed by three inches."

Damian laughed and moved the file on his desk.

"In truth, the club are being fantastic because Matt knew in his heart that he was not going to make it. They have a link with the university and are paying for him to take a degree in history: he's going to be a teacher."

"History!"

"A man of hidden depths, Damian. He'll make a great schoolmaster. He's already started telling baby Smith about the kings and queens of England: he can name the lot."

"Where does this leave you?" he asked.

"It makes me the main breadwinner: we don't even

have the money to buy Matt a car."

"Perhaps Glen has a spare bike."

"We knew last night that the deal was off. The atmosphere changed throughout the day and Glen and I stayed behind. You thought I had gone home but I came back: for the first time I felt a warmth. I'm not sure I'd want to be on a desert island with him but he's genuine. Have you accepted his terms?"

"Yes, exactly as he wanted."

"Harry Kane! At last, you are beginning to make some right decisions." She smiled. "Lead me to my desk, Damian, and watch me earn fees." She hesitated. "I'm going to take three months maternity leave for the sake of my baby but I've spoken to the audit team and they'll send me any priority work."

"Please stay for a few minutes, Rachel," he requested.

Damian talked through the effects of Glen's move sideways. His concern, emphasised by their brush with Malkins, was that they were thin on the ground at senior level. He said that accountancy was changing and they needed to get up to speed.

"Buses always come in threes, Damian," said Rachel. "I have a friend who's looking for a job."

"What's her name?"

"Lydia Pennington. She can be here at three o'clock."

Marie spent her fifteen minutes break sitting on the wall where Damian had first collected her. However hard she tried she could find no way to break her self-imposed agreement. Six days, perhaps a few hours less, and she wanted to hear his voice as her anxiety grew that it was giving his wife far too long to secure their marriage. She was certain that eventually they would split but that might take months and, from her viewpoint, Damian would be lost to her. She went through her options but there was simply no way she could act before Sunday evening. She imagined their dinner together tonight as Cathy used her culinary skills to eradicate the remains of his keto diet. He would put on the pounds but he'd still have the physical allure that would attract any woman and the problem was that it would be to Cathy's bed where he was heading. She slapped her thigh: six days! What had she been thinking?

"My name is Lydia Pennington and I want you to explain, in as much detail as you can, your business plan for the next two years."

Damian stared at Mrs Lydia Pennington FCA and then at Rachel.

"I thought I was interviewing you?" he said.

"You should be leaping around in relief that I'm available," said the interviewee, "although from what I hear you have been doing just that."

He looked her up and down and decided that she was pencil thin and bodily straight from the top of her glossy black hair, she wore a pair of Dior Stellaire 01 glasses, was dressed in an immaculate business suit, and she had a posture that would have pleased an army sergeant on the parade ground, down to her Dangle Anklet: he was not to know that she had been attracted by its name: 'Silver Dreamcatcher'.

"I've been in touch with my friend Rachel for a long time and she had suggested I might want to consider joining her at this practice. Apart from the fact you can't afford me I had intended staying in London with one of the big four firms. However, lockdown changed all that and my husband and I have decided to make lots of money, retire, sail round the world in our catamaran and retrace the voyages of Captain Cook."

"Good luck round the Cape of Good Hope," said Damian. "How many job interviews have you undertaken."

"Seventeen."

"How many offers have you had?"

"None."

"Any reason why?"

"I speak my mind and accountants like you don't like it. May I please ask you some questions? Where's your entrepreneurs' club?"

"What entrepreneurs' club?"

"The one you should be leading in your business community. The Treasury is pouring money into the revival of the economy and you are at the top of the tree. You have a massive personality and the ability to help entrepreneurs develop their fledging businesses and what about your computer system?"

"What about our computer system?"

"It was designed by Methuselah. You seem not to understand that the modern world is about information sharing: do you recall the Prime Minister's adviser Dominic Cummings? He was ahead of his time and some of the papers he has written have been visionary."

"What a pity he decided the rules did not apply to him?" said Damian.

"And what is the firm's policy about climate change? Are you discussing with your clients about their own responsibilities?"

"I'm a fucking accountant, Lydia," he snapped.

"The business employs thirty-seven people, we act for around one hundred and seventy clients, we pay our taxes and I am treasurer of our local rugby club."

"Pathetic. You're a dinosaur, Damian. You've been adding up columns of figures for too long. Auditing is a process and the rules are very clear and understandable: just make sure you are always polite to the regulators."

"So, what am I?" he asked.

"Take that incident with Rachel and the brothers. That's what you are: it was totally responsible to make the decision you did and, from what I hear, when you could ill afford to lose the audit fee. You are a leader, a consummate professional and it's about time you started acting like one."

"Who does the work, who earns the fees?"

"Your thirty-seven members of staff. You empower them, form cluster groups so that all aspects of the business are covered: you are a figurehead. Auditing is a licence to print money providing you create elite teams who trust each other. The objective is to build a reputation where every business in the community wants to be able to say "we're audited by Hannon, Shannon and Smith" and they'll pay the fees. What car wash to do you use?"

"Car wash! Er … the one on the by-pass."

"Why?"

"To suggest having the car cleaned is too simplistic for you."

"How much do they charge?"

"I've no idea, except I do remember because I was a pound short last time: I must pay it when I call in. It was twelve pounds for just a wash which is quite expensive."

"There will be cheaper car washes in the town. Why do you go there?"

Damian looked at Lydia and noticed that Rachel was absorbed by their banter. He recalled that he went to this particular carwash because there was a foreman, a rotund East European who ruled the business with a rod of iron. He seemed to know every client and when the car was ready, he'd inspect it and ball out his staff if there were any defects. He told Lydia about him.

"Does he clean the cars, Damian?"

"No, he creates the whole atmosphere."

"I rest my case."

He paused and read several sheets of paper in front of him.

"Your career record is seriously impressive and your fellowship of the institute at quite a young age suggests others have thought that. What salary do you want, Lydia?" asked Damian, "and when can you start?"

"Here's a list of my requirements" she said pushing a piece of paper towards him.

Damian scanned the sheet and put it down. He said that he'd pay a salary of sixty per cent of what she was asking, holiday entitlement would be five weeks, he'd been thinking about health insurance and he would action that once she became a permanent member of staff and she'd report to Rachel. She would, initially, be on a three-month probation and Rachel needed to obtain her references. She stood up and glared at him.

"I'll start in the morning," she said. There's work to be done."

The two friends left his room allowing Damian to dictate a contract into his dictaphone. As he finished, Rachel came back into the office.

"Fancy living dangerous, Rachel?" he smiled.

"She's a pussycat," she replied. "That's one hell of a good decision you've just made, Damian." She turned but stopped because Damian had a request to make.

"Can I have the rugby shirt back, please? I'm due to see Arthur."

"It's in the car," laughed Rachel.

Marie arrived home at around five o'clock and decided against pouring herself a glass of wine. The last patient had been challenging: the lady was, perhaps, a little plump and made it clear with a series of moans and groans that she did not feel comfortable in the chair. Marie was not sure how it happened but, at one point, she was cleaning plaque away from the patient's upper teeth when the lady seemed to jump up and the scaler sliced into her upper mouth.

Mayhem followed and Mr Choudhary was called in, initially calming the situation and then reassuring the customer that there was no laceration of the skin and just some soreness on which he pasted an antiseptic cream. That was not sufficient for the injured party who proclaimed that she'd never allow the hygienist to treat her again. As she was leaving the building Marie saw that Mr Choudhary was watching her.

After returning home she changed into her running gear, locked up the house and covered around ten miles along the side of the canal before reaching back home, showering and finishing the bottle of wine. She went to her piano and played several Chopin Etudes before bashing out on the keyboards three jazz classics. When she finished, she realised that she was crying because there was absolutely no way that Cathy Hannon would let go of her husband.

Mrs Hannon was not in the mood to take prisoners.

"You're a pathetic sex-obsessed fool," she yelled. "You've lost our future: I had secured the deal: Stuart Oliver gave me his word."

Damian had told Cathy about the day's events emphasising how he'd taken command and secured the support of the staff but he managed to underestimate her venom.

"You've given away the route to our future," she yelled. "The three hundred and fifty thousand pounds was our passport out of the financial mess you've created. You've lost our savings, taken on bank loans and credit card debts, you're behind on the pension payments, you've reduced your drawings and Glen Shannon has seen straight through you with a clever deal that leaves him well placed and with no partnership liabilities." Cathy had more to say. "As for Mrs Smith! She's wrapped you around her little finger and she's still taking three months maternity leave. Chinese women drop their children in the fields and carry on farming the rice."

Damian decided the conversation was becoming hysterical but made yet another misjudgement and told Cathy about Lydia Pennington in glowing terms.

"Oh please, Damian, save me the details. She's blonde, busty and told you that you are wonderful."

"Not quite," he said, "but Cathy, it was you who talked on Sunday about rebuilding our marriage. I now have Glen's share of the partnership and a clear vision on how we'll create our future. Did I tell you that we are launching an Entrepreneurs' Club?"

"I'll phone Stuart Oliver in the morning and revive the deal," she said.

"Course you will," acknowledged Damian.

He went out, got into his car and drove around the streets of the town. He stopped near to Marie's home and agonised on whether to call in. She had been emphatic about the six days and he was not prepared to take any risks.

Nurse Catherine Margaret Hannon was starting a journey of fulfilment empowered by a single word. She had been mandated by Dr Martin Armstrong to write a confidential paper on the issue of overweight patients and it was to be 'brutal'. She pushed away her freshly made pot of tea, opened up the laptop and created a new document realising that it needed a title. The words began to appear on the screen: 'The Obesity Crisis'. This is what she faced every day in the surgery as patients experienced the consequences of carrying too much weight and she was expected to help them lose the pounds. Cathy had been playing around in her mind with a structure for her dissertation and shrewdly rejected any personal narrative. She decided to go back to basics and question the whole rationale for labelling the situation as a 'crisis.' She gathered together the notes she had written when searching the internet for the information she required.

Following an introduction, which was addressed to Dr Armstrong, repeated his request and set out her objectives, she input her first heading: 'What is Obesity?' She groaned as she reflected on the human bodies she was expected to deal with in her clinic. To her surprise the words flowed as she explained that obesity is a medical condition in which excess fat has accumulated to the extent that it might affect the patient's health. She knew that the problem was that obese people generally stored much of their surplus fat deep inside the abdomen where it wraps around the pancreas, liver and other vital organs.

Called visceral fat, it may pollute the blood with molecules that can cause inflammation which, in turn, can lead to cardiovascular health issues.

She took her refreshments to the draining board, went to the cabinet and poured herself a vodka and tonic as she wondered when Damian would return home. She re-read her opening paragraph and awarded herself a silver star. It was a good start. Her mind wandered as she recalled a man of about fifty-five years old who was desperate to lose weight. She believed that his best hope was a gastric band but this optimum remedy was not available following the pandemic and the lengthening of hospital waiting lists and he did not have the ten thousand pounds in personal assets to pay for it privately. He had sat on her couch with the rolls of fat pouring over his shorts and had pleaded with Cathy to help him.

She added her next heading: 'How do you measure obesity?' She hesitated because she reflected that Dr Armstrong might take offence at this as every day in his surgery, he used the NHS Body Mass Index (BMI) calculator to ascertain a patient's condition which was achieved by relating the individual's height divided by their weight with the computer programme adding in age, sex, ethnic group (optional) and activity level (less than thirty minutes a week is inactive). A reading of over thirty defines obesity and Cathy now let rip. She had serious doubts about the efficacy of this method which she believed led to unnecessary patient suffering. She input her concerns including the conundrum that the BMI did not differentiate between excess fat, muscle and bone. One of her patients had panicked when she had used the NHS calculator on its website and found that she had a BMI of thirty-two when, in fact, she had a serious eating disorder.

Cathy had experimented with the waist-hip ratio (WHR) which used a calculation involving the circumference of the narrowest part of the waist and dividing it by the measurement round the widest part of the hips. The tables defined normal weight as below .80 for women and below .90 for men, the difference being that the female pelvis is wider so allowing the passage of a baby's head during childbirth. When one of the doctors in the practice discovered that if obesity, as defined by WHR, was used instead of the BMI, the proportion of people categorised as 'at risk' of a heart attack increased threefold and he banned its use.

She saved her document and closed down the laptop feeling well pleased with the start of her paper for Dr Armstrong. She was looking forward to letting rip on her favourite medical topic, 'losing weight'. It was so simple: the male needs two thousand, five hundred calories a day to maintain good health and a woman two thousand. Excess calories are stored as fat and so dieting is simple. All the individual has to do is to consume less than their daily ration of calories and the body will use its stored fat to main its energy, in effect its heating. Why then could patients not lose weight?

She thought that she had heard every excuse known to man (and woman) but of one thing she was certain. Patients lied to themselves let alone to her. She went into the lounge and watched the news headlines before she was aware that her husband had arrived home. A few minutes later he joined her and gave the impression of being jaded, which, Cathy judged, was his own fault for losing their deal.

Damian's mood did not improve on hearing that Cathy had phoned their son and told him that his father was coming to see him on Thursday.

"I've a business to run," he pleaded.

"We agreed that you would see Arthur and if you've time to have relationships with younger women you must have time for your son?"

A few minutes later Cathy announced that she was going to bed: Damian followed her up the stairs to her bedroom where she opened the door, went in and closed it in his face, so he went back downstairs and sat in the lounge. The silence seemed to accentuate his feeling of desolation: his approach to life was to be orderly and on top of management responsibilities as demonstrated by his office which was a model of organisation. His mental checklist was a way of deciding priorities but the list at the moment was conflicting; Cathy, their relationship, the business, the upheavals, Rachel and Glen moving the goal posts, the arrival of Mrs Pennington, Arthur, his situation and financial problems, his imposed decision to give up the keto diet and Marie.

Marie and five days to go until he made his decision. He tried to rationalise how he had arrived at his present position, had he made mistakes and how did he regain the initiative? He decided that tomorrow would be a new dawn: Damian Hannon would be back in charge. It was the only way he could live his life. He climbed the stairs to his bedroom and prepared for bed. But sleep would not come as he thrashed around trying to create order from chaos. He sat up and stared out of the window at the stars in the clear sky.

"Hell," he cried out, "I'm in a mess."

He settled down again but found that sleep was some time away.

Rachel was cradling Matt's head in her lap as they tried to work out their best option for purchasing a car which they decided was solved by taking out a personal contract plan on a Vauxhall Astra.

"Not quite my image," he laughed "but ideal for a history master."

"You're happy about the way things are working out?" asked Rachel.

"I had been coming to the realisation that modern rugby was becoming a step too far for me, Rachel. The speed of decision-making is such that a fraction of a second, a delayed pass, a missed tackle, a high ball fumbled can all lead to the loss of a match and the atmosphere afterwards in the changing room with the coaches, the fitness staff, the medics: winning is everything." He pulled himself up. "Then the chairman comes in. He's bankrolled the club and getting into Europe is everything. The pressure is unrelenting."

"But isn't that modern life, Matt? Everything is about winning: look at our politicians, being in power is the sole criteria." Rachel hugged her husband.

He patted her bump, said that was a bit profound for him and reassured her that becoming a history teacher was good to go as far as he was concerned.

"How many wives did Henry the Eighth have?" he chuckled.

Rachel suggested "too many" and reminded Matt that he was only having one. She then told him about the events at work and the appearance of Lydia who they had met in London at various times.

"That's an interesting development," said Matt. "I

thought that she was a high-flier?"

"You and me both," said Rachel, "but something has happened. She certainly gave Mr Hannon a run for his money although he did deal with her rather well. It's a risk, Matt, but she has the capacity for giving us all a kicking which is what we need. Tomorrow should be interesting."

+ + +

CHAPTER SIX

They had been courteous at the breakfast table although he felt that Cathy's thoughts were elsewhere. She left for the surgery before him because he wanted to take a detour to the office. At nine o'clock he was at the carwash situated on the by-pass and was enjoying the fresh air. He had handed over the keys because he wanted a full valet of his vehicle despite the advertised cost of eighteen pounds: his phone was turned off and he was watching the team of men and women go to work. When the interior had been thoroughly overhauled, and he watched one of the cleaners hoover the carpets until they were as good as new, the car was taken into the wash area. He spotted the foreman who was controlling the process and pointing with his finger. Kaspar Koppel had arrived from Estonia seven years earlier after a phone call with his cousin and, despite his home country prospering in the European Union, he was on the cross-channel ferry two weeks later to take over the business: his wife and three children followed him a year later. The only visible change was his waist-line.

Damian realised that Kaspar was standing by him holding out a carton of steaming coffee: the closure of the keto diet was making his life somewhat easier. He thanked him and the Eastern European moved over to his car, opened a back door, stopped the washing, shouted at the girl who had come running over and who was on her knees rubbing furiously at a previously unobserved stain in the carpet. The washing was completed and the drying team took over producing a result that took Damian's breath away. His black Mercedes looked immaculate as he handed over a twenty-pound note and told Kaspar to keep the change. As he drove to his office, he decided that Lydia had made a good point.

The first thing that hit him was the flowers on Louisa's reception and the desk which he sensed had been cleaned.

"Secret admirer?" laughed Damian.

"Mrs. Smith."

"The flowers are from Rachel?" he queried.

"Mrs Smith telephoned me last night and asked if I would mind coming in at eight o'clock: these were on my reception when I arrived. I'm glad I did because I was able to have five minutes with Giddy Liddy."

"Who is Giddy Liddy?" he asked.

"Mrs Pennington. She said that I have an important job in the office: "you only get one chance to make a first impression" she told me. The lads have already named her 'Giddy Liddy'."

Damian hurried to his office, turned on the computer, looked at his appointments, checked his mobile and registered one recorded message. He went into the main office, which was pleasingly industrious, and spotted that his new recruit was working at a desk in the middle. He rushed up, apologised and told her that her office on the first floor was being made ready for her. She stood up and operated a small hand-held air hooter which emitted a piercing noise: there was laughter and applause in equal measure.

"Team, Lydia speaking," she said in a firm voice. "Decision time: do you want me to relocate to an office on the first floor: if so, please cheer?" There were two muffled sounds in the room until a phone rang. Lydia was in full flight. "Do you want me to remain here watching what you are doing and making your lives a misery?" There was an explosion of whistles, cheers and laughter. "Decision made," she announced. Damian saw that Rachel was standing at his side and nodded towards his office.

"What is going on, Rachel?" he pleaded.

"Mrs Lydia Pennington FCA has arrived," she said. "We agreed to meet here at eight o'clock this morning and it gave me the chance to introduce her to our people as they arrived." She laughed. "I've never worked with her: we met at a conference some years ago, became friends and have followed each other's careers." Rachel laughed again. "She never walks, she strides around and she already knows many of the names."

"Did you believe all this stuff about making money and sailing round the world in a catamaran?" asked Damian as Rachel sat down.

"Just before lockdown, in fact the previous autumn, she went missing and we lost contact. When she did re-appear, she offered no explanations and I did not push it. In truth I was pleased to get her back: she's seriously bright and can be funny."

"What happened to her?"

"I don't know, Damian, but I can tell you one thing. I think she's looking for a home."

At that moment there was a knock at the door and in came their new recruit. Lydia sat down and said that she was surprised that Damian was late for work which resulted in an accusation that it was her doing because he wanted to check out the carwash. He continued digging a hole because she pointed out that eight-thirty, his usual time of arrival, to the present time, two hours was four point seven per cent of his working week and, so far, he had contributed nothing to the business.

"It's my bloody business, Lydia," he yelled.

"No, it isn't, Damian. It's our business, all thirty-eight of us."

"You're including yourself in the staff numbers?"

"From eight o'clock this morning, yes I am," she snapped.

"May I please point out, Lydia, that you are on three months' probation." whereupon she smirked and returned to her desk.

Rachel stood up and moved towards the door.

"Damian, excuse me being blunt, but I think it is you who's on probation."

Damian stared at her and then remembered that he had something to ask her.

"I'm not in tomorrow, Rachel, I'm away for the whole day."

Rachel laughed, and said he must make sure that he brings back some decent business.

"That's rather the issue," said Damian. "I'm away on a personal matter."

"Ah," said Rachel. "I suspect that Giddy Liddy will be going into super orbit!"

Marie's day started well following a decision to read an online newsletter to which she subscribed as part of her research and understanding of the complexities of climate change. The article was centred around the phenomenon that polar whales were rediscovering their old habits in the Arctic and Southern oceans after centuries of being hunted near to extinction. She shuddered as she read that over a period of seventy years more than one million whales had been killed but following the end of commercial whaling there were signs of recovery. Marie felt her spirits lifting as she studied the photographs of the western Arctic bowhead whales rising out of sea.

She had washed her uniform last night following the afternoon's catastrophic incident with her patient: she went over and over the flash point where the scaler slipped into the roof of the patient's mouth: it had never happened before and it shouldn't have occurred with all the safety procedures they followed. The remaining memory she was dealing with was the action of Mr Choudhary in watching her leave the building. She convinced herself that with her record of service and regular testimonies from her patients, the matter would be forgotten.

Marie went in early and cleaned her clinic from top to bottom, checked all the equipment and read carefully the notes of her six appointments for the day. Mr Choudhary had smiled at her and the day's agenda went well including one patient where she called in a dentist following the discovery of a black scab almost hidden from view at the back of the mouth. Her colleague, Freddie, who was rapidly becoming a key member of Mr Choudhary's team, patted her on the back after the patient left to book an appointment with her doctor. "Not sure, Marie, but definitely needs investigating. Good spot, kid."

"Kid," Marie mused. "I'll take that" she thought to herself. She completed her work and was pleasantly surprised to find Mr Choudhary waiting outside her door. He asked if she could spare him a few moments.

"Why?!" she exclaimed as Mr Choudhary sat back

after delivering the news. "You've never done this with anyone else?"

Marie was told that as part of her continuous professional development she had been booked in for a week at Portsmouth University. He'd a friend who ran the degree course in dental hygiene and dental therapy and he had agreed that Marie could join the programme.

"But I could teach them!" she argued.

"My friend thought exactly the same and is looking forward to having you in his class," said her employer. "All your expenses will be paid and Mrs Choudhary has found you a pleasant hotel which is a mile away from the university."

"When does this happen?" she asked.

"They are expecting you next Monday," he said. "Mrs Choudhary has organised for a relief hygienist to come in."

Marie stood up, considered resigning her position, rationalised that resistance might prejudice a future employers' reference and realised the idea was beginning to resonate with her: it was a clever move and she'd maximise the benefits of the course. She said that she'd work up to Friday only to hear that she was to leave now to give her time to prepare for her trip. Within minutes she'd decided to travel down the next day and spend three days on the beach sunning herself in the improving temperatures. As she was leaving the practice Mrs Choudhary came up, hugged her and promised to look after her patients until she got back.

Damian decided that the day had provided enough excitement and was preparing to travel home to watch a day/night one day cricket match on television when his mobile buzzed. He read the text message: '*See me at 7. Mx.*' He sent a reply. '*6 ok?*'. Marie answered in the affirmative and so he stayed at the office until it was time to leave. He looked around the main building and saw that Lydia and Rachel were with a group of staff. He reviewed a pile of files, checked his phone and drove out of the car park reaching Marie's road within thirty minutes. He parked at the side of the house and entered the kitchen where he found her vigorously spring cleaning the whole area. She grabbed a half empty bottle of cider and poured him a glass before sitting on a stool.

She told him the whole story without missing out any of the detail, finished her drink and went to the refrigerator for a second bottle.

"You are leaving in the morning?" he asked.

"Mr Choudhary forced the issue," she replied. "I wanted to see my list through until Friday but I was told to leave immediately. I can see his position because he's responsible for health and safety as well as clinical standards and the accident with the patient has unnerved him."

Damian sipped his cider and stared at his companion.

"What did happen, Marie, I don't understand how the accident occurred?"

"My assistant was not watching at the precise moment and so we have no independent witness but I think the woman jumped up because she was jittery but she says not. The other explanation was that I lost concentration."

"Did you?"

"Possibly," she snapped. "If so, it's the first time in my career."

"Any reason why?" asked Damian.

Marie jumped off her stool and led Damian into the garden. She began by saying that she had been a fool to herself and possibly to him because she realised that in giving Damian six days to make a decision, she had handed the initiative to his wife. She was spending her time imagining the spells that Mrs Hannon was weaving and she was certain there would be the offer of a return to the matrimonial bedroom before too long.

They sat down and Damian began to tell of the events at the accountancy business, explaining the loss of the Malkins deal, the upheaval with his partners, Rachel's news and the explosion from his wife. He stood up and expressed his anger at the changing attitudes.

"One minute we're rebuilding for the future and the next I'm being pilloried for losing three hundred and fifty thousand pounds. She had no sympathy for the stress I'm feeling."

"She's under similar emotional upheaval, Damian: she's fighting for her marriage."

"Is she, Marie, because I'm still of a mind that her direction of travel is to the lawyers?"

He brought some levity to their conversation by detailing the arrival of Mrs Lydia Pennington FCA and her portable air hooter only to face a series of questions. Marie wanted to know everything about 'Giddy Liddy' and didn't bat an eyelid on hearing her nickname. When she heard that Rachel Smith had told him that he was on probation, she nodded her head.

"She's right, Damian," she said. "I like what I'm hearing, and you deserve great credit for the decisions you are making. You've got Rachel back and I accept her situation has changed but she would not have cut her leave unless she was convinced about the future." She paused while she looked out at her inlet and the moored boat. "Mr Shannon is sitting there making you money: smart move Mr Hannon."

"He gave me no choice!" exclaimed Damian.

"He's the smart guy because he worked out what was best for him and thus right for the practice. How's he adapting to Mrs Pennington?"

"I'm not sure that they've met but I would think it'll make the Battle of the Bulge seem like a children's tea party."

"What's the Battle of the Bulge?"

"In the second world war when the Germans fought back after D-Day. Great movie."

"I was born in nineteen hundred and eighty-three, Damian. Why should I know about wars that took place almost forty years earlier and who won?"

He laughed and said that it was a question, following the painful Brexit years, that some people still ask."

They decided to walk along the towpath and became lost in their individual thoughts until he asked the key question.

"Where does all this leave us?" asked Damian.

"I never imagined that things would work out like this," she said as they arrived back at her garden.

"You are leaving tomorrow morning," surmised Damian," and will be away just over a week. All I can suggest is that we get together on your return and talk things over."

Marie came up to him and put her arms around his neck.

"How did we get ourselves into this mess?" she

asked. "Will you stay in contact with me?"

"Every day," promised Damian.

"I've made the bed," she said.

"That's for when you return," he said, kissing her gently, giving a final hug before moving towards the exit gate.

Cathy Hannon opened up her laptop and called up the document 'The Obesity Crisis', re-read her work from the previous evening and was pleased with her efforts: she had set the scene and now she was reaching the section that mattered most to her: the issuing of losing weight. The Department of Health and Social Care, before the pandemic had really taken hold, published a paper which stated that sixty-three per cent of the population were either overweight and/or obese which worked out to around thirteen and half million people. She related that to her own environment: her surgery had around eight thousand patients of whom six and half thousand were over the age of eighteen. Her fingers flew over the calculator and she established that perhaps two thousand of the patients were obese.

During the working week she met with about eighty to ninety men and women (perhaps on a ratio of one to two) of whom about thirty were referred to her for weight loss counselling rather than specific illnesses such as type two diabetes where the doctor would have already set out a treatment plan or hospital referral. There was a standard procedure of weight measurement and calculation of the BMI, establishing the wishes of the patient, dietary advice, local slimming clubs, walking groups, swimming classes, gyms, cycling, weight-loss apps and other newly designed methods. She spent much of her time explaining specific dietary options and then there was the issue of alcohol consumption.

Cathy's favourite patient challenge, especially for the men, was to establish how many units of alcohol they drank each week, multiply by two or three depending on her assessment of the individual (most lied over the amount they drank) and convert the result into calories. She'd then show a picture of a pint of lager and of a piece of pizza and ask which contained the more calories? The answer did not matter (both have around two hundred calories) because all she was attempting was to get the patient to think statistically: her approach was to get the individual to think two and half thousand calories for men and to discipline their consumption within this limit. She knew that most men would promise to adopt her approach before leaving the surgery and going to the pub.

Her female patients were more demanding and knowledgeable and in general offered greater commitment to the losing of weight. She had more success particularly as she had the personal quality of gaining an empathy but the tragedy was that, time and again, the patient would lose weight and then put it back on again. Cathy thought there were more tears shed in her clinic than at a showing of Romeo and Juliet.

She set out to summarise her musings for the paper to Dr Armstrong and focused on the more meaningful section which was where she offered solutions, the problem being that she didn't have any. This was not going to be as straight forward as she had at first imagined.

What Cathy Hannon did not know at that moment in time was the remarkable achievement of one of her patients in losing around eighteen pounds with the potential of reducing much further. It was a story where the seeds of success were sown in a staff canteen. The individual was aware of talk which had circulated the rumour mill but it was a chance meeting when attending a motorway crash involving three HGVs and a number of cars and resulting in three fatalities that a comment, in answer to a question, led to a hospital in Latvia.

Inspector Paul Marston of the Bedfordshire constabulary was not long out of hospital and back on duty partly because of a need to retain his salary in order to settle his maintenance payments to his ex-wives. He was called to the incident to assess the length of time the motorway needed to be closed and found himself in conversation with a paramedic who was waiting for the fire crews to open up a car wreckage to allow them to attend to the crushed driver. The medic made a joke about the inspector's physical size only to find that he was required to hear about Marston's brush with hospital and the news that there was no funding for bariatric surgery. He proffered a possible solution which grabbed the inspector's interest and, later that night, he used the internet to ascertain the information he needed.

Events moved quickly in that he filled in the questionnaire and two days later had an online consultation with Dr Troickis, clinical director of surgery at Riga hospital in Latvia. His BMI, which the hospital had recorded at 36, qualified him for surgery and there followed an explanation that the procedure would not involve a gastric bypass, despite its high rate of success. The operation was complicated because it required two joins in the stomach. This could lead to absorption issues and a requirement for the individual to take supplements to provide the necessary nutrients needed by the body. Dr Troickis recommended a sleeve gastrectomy involving the stapling off of a portion of the stomach and removing the excess, effectively turning it from a pouch into a sleeve. The medical practitioner, speaking in near perfect English, explained to his potential patient, that because no part of the stomach is bypassed, nutrients are absorbed in the usual way. Dr Troickis cautioned that because food consumption would be less there would still be a need for some supplements.

Paul Marston became convinced that this was a route for him to follow especially when he was told that the success rate could lead to seventy per cent excess weight loss which was better than the figures for the gastric bypass with the added attraction that the recovery period was shorter.

It took the police officer nearly two weeks to raise the finance required. He used his three credit cards up to their maximum limits, borrowed various sums from several younger police officers two of whom felt a degree of intimidation, sold some furniture, cashed in his premium savings bonds and secured the remaining amount from his girlfriend. Two weeks later he paid the fee of just under five thousand pounds, flew to Riga on the southern shores of the Baltic Sea, had the operation, spent five days in hospital and returned home. He consulted a private doctor when back in England because he did not want to chance meeting up with nurse Cathy Hannon for whom he had other ideas. The operation was a success and his recovery remarkable albeit he was driven by his plans for revenge.

He had a daughter, Scarlett, who he had not met although he had her address, as a result of sex with a woman twenty years ago whose husband drove around the town in an expensive Mercedes and was held up as a leading business man. Marston's girlfriend was delighted with his physical improvement and change in self-confidence, so much so that she agreed to pay for them to have a week's holiday in the Mediterranean sun.

As he recovered Marston continued to be obsessed with the words which nurse Hannon had spoken to him in the surgery which insulted him. He recalled the evening in the garden: he was forging his career in the police but accepted he was a willing partner. She was frantic and almost clawing at him: it happened and then she came to see him which is when he realised the possible damage to his promotion prospects. He threatened her, or rather her husband, and heard no more although he learned that she'd given birth to a baby daughter.

When he met Cathy again in the surgery nearly twenty years later, at a time when his health was a worry, he was at a low point. He regretted pinching her bottom but nothing justified the words she had spoken humiliating his sexuality. It was time for revenge and he wrote his letters managing to find Scarlett's address through the misuse of a police computer. Then his medical journey took over but now he was back and in receipt of several legal demands from lawyers acting for one of his ex-wives whereupon he was, effectively, told to take early retirement from the police force. He was able to cash in a lump sum from his pension and pay off his debts.

He and his girlfriend caught a plane to the Costa del

Sol where, after two days, they had a massive row, he slapped her face, she flew back to England, collected her belongings and moved out of the house leaving behind a written demand for repayment of the money she'd advanced to him.

He stayed on and, by chance, met a criminal, now out of prison and living in the sun, who he'd arrested some years earlier. There were no hard feelings and the beers flowed at the night-club bar. As he listened to tales of retribution and the simplicity when it came to removing rivals an idea began to grow in his mind as he blamed all his misfortunes on Cathy Hannon. She should have got rid of the child as he had argued. The following day, as he applied suntan cream to his flattening stomach, he decided that he would remove one of the three: Cathy Hannon, Scarlett Hannon or Damian Hannon. But which one? He pondered on how he would make his selection and started to look forward to the next few weeks.

CHAPTER SEVEN

The informal meeting took place in the Board Room at the offices of Hannon, Shannon and Smith. Lydia Pennington was the self-appointed chairperson and neither Glen Shannon nor her friend Rachel seemed unduly concerned. She had told Lydia that Damian was away for the day and watched a shrug of the shoulders. Lydia announced that there were several matters which required immediate discussion and review.

Glen Shannon was enthused by the first matter which involved Lydia holding up a copy of the monthly practice newsletter which was emailed to all clients and asking what were the benefits of the exercise? Glen said that it was a total waste of time and money but Damian was never willing to discuss it with him. She asked if there were any contents in this edition which could benefit a client and on receiving negative responses pointed out that any self-respecting business would be using the internet to obtain current information. She said that the HMRC website had improved out of all recognition and their clients, in the main, would be using it to obtain their tax and other information. She stood up and walked around the room.

"The modern world is moving at a pace that we've never seen before and this newsletter makes us look like out-of-date provincial accountants," she said.

"Which is what we are," agreed Glen.

"No, Glen, what you meant to say is 'which is what we were'".

"Tread carefully, Lydia," cautioned Rachel, "this is something dear to Damian's heart. He won't agree with you."

"It's a good job I'm not asking him. We pay two thousand pounds an edition from the publishers and there are ten in a year." She almost snorted. "Twenty thousand pounds, I ask you! Glen, how many clients pay more than that in annual audit fees?" She smiled. "I'll save you the trouble because the answer is thirty-six."

"Shall I add it to the agenda for the next partners' meeting?" asked Rachel.

"No point," said Lydia. "There's three of us and we all agree to discontinue it, so the decision is made."

"Will you tell Damian?" asked Rachel who decided not to point out to Lydia that she was not yet a partner.

"He already knows because I've emailed him. He must learn not to take days out of the office unless he's bringing in new business which takes me to item number two. I worked through the night but don't let that concern you, I don't need much sleep, so here's a list of our clients and an annotation as to who is the partner in charge. You'll see on the right-hand side, I've re-allocated each client but Glen, let me explain, because you face changes. I've moved your bottom five accounts and allocated them to Rachel. I've given you nine of Damian's accounts because you're our big hitter."

"Fantastic," responded Glen. "I've suggested this approach many times: my immediate reaction is that I'll increase my chargeable earnings by perhaps seven or eight per cent."

"Don't undersell yourself, Glen, because this is your revenue target for the coming year," continued Lydia as she placed a piece of paper in front of him and handed one to Rachel. Glen nodded albeit cautiously.

"Rachel, I've given you several of Glen's accounts and two from Damian."

"And you've taken all but five of Damian's accounts," she exclaimed.

"Of course, and you'll see that my own new business target is ambitious."

"But," said Rachel, "what about Damian?"

"Damian is our number one new business getter. Instead of messing around with client newsletters, he'll be out there chasing the big accounts and so I have expressed his target differently because what I want him to do is to bring in four new accounts each with a minimum audit fee of fifty thousand pounds."

"Where does he find those from?" asked Glen.

"I promise you they're out there," said Lydia.

Damian drove down the motorway towards north London listening to the early news bulletins and reflecting on his mission which had been agreed during his discussion with Cathy. It was time to bring matters to a head with their son, who was becoming increasingly wayward, not only to meet their parental responsibilities but perhaps more so due to their perplexity over his behaviour. He reached the Finchley Road and turned off toward Maida Vale before parking in the road where Arthur rented a flat.

He climbed down some steps to the basement flat, rang a bell which was out of order, knocked on the door which was answered, he entered and fell over a bike in the hallway. He found himself sipping strange tasting coffee and staring at his son who was scruffily dressed. Arthur explained that it was rather early for him as he did not usually get up until eleven or even later. His father simply did not know where to begin but was saved from further indecision when Arthur began talking.

"I did not want you to come, Dad, because it is inevitable that you won't be able to resist giving me the parental lecture which I don't want to hear."

Damian already had his back to the wall and so he decided to go on the attack. He began with several half-hearted compliments, which were disregarded, said that he and his mother loved him but he was to stop asking for money. This backfired because his son nodded his head and said that was agreed.

"I only ask you for money, Dad, because you always say "yes". If you didn't, I wouldn't come to you but it's worth the patronising sermon if you send me the funds. Mum always says "yes" without any fuss because I ask her for small amounts."

"Your mother sends you money!? He paused. "You've been asking your grandparents as well: I understand they paid for your weekend in Spain."

"They did and they were thrilled to do so providing I told them all about our time there. What you must understand is that when you give me money, you do so because it's part of your middle-class image. Mum told me that you felt a sense of shame when I left university. She actually said, "your father does not know how to tell his friends." He stood up and poured himself a beer. "Stuff your friends, you never asked me why I had left and, in truth, I doubt it crossed your mind. Scarlett and I were part of your place in society: successful businessman, lovely house, wide circle of friends, political influences and, in Mum's case, her reputation at the church and two perfect children going through the school system to university, marrying, producing grandchildren and taking care of you in your later years. No wonder you give me money."

Damian stood up as he was reaching the point where he was going to leave the flat and go home. He asked Arthur how he was managing for money and blinked as he was told that their joint income from his job as a barman in the Paddington area and Faria's job in a bank more than gave them a decent living. He asked about Faria only for Arthur to laugh when he said that he knew his father would be impressed by her bank job.

"Are you two serious?" he asked, "You and Faria."

"You wouldn't understand, Dad: there's no point in me trying to explain," he said as he watched his father sit down again.

"Arthur, tell me what you think about your mother and myself. You seem to be keen to, shall I say, denigrate us?"

"Interesting choice of word: 'denigrate'. To be honest I never think about it."

"I've a rugby shirt in the car for you from Matt Smith," said Damian.

"Thanks, I don't want it." He laughed. "I don't play rugby anymore because I need to earn a living." Damian stood up and looked around the flat which was in fairly good condition.

"Do you follow politics?" he asked.

"Both Faria and I are active in the Labour Party. I know that the next General Election is several years away but the Conservatives will not be able to hold on to their northern seats and London will be awash with Labour MPs."

Damian was now facing his son.

"Arthur, would you like to see me again?" he asked.

"Why don't you and Mum invite us for Christmas," he suggested. "I'll let you know when the baby is born."

"What baby?!"

"Faria is four and a half months pregnant which is why we went to Spain so she could have some rest and sun. She works very hard at her job."

"When are you getting married?" Damian asked and added fuel to the fire by pointing out that his son was only just twenty-one years of age.

"We've never discussed it," laughed Arthur. "Sorry Dad, another black mark on the middle-class chart."

"Stop talking about this fucking middle-class thing," he shouted. "We simply did our best for you and Scarlett. You think everything was easy for us but that's because your mother and I did all we could to protect you and to give you the best chance in life. How many of your friends have experienced parental divorce?"

"From what I hear I may be joining them," he said. "How are things with you and Marie, I think that's her name?" He paused. "Don't bother Dad, one of my friends emailed me: apparently the whole town knows. That's fucked your middle-class image, hasn't it?" said a smirking Arthur.

Damian stared at his son and asked to use the bathroom which he discovered was, at best, unhygienic. When he came back, he shrugged his shoulders and moved towards the door.

"I will, obviously, be telling your mother about our conversation and I want to ask you a favour. She'll be the baby's grandmother and I want you and Faria to allow her access: don't cut yourselves off and please let

114

her see her grandchild."

Arthur did not answer his father's request simply opening the door of the flat and walking with him to the car. Somewhat to Damian's surprise his son shook his hand. He drove away, not looking back, towards the M1, joined the motorway and stopped at the services where he bought himself a café latté which he took outside before checking his mobile phone. Rachel asked that he contact her as soon as possible and there was another message:

On way to Portsmouth: there's nothing we cannot achieve together Mx

He stared out at the packed facilities and watched people enjoying themselves. He was running over their conversation and wondering who was the person with whom he'd been in discussion and how could he have handled things better? He found himself becoming emotional as he realised that his world was coming apart and he had no idea how to stop it doing so. When he reached his home town he drove to the canal and walked along the towpath until he reached the inlet and could see into Marie's garden. He desperately wanted her to appear so they could be together but that was not going to happen. He returned to his car and went home after deciding against going to his office. Cathy was in the back garden allowing the sun to start tanning her skin. Damian could not help nodding in admiration of her lithe figure.

She had prepared some refreshments for them.

"Arthur phoned me and said that you would be in bad shape when you arrived here," she said. "I'm going to be a grandmother."

"What else did he say?"

"He thought that you and he had managed your first

115

ever honest conversation."

"Is that what he said?"

"He also said he had challenged you about your girlfriend and he was impressed when I told him that it was out in the open between us."

"Did he ask for any money?"

"Yes, two hundred pounds to buy some things for the nursery."

"And you said "no" I assume."

"I've already sent the funds. It's my grandchild."

"But we agreed that we'd say "no" in future."

"Frankly, Damian, I'm not sure what you and I are saying to each other. It's my money, I've earned it and I have sent it to my grandchild, not for Arthur!"

Marie arrived in Portsmouth during the afternoon, located the University, booked into the Holiday Inn and parked her car having decided to walk everywhere during her nine day stay. As she signed the register, she was pleasantly surprised to be told that all her costs, including breakfast and dinner, were being paid for by a Mrs Choudhary, she unpacked and went downstairs to use the swimming pool. Later on, she walked round the port area and decided to base herself the next day on Southsea Common where, according to the weather forecast, she would be able to absorb a number of hours of sunshine.

She had dinner in the hotel restaurant and moved into the lounge and bar area having ordered a large gin and tonic. She raised her glass to Mr and Mrs Choudhary and silently thanked them in the realisation that they were giving her another chance. She made a vow that she'd maximise the time in the dental classes at the University and ensure that her lecturer's report (she knew that Mr Choudhary would expect that) contained comment on her commitment and enthusiasm. She relished working as a hygienist, was determined to keep her job and realised that she had to achieve her aims.

The stranger did not ask if he could join her, choosing to sit down on the opposite chair, staring at her and then smiling. Marie waited for the inevitable opening line but, to her surprise, he said nothing. She liked his suit and open neck shirt but this was not how it was supposed to play out and she began to feel uncomfortable; it was time to break the ice.

"Are you going to offer to buy me a drink?" she asked.

"Why would I do that?" he asked. "My name is Eric."

"Tell you what, Eric, I'll go and fetch you a drink so what would you like?"

"An orange juice, please," he said looking at his watch. "Ten minutes to go," he murmured.

Marie reached the bar, was delayed by slow service and arrived back as Eric was again studying the time. She apologised for being slow and he dismissed her words saying that he must begin.

"Begin what, Eric?" she asked.

"I'm the pianist here," he said. "I'm due to play from nine until ten-thirty." He finished his drink, nodded towards Marie and walked off: she followed him with her eyes. He reached the baby grand, settled himself on the double stool, flexed his fingers and started to play a Beethoven sonata not flinching when she arrived and sat down with him. As he finished, she asked that she choose the next rendering: he nodded and heard her selection. He began to play Franz Liszt's

Hungarian Rhapsody No 2 which not only began to attract the attention of some of the hotel guests but was added to by Marie playing along with him as they aired one of the world's greatest ever piano duets. They finished with a flourish which resulted in Eric nodding towards her in approval which was the encouragement Marie needed.

She did not ask about their next piece because she was already into The Beatles 'Let It Be' which the people now surrounding them asked to be repeated. This time she not only received a nod from her playing partner but also a glass of champagne which was handed to her by an American judging by his vocal endorsement of the musical pair. Eric took the initiative and commenced playing 'I've Got Rhythm', a Gershwin classic that she adored and joined in, finishing with an arm round her shoulders and a hug. This was cut short as Marie was starting to play Bernstein's 'West Side Story' which caused her to remember the night with Damian and, as the hotel guests started to sing along and they reached 'Somewhere', proved too much for her emotions. She stopped playing, hurried out of the lounge and into the reception area where she slumped into a chair. She wiped her eyes, looked up and realised that Eric had followed her.

"Are you feeling unwell?" he asked.

"Sorry Eric, you must get back to your guests. I loved that session and thanks for allowing me to play with you."

"Best night I've had for ages" he said. "I don't know your name."

"Marie."

"I'll dedicate tomorrow's performance to you,

Marie."

"That's very kind, thanks."

She watched as a woman walked over and kissed Eric on the cheek. He immediately introduced his wife Elaine to Marie and told her about their piano duets. Elaine was polite but said he must finish his playing session, walked off and left Marie on her own.

She sat down and reached for her mobile phone, checking her messages. There was nothing from Damian.

Former police Inspector Paul Marston sat in his lounge and pondered the key question facing him. The examinations he had passed to achieve promotion gave him a sound legal understanding and three years in the CID, a knowledge of forensic procedures. The removal of the individual was the easy bit: getting away with it was somewhat harder. He had already answered the three key questions: how was the elimination to take place, where would it happen and when? He had yet to decide which of the three potential targets he would select. He knew that police the world over feared the sole killer and as he had no police record, he was as elusive as could be.

The first of his three questions he had settled because he wanted to avoid any physical contact with the victim and, even though strangulation was relatively easy, he had decided to use a shotgun with a sawn-off barrel. Since the Dunblane massacre in Stirling, Scotland in 1996 when Thomas Hamilton had shot sixteen pupils and a teacher before killing himself, gun control had significantly tightened up, thus leading to his choice of a shotgun with the additional advantage that the pellets cannot be linked to any particular weapon. He had enough contacts and knowledge to obtain one and to ensure the weapon had not been fired before. He would dispose of it afterwards in a local lake thus eliminating any potential forensic evidence. The location of the hit could not yet be chosen because he had not decided on the victim. He was fairly certain that one of the three would be spared but choosing between the remaining two was more problematic: he could take out two but that increased the risk and defeated the purpose of making the survivors suffer. The third answer he was searching for was more straight forward in that he wanted to kill as soon as possible.

His bitterness was increasing partly because his pension was proving frugal, he had spent all the cash taken out and because the legal letters kept arriving. His stomach sleeve was not healing properly and he was forced to consult with his private doctor who wanted him to go back to Riga and have a second operation. In the interim he was on antibiotics and anti-depressants and becoming increasingly irritable. The doctor's bills were hurting but he could not risk going back to his NHS surgery for fear of coming across Cathy Hannon.

He drank his glass of whisky rather quickly and decided that he'd give himself a week in which to make the final decisions.

Cathy Hannon opened up her laptop and re-read her paper on 'The Obesity Crisis'. She awarded herself another silver star and nodded approvingly at the early paragraphs setting the scene for the key section, 'Some Possible Solutions', before inputting the next heading, 'The Nature of Hunger' which was a topic which never ceased to perplex her. In essence, losing weight was straightforward and she thought back to the patient she had attended during the morning surgery. Amy Rowan was a forty-six-year-old mother of two children whose main burden in life was the caring of her parents. She was well placed financially as her husband was employed at a senior level in the local council, the local schools were respected and Amy had a comfortable lifestyle except she was, according to Dr Armstrong, two stone, twenty-eight pounds, overweight which gave her a BMI of thirty-two and a developing problem with hypertension. She was an only child: her parents were in their eighties, relied mostly on their pensions and had continuing health problems. The bigger dilemma was that they took full advantage of Amy's goodwill which had reached a point where her husband was deriding her willingness to respond to any and every call for help.

Cathy related rather closely to her patient's situation except she did not have a weight problem. They had discussed during a number of visits Amy's inability to adhere to a diet despite nurse Hannon's efforts involving introductions to slimming clubs, innovative diets which they discussed at length, exercise routines and the possible consequences if she did not manage to shed some pounds. To add to the situation Amy was fully aware of the issues but said that, whatever her determination, the moment the telephone rang, it was a signal for a collapse in her resolve. She would drive the three miles to her parents' home, deal with the matter at hand, provide the care needed, drive back and binge eat. To add to the conundrum, her mother in particular, rarely asked for help unless it was needed but it was the second issue that was the real showstopper. On almost every visit her father pleaded with Amy not to put them in a home for the elderly and, on this matter, he was supported, at a distance, by his son-in-law who told Amy lurid stories of events at the several homes run by the council.

This was a situation where logic flew out of the window because all parties understood the position and, in particular, the psychology behind Amy's binge eating: she told Cathy that she almost welcomed her parent's calls because she was spending her evenings waiting for them: thus, on her return, food was the comfort factor especially as she consumed a limited amount of alcohol.

The section on 'The Nature of Hunger' was nearing completion: 'Hunger is controlled by the brain whose objective is to ensure that the body avoids running out of energy which it achieves by generating hunger pains telling the person to consume food. The brain may take the opportunity to seek additional food so overcoming the feeling of fullness.' She pressed 'save' and poured herself a glass of wine before completing the section: 'Assisting the brain is Ghrelin, often called 'the hunger hormone', which is produced by enteroendocrine cells of the gastrointestinal tract mainly in the stomach.'

She paused and reflected on how she was expected to use this knowledge in the brief periods of time she had with each of her patients. She continued writing: 'Ghrelin increases food intake because blood levels are highest before food when the individual is hungry. It helps prepare for food intake by increasing gastric acid secretion and it can promote fat storage'.

Cathy had discussed with her colleagues the prescribing of appetite suppressants but generally, because of the possible side effects, it was not a route taken by the GPs: just occasionally they would prescribe orlistat which worked by reducing the amount of fat absorbed by the body and needed to be part of a low-fat diet.

She closed down her laptop and thought about Amy Rowan because absolutely nothing she had written was of any help to her patient.

+ + +

CHAPTER EIGHT

The attack on the bank, in broad daylight, was as brutal as it was audacious. Two motor cyclists drew up outside the premises, the pillion passenger on the one held the two machines as the raiders ran into the building, one firing a shotgun into the air, shattering the lighting system, while the other grabbed a middle-aged woman at one of the machines and held a handgun to her head.

"Fucking lie down," he screamed at the other four customers who did exactly as they were told. He nodded at his partner in crime who was now at the cashier's screen demanding money. He immediately sensed the staff were delaying following his instructions and fired his shotgun again at the screen which shattered, leading to one of the younger cashiers crying out and collapsing to the floor. This caused the gunman to become even more angry.

The first robber dragged the customer with him to the bullet proof screens and shouted that she'd die if they did not give them money. A dark-suited man was trying to operate a small safe at the rear of the banking hall but was fumbling with the code. The helmeted thug shouted again his warning that unless they were given money someone would die and still the bank official struggled to open the safe door. Suddenly there was a blast from a handgun and the female customer fell to the floor with part of her face missing. Two bags of bank cash were thrown over the screen to the robbers who each grabbed one and ran outside to their bikes being held by their accomplice.

They sped down the high street straight into a police car coming the other way and which was turning into their path. One motorcyclist went straight over the top of the vehicle and suffered broken ribs while the other braked and turned into a side road where he disappeared. He was located, an hour later, by a police helicopter which tracked him hiding in a warehouse and, after a forty-minutes siege, was apprehended by armed police officers. The badly injured customer was taken to hospital where she was pronounced dead on arrival. She was later identified by her husband, a local business man.

Later that afternoon two detectives arrived at the home of former police inspector Paul Marston who had been drinking. They invited themselves into his house and confirmed that he was aware of the events which had taken place earlier in the day. They exchanged some banter and the senior officer gave Marston the names of the two bank robbers which he immediately recognised. They were two local petty criminals, more usually drug trafficking, who had been arrested and charged by the former inspector on several occasions. He thanked the two detectives for informing him about the crime but why were they involving him?

"Because, Mr Marston," said the one, "when we asked the one laddie why he had robbed a bank he said because you told him to do just that."

Paul Marston's memory was in overdrive as he recalled the McMahon Brothers who caused so many problems several years ago and who managed to drive a coach and horses through the station's crime figures. Late one night they had been brought in for theft offences and the inspector found himself in a cell with the younger of the pair. He told the probationary police constable, who was on prisoner watch duties, to look the other way as he kicked Conor McMahon in his thigh. As he rolled around the floor, Marston shouted at him: "Bleedin' two hundred quid you've stolen, and I've got to put you through the soddin' wringer and you're wrecking my figures." He saw that the constable was staring at him and so he held back his second intended assault but continued swearing at his prisoner: "Go somewhere else but don't come back here, you little shit," he shouted. "Alternatively, why don't you do some real crime. Rob a fucking bank."

As the cell was secured and the lock turned, Inspector Paul Marston walked out with the young police officer.

"What did the constable see happen in the cell?" he asked.

"The constable saw the prisoner attack the inspector who defended himself and suffered a blow."

"Write it up in the custody book," he instructed.

Marston recalled the whole occasion and related most of it to the two detectives.

"It was said in the heat of the moment and even the Irish thug would not have taken me literally," he explained. "You surely don't think I had anything to do with the hold-up?"

"It would appear you were taken very seriously," said detective inspector Mark Whitehouse. "Very seriously," he repeated.

Their questions continued for some time as an attempt was made by the officers to ascertain a link between the McMahon Brothers and the former police officer. They decided to leave, asking Marston to come to the station the next day to make a statement.

Paul shut the door and went back into his lounge where he reached for the bottle of scotch. There was no connection between him and the McMahon brothers and he was relaxed about that but what was causing him to panic was that his name was now in front of the local police. He held his stomach as the problem secretion became more painful. He had booked an air flight to Thailand for two weeks ahead and he had around twelve nights in which to kill his target. Thus, he had the 'how' and the 'when' and was nearing a location to answer the 'where'. He needed to decide on his victim.

Late on Friday afternoon, the three partners of Hannon, Shannon and Smith found themselves in the boardroom being addressed by Mrs Lydia Pennington FCA who was expressing her pleasure at the progress they had achieved in such a short time. She added a concern that Damian had not come into the office until mid-morning and explained that there were several matters that needed to be aired so that they could begin work on Monday morning "all systems go" providing everybody was on time.

The first item was the cancellation of the practice newsletter which resulted in Rachel staring at her mentor and awaiting the explosion.

"You're right, Lydia, this business is behind the times and I need to understand modern communications much better, so well done and thanks," said Damian.

Glen Shannon looked to the skies and Rachel

seemed relieved albeit her phone call with Damian had paved the way.

"The redundancies," Lydia continued, "we have paid well over the statutory limits which I find surprising at a point in time we're fighting to re-establish ourselves."

"Which is not the fault of the individuals who we've had to let go," snapped Damian. "If you want to screw the last penny out of the business go and work for Goldman Sachs."

"I might just do that, Damian," she smiled, "but let's concentrate on matters here. This is the allocation of customers which we've agreed and our individual revenue targets which have also been sanctioned."

Rachel was gripping the edge of the table because they had reached the point where she thought that Giddy Liddy was pushing the boundaries just a little too hard: Damian seemed cool.

"Fine by me," he said, "except that Glen and I have agreed that Mortimer and Bland will stay with me. Their overseas dependencies and the exchange rate complications means it's one where my experience is valuable."

"But that does not count against your target, Damian. You must bring four new audits each over fifty thousand pounds."

"Absolutely fair and proper, Lydia, and it's a challenge I'll relish especially as I've already achieved it!" Damian went over to the side table, picked up a bottle of water and poured them all a glass. "It's amazing how productive one can be when one's late for work."

"I smell a rat," said Lydia.

"Just your suspicious mind, Lydia," he laughed.

"Glen will recall that when the partnership broke up in very acrimonious circumstances, he and I formed this business, together with, later, Rachel, and the other four partners went off to make their fortunes. I take no pleasure in telling you that it's been a disaster and they are splitting again. But Glen will remember that there was one other partner, Gerald Kimberly, who went off on his own. He was a safe, solid man who, a bit like Glen, hated the politics. We've always stayed in touch and I telephoned him yesterday. Just for once fate was on my side because he wants to retire and I have agreed to buy his business." He paused to allow the others to gasp their surprise.

"Here's the deal: you'll see on this piece of paper that there are two figures: annual revenues and the amount we pay. This will be over five years and Gerald will stay on to complete the handover which we agreed will take perhaps six months although he does not want to come here. I told him that you, Lydia, will oversee everything."

"Are we going to discuss this, Damian?" she asked.

"No."

He left the room wishing everyone a super Spring weekend.

He drove out of town, parked in a concealed layby and telephoned Marie who wanted to know what the local reaction had been to the bank robbery. They discussed her hotel and anticipation of the week ahead at Portsmouth University and he told her about his new business partner: Marie thought that Giddy Liddy sounded a handful! There were several silences as they struggled to avoid bringing up their relationship before reaching common ground and agreed that it must wait until she returned home. Damian said that he would telephone her on Monday evening and was not to know that this was received with a certain amount of relief. They concluded their call together and Marie decided to buy herself fish and chips and wander around the marina.

It was Cathy who suggested that they have a barbecue lunch together in the garden which appealed to her husband who was keen to unwind from a demanding week. Her mood was influenced in part by a phone call with Scarlett, who seemed in good spirits and did not follow her usual tendency to try to cut the call short, and because she was pleased with the news of the Gerald Kimberly transaction which she immediately understood and could appreciate the benefit to the business.

She busied herself in the kitchen with the preparation of salads and sauces leaving Damian to drive to the market to purchase chicken pieces and burgers which he took home to start cooking after firing up the heating blocks in the barbecue. She produced a fresh crusty loaf, butter and a bottle of chilled Sauvignon Blanc. The weather was kind and Cathy wondered about using suntan cream but decided it was not quite warm enough. The meats were cooked, served and the side dishes added. Initially they were subdued but, as they ate the meal, their conversation gathered pace as they expressed their shock at yesterday's bank robbery. They left everything on the table and retired to their individual sun loungers having opened a second bottle of wine which she placed on a small table between them.

Cathy revisited his meeting with Arthur and tried to

reflect on it in a positive way before revealing to Damian that her efforts to secure the return of their savings seemed unlikely but she doubted if any legal force could be brought to compel them to invest any additional amounts: she intended pursuing the matter further. He already knew that as he had taken his own legal advice but he was impressed by her diligence.

Their conversation moved on to the paper that Cathy was preparing for Dr Armstrong and she explained that she was trying to produce conclusions on the best way for patients to lose weight. She asked him about the keto diet and why it seemed to take over his whole life?

"In many ways, Cathy," he answered, "you've put your finger on the key point. Keto takes over everything. If I had not met my acquaintance at the conference, perhaps I would have wavered but he set it out without equivocation." He paused and refilled their glasses. "Like so many people I wanted to lose a few pounds especially as the years advance it becomes more challenging. But keto was totally different and I think there's an important point there. People like acquiring knowledge and, as I went further into the science, it began to consume me." He stepped off the lounger and pulled up a small seat which he placed by the other sunbed to talk further with his wife.

"Keto is so contradictory to conventional wisdom, eating fats alone, that it makes you feel part of an exclusive club. The membership qualification, if you like, is trying to reach a state of ketosis which is achieved by eliminating all other foodstuffs from your body. You then have to maintain that balance by eating only keto foods which you have seen me do." He paused. "I should add that once I sensed weight loss gathering pace and I started feeling better, my self-confidence soared: the feeling of putting on a suit that fits loosely is amazing."

Cathy explained that although she understood the complexities of conventional dieting, she was struggling to find ways in which her patients could lose weight. Damian stunned her by suggesting that it was because she was looking in the wrong way and, when asked to explain his statement, he argued that the keto diet was successful, in his case, because it made him feel part of an exclusive club.

"Isn't that what a gym or a slimming club is?" she asked.

"Perhaps, but they have little success because there is no focus from the members as I experienced with keto."

"So how do I make my patients feel part of an exclusive club" she asked.

"You pay them."

"Pardon!?" she exclaimed as she came off the lounger. "Are you mad?"

"Offer them an incentive to lose weight. You keep telling me it's about overcoming hunger pains so help them do that. Offer them, say, one hundred pounds for every pound in weight that they lose."

"And who is going to pay for your madcap idea?"

"The NHS. Patients losing weight means less demand for hospital services and now I am thinking about it, the probability is that it could be financially positive to the NHS. Diabetic patients can end up needing amputations which cost what, ten thousand pounds. If you've paid out five thousand pounds to help that patient lose weight the NHS is getting a good deal."

He paused because he could hear the telephone ringing in the house. He hurried in and listened carefully to the message he was being given. He put down the receiver, took a deep breath and hurried out to speak to his wife.

"Cathy," he said. "It's your father."

After much debate at six o'clock the next morning Cathy Hannon drove out of their driveway after an emotional embrace with Damian. She crossed over to the Isle of Wight in the afternoon and reached Ventnor General Hospital in the early evening where she found her mother sitting by a bed. Even though it was partially hidden by the intensive care unit equipment she could see vivid bruising over his face. Her mother explained that he had been acting strangely and trying to reach the path down to Luccombe Bay and, when her attention was distracted, he'd managed to struggle down the road before falling into a gully.

An hour after her arrival, Henry, Harry as he was known, died without regaining consciousness.

The following week was disappointing in that the Spring weather faded and heavy rains came in from the South-West causing flooding in Wales and the North-West of England. Nothing, however, could dampen the enthusiasm of Marie Cameron who slipped smoothly into university life. Her initial strategy of being attentive and not talking about her practical knowledge and experience, lasted less than a day as the professor urged her to illustrate his theoretical lecturing with the reality of the dental clinic. At one point there was a discussion on the importance of understanding the personality of the patient and Marie, briefly, stumbled when her memories of her first contact with Damian came flooding back. To her credit she managed to explain the issue of close bodily contact and found herself answering some sensible questions. She also managed to tell Rebecca, who she warmed to almost immediately, that she had a partner as she realised that several male undergraduates were planning to take the concept of bodily contact more seriously.

Her phone calls with Damian did not change as they found it difficult to overcome the impersonal nature of distance: she tried hard to find words and phrases that might lift his morale as he struggled through a difficult period. She knew that Cathy was in the Isle of Wight but did not really want to discuss the matter and agreed that they would meet on Friday evening when she would be back in the town.

The attractions of the harbour took over her evenings and she knew she was putting on some pounds through the daily consumption of fish and chips. On one evening she went to a wine bar with the professor and the following day agreed to meet Rebecca who gave her a guided tour of the great vessels. Her companion quickly understood her musical talents and they devised a plan that as they visited each ship, they had to hum a nautical composition.

Their time viewing HMS Victory was accompanied, a little illogically, with Debussy's 'La Mer' and when they reached The Mary Rose, Marie saluted Henry VIII's flagship by humming Mendelssohn's overture 'The Hebrides' but it was HMS Warrior, Britain's first iron-hulled battleship, that launched the rendering of Khachaturian's ballet music for Spartacus. Somehow, they hugged each other while laughing and managed to link, dubiously, the captive king of Thrace with the television seafaring series, 'The Onedin Line' when Rebecca claimed that she'd watched all the repeats. As they walked back to the hotel Marie experienced a freedom which she was beginning to relish.

The intensity of university life and the friends she was making took her away from the dental surgery, from her broken relationships and perhaps from Damian, at least until Friday evening.

Lydia Pennington took to Gerald Kimberly almost immediately as she and Damian arrived at his small offices early on Monday morning. He had spoken to Glen over the weekend and was prepared for her arrival which he celebrated by teasing her from the beginning – and she loved it. By lunchtime the takeover was well underway and Damian returned back to his office. He went home for lunch so that he could phone Cathy in private. She was dealing with matters in her usual efficient way and had spoken to Scarlett who would be coming to the funeral in three weeks and Arthur who could not take time off work but would send some flowers if his mother could make him a small advance.

At a later stage Damian would realise that he did not pick up the vibes coming from Luccombe Bay. He understood why Cathy was so concerned about her mother's future but assumed the retirement home would be where she could build a new life but why was Cathy having second thoughts about its suitability?

He returned to the office to conduct meetings with two clients one of which involved Rachel whose pregnancy was now showing and who seemed to be glowing with health. After his door was closed, he reflected on the births of Arthur and Scarlett and, for no obvious reason, wondering if he and Marie would have children and if he was too old for parenthood?

Former police inspector Paul Marston had now decided on his victim which proved more straightforward than he had imagined. He was clearly not going to select his daughter Scarlett who he had not met, and to whom he wished no harm, leaving a choice of two. He had been shaken by a second visit from the two detectives investigating the bank robbery who were annoyed that he had not attended the station to make his statement and who were insistent that he accompanied them immediately. When he arrived, he realised that former colleagues were avoiding making eye contact as he was hurried into an interview room.

He left two hours later infuriated by the reluctance of the two detectives to disclose exactly what the McMahon brothers were saying except that they considered it to be material. He went to the pub and ordered a large scotch and soda as he began to prioritise catching the plane to where he would begin a new life. The tenants for his house were waiting to move in and he was pleased with the rental that the agents had secured. He smiled as he imagined his ex-wife's lawyers struggling to find him halfway across the world.

Now that he had selected his target, he was finding that the desire to kill was greater than ever before: the victim had caused the whole situation wherein he fathered a child who he had never met. He did not have any decency left in him to recall his anger on hearing of her pregnancy and of his threats to wipe out Damian Hannon.

He had been continually overlooked throughout his career with the police despite the success his old-fashioned methods produced and yes, there had been a number of complaints but none was ever upheld. His loudly spoken dislike of the Masons did him no good whatsoever and there was some fallout from his one divorce from those who knew what he had done to his then wife.

There were several officers who had watched him risk his own life when he pulled an illegal immigrant from out of the path of a lorry on the motorway.

His thoughts were envisaging the moment when he lifted the shotgun and killed his victim before catching a flight to a new life. He felt pain from his stomach and wondered if he needed to see his doctor but he knew they would have medical centres where he was going and he decided to brave it out. He ordered another drink and began the countdown to his moment of ecstasy when he would right the wrongs of the past. He held up two fingers and fired his weapon aiming for the victim's stomach where he knew he could cause the most pain and a slow, agonising, lingering death for the person who deserved it the most: he laughed and finished his drink. He remained seated as he watched the pub's television screen inform the public that Bedfordshire police had arrested two McMahon brothers one of whom was charged with murder and robbery and the other with robbery.

Her week was complete and Marie reached the motorway which would take her back to her home with the best wishes and hugs of her new friends which gave her so much pleasure: Rebecca handed her a present and one of the lads gave her flowers: there were the words of her professor who suggested it was not au revoir. Her imagination was turning to Damian and she began to feel stimulated by the thought of their evening ahead. Now she knew the truth: she had missed him more than she had anticipated and she hoped that he had not been discouraged by their hesitant telephone calls. She reached home, unpacked, flicked through her mail, cleaned the kitchen, showered, changed, sat down at her piano and played 'Imagine' along with John Lennon.

CHAPTER NINE

The week progressed well for Damian who was relieved that Lydia was settling in with her 'team' as the initial brashness developed into a warmth and commitment together with her growing friendship with Gerald Kimberly. In a surprising decision one of the staff who had been made redundant was re-employed, a move that went down rather well with the members of Hannon, Shannon and Smith.

Damian went home late on Friday morning to prepare for the return of Cathy from Luccombe Bay which necessitated a visit to the supermarket, the cleaning of the kitchen and some housework. She arrived early afternoon and they were soon in the garden enjoying the re-appearance of the sun. She asked for an hour to settle back home, shower and change. When she joined her husband in their garden, she found a Greek mezze platter awaiting her, courtesy of Annie behind the continental counter at the supermarket although the white wine was his choice. He thought that Cathy's eyes suggested a lack of sleep and perhaps weariness.

She began to talk about the brief time with her father, looking after her mother, the funeral arrangements and the sale of the property which was proceeding as contracts had been signed before Harry's death. She commented that this made things much easier, a remark that Damian let pass although it was not too long before the bombshell detonated.

"Mother cannot live on the Isle of Wight on her own, even in a retirement home, can she?" she said.

"Is that something we're going to discuss?" he asked.

"What is there to discuss?" replied Cathy. "I'm her only living relative, she's in her eighties and it's obvious that she'll be coming to live here."

"As I said, is this a matter we'll agree together?"

"We are agreeing it. The retirement home is happy to release Mother from the contract that they signed albeit there will be a penalty payment. She'll have a substantial amount of cash from the sale and I'll be applying for power of attorney. I've spoken to a local nursing home about a mile from here and they are able to take her in whenever we wish: she can move in after the funeral. It will take about six months to build a granny extension onto this house then she can move in and be with us. You know my friend Gillian at the church: she's done exactly that for her parents and it's working well."

"Is Gillian's husband the art teacher at the middle school who follows her round with a hangdog expression?" he asked.

"I've given it a lot of thought and I'm willing to make the sacrifices necessary. Mother will need some care which I can arrange at the surgery. She could easily have another ten years of life which will be lovely: she's talking about taking up bridge."

"Professionally?" he asked.

"Scarlett says that she'll come to see mother and I'm hoping Arthur will bring Faria and the baby in due course."

"Providing we send him enough money."

"Damian, I'm sensing some resistance from you. Why would you not agree with my plans because I'll be doing all the work. I'm not asking you for anything."

"Except I live here or rather I did live here but now I'm having to share it with my mother-in-law."

"You won't notice any difference because mother will have her own home, separate from us."

He snorted and stood up.

"Will she have Sunday lunch with us?" he asked.

"Definitely. There's no way we can leave her alone when it's no trouble to cook for three," she said. "It's me who'll do the cooking."

He continued their debate by wondering whether on the occasions they were in the garden would she join them? Cathy gave him short change by pointing out it would be selfish to leave her on her own because once the extension was constructed there would be less garden.

"What happens if you're ill?" he asked.

"I'm never ill, you know that. My health is excellent because I take care of myself."

He continued mulling over their conversation.

"Let's suppose your mother has a hospital appointment," he continued, "and you're on duty at the surgery. How will she get there?"

"You'll take her, of course. She'll love that."

She ate a final selection from her mezze, thanked him for his support and said that she was going to close her eyes because she was exhausted. He cleared away the plates and went inside to shower and change because he had another important matter on his mind.

They both struggled to break the unfathomable atmosphere which existed between them. Even the initial hugs lacked their usual passion and it was not long before they were in the kitchen with Damian resting his arms on the surface of the island sipping a cup of green tea. Marie picked up the pace which gathered in its intensity as she described the events of her week at the dental school within Portsmouth University although he became confused by the various personalities including the professor, Rebecca, Khachaturian (mention of whom caused her to giggle), the lad with the flowers and Eric. The delivering of her news seemed to ignite Marie who changed gear and wanted to know about his week and was Giddy Liddy still employed by him?

Damian went straight into the return of Cathy and the revelation that her mother was coming to live with them leaving out none of the details: he tried to moderate his anger.

"Seems right to me," said Marie, "because what else can Mrs Hannon do? She can't leave her mother on the Isle of Wight and do you want the responsibility of going down there to see her? There's plenty of money available, so you say, and I can imagine a nice home for her annexed to you. Cathy will look after her and once she gets into a bridge circle, you'll never see her!"

"How do you feel about the situation where I've been told what is going to happen: no discussion, no chance to give my opinion, in fact not to be asked what I think?" He paused and wiped his face. "She just sat there and laid down the law as though I was a servant."

"As you're leaving her, so that we can share our lives together, it seems a great development," said Marie.

Damian stood up, went a few paces away, turned and faced her before he exploded with frustration because, as he explained, there was now no possibility that he could quit the marriage and leave Cathy on her own. The construction of the annex was a significant undertaking and he would need to oversee the building contractors and ensure that agreed budgets were followed.

"At last, we have some clarity, Damian," snapped Marie. "Mrs Hannon has won and I withdraw my application to be your partner which is a fucking great shame because I think we had everything going for us." She threw her glass across the kitchen and tried to hide her tears.

"She's won," she continued. "I always feared that she would because at heart you are perhaps the most decent man I have ever met." She moved towards the door. "I'd like you to leave please Damian because I'm going to play my piano."

"Am I allowed to ask you to give me time to reconsider my position?" he asked.

"And what could possibly happen that would make you do that?" she said.

Damian and Cathy had Sunday dinner together and then Damian surprised his wife by referring back to their discussion on helping patients to lose weight: he handed her a sheet of paper. He explained that he had used his time to think through the possibility of offering financial incentives and acknowledged that it was controversial but, to use her own words, there is an obesity crisis. He said that she had given him a clue when she was talking about hunger pains and the inability of a vast number of overweight people to avoid breaking well intentioned diets because of the seduction of food. Expressed in those terms the challenge was to create rewards that are greater than hunger pains.

Cathy had become absorbed in his train of thought and studied his presentation.

"The one subject on which I know my stuff, Cathy, is money. I have seen people do the most outrageous things. One of my clients was a model of propriety until his business hit the rocks and he thought he was going to lose his house: he became an animal and secretly sold off all the assets of the company breaking every rule in the book except that he saved his home."

She re-read the paper and asked Damian to take her through his calculations. He said that it was relatively straight forward and started to explain his proposition.

"A patient comes into the surgery with a health problem. In diagnosing the complaint, the doctor ascertains that the individual, it makes no difference whether it's a man or a woman, is two stones overweight and nearing a BMI of thirty and thus obesity. The patient's notes reveal that the medics have offered various alternatives but none have proved effective. The doctor then says that they have access to a new scheme whereby the patient will receive financial incentives to encourage them to lose weight."

Cathy held up her hand and looked again at her piece of paper before asking Damian to continue.

"They agree between them that the patient needs to lose twenty-four pounds and is taken into the nurse's clinic who weights the individual and confirms the target. Every two weeks the patient comes in and is weighed. For every pound lost they are paid one hundred pounds. For example, at the first weigh-in it is found that the patient has lost three pounds. The practice manager transfers three hundred pounds into the bank account of the patient. When the person loses a stone, fourteen pounds, they will have received fourteen hundred pounds and are paid a bonus of five hundred pounds, a total of nineteen hundred pounds."

She leaped up out of her chair and exclaimed that if the patient loses the full two stone, they will receive three thousand eight hundred pounds of taxpayer's money."

"What a deal for the taxpayer," said Damian. "The NHS has one less patient to treat for diabetes."

"As soon as they have their money, they'll put the weight back on."

"Read on," suggested her champion, "I've built an incentive to address that possibility. The patient carries on being weighed by the nurse and if they retain the weight loss to within three pounds of the target, they receive another five hundred pounds every six months for three years."

"The NHS pays out another three thousand pounds!" she yelled.

"How much does a stomach band operation cost, Cathy?"

"You'll not get much change out of ten thousand pounds," she answered.

"I rest my case," he smiled as he hugged his wife.

"You're stark raving bonkers, Damian!" she exclaimed. "They'll be queuing at the door."

"Sounds as though I've just solved the obesity crisis," he said.

There were no further words spoken as they climbed the stairs and approached her bedroom. This time her door stayed open.

Former police inspector Paul Marston brought forward his flight ticket and decided that he would kill them on Monday night. He was struggling to remember his prescriptions schedule and was mixing up the tablets which caused him to experience dizzy spells. His suitcase was packed and he would travel to the airport by public transport, avoiding the CCTV as best he could, after leaving his car in a garage he had hired separately. His tenants were moving in on the following Friday and the agents had agreed to handle all matters. He would walk to their house, which was an exclusive detached property and almost certainly out of range of neighbouring CCTV, staying within the trees wherever possible.

He would execute them both. He could not decide which one of them had damaged his life more and he could not afford to leave a witness. He knew the routine well enough: he would throw the shotgun and his shoes into the canal, strip off and deposit his clothes in one of the many refuse bins people left outside their homes, and he'd shower carefully. Because he was familiar with the police procedures known as Locard's Principle of Exchange he knew that, ideally, he should burn his clothes. They stated that every contact leaves a trace on both sides of the contact and so his victim, or victims, might leave their contact on him but he also knew that time was on his side as the longer the gap, the more the possibility of legitimate reasons for fingerprints and blood stains. To add to the risks he was taking, the police's Murder Manual included, as a first post-incident action, the securing and searching of local dustbins, public areas and gardens. He also knew they were desperately short-staffed.

He'd fly out to the East and begin a new life. He had answered one of the many websites available and was dazzled by the array of girls available to him, selecting several of the dark-haired candidates. He drank deeply and threw the empty scotch bottle onto the carpet. He went to bed for the last time in his home.

Marie stared at Mr Choudhary who was not reacting in the way that she'd expected. She'd received a warm reception at the practice, a hug from Mrs Choudhary and had a number of people booked in to see her. She had responded to his request and provided a full assessment of her week in the dental class but could not draw his attention away from an email which he was re-reading.

"Am I right in assessing that this has been a success?" he asked.

"I'm grateful for your wisdom, Mr Choudhary" she said, "because it was exactly what I needed. There will be only top-class dental treatment from me from now on for my patients, that I can promise you."

"Perhaps," he said.

"What do you mean? Have I had a bad report from the professor?"

"My friend Professor Warnock certainly has a lot to say but I'm not sure that it's what I wanted to hear," continued Mr Choudhary.

Marie was stunned by this information. Rebecca had said that they all loved having her in the class and her dinner with Professor Warnock had been enjoyable even if he did ask rather too many personal questions.

"I'm going to let you read the email I have received from him. You were a great success and, in his opinion, added considerably to the practicality of the student's training." He smiled. "He says that you and he had an interesting time together and he understands your circumstances including your qualifications and career details."

"Career details?" asked Marie.

"He's asking my permission for him to offer you an assistant professorship at the dental school of the university starting in September." He paused. "You'll be working directly under his guidance." He paused. "The money is breath-taking."

She took the email off her boss and read it carefully before looking up at him.

"I never expected this, Mr Choudhary, and I promise you all I tried to do was use the time properly."

"We don't want to lose you, Marie," he said, "but the decision is yours. It's an amazing offer." He paused. "Take the day off. Mrs Choudhary is going to cover your list and when you are ready, make your decision." He stood up and shook her hand. "If you decide to accept the offer, you'll bring great honour to our practice." He paused again. "You'll see that Professor Warnock is suggesting that if you are interested you might go back down to Portsmouth to see him before term-time finishes."

Marie left the building and stood in the car park with the tears pouring down her face. She used a tissue to wipe her eyes before sending a text message:

Hi ' becca. The navy's coming!

Monday proved to be a particularly successful commercial day for Hannon, Shannon and Smith with the news that Lydia had persuaded Gerald Kimberly to move into their premises and commit to another two years thus providing the additional senior support that they needed.

"We're on a roll," she had announced to the meeting of the partners. Damian had nodded in agreement and with a certain amount of relief that stability had returned to the business. He spent the rest of the day with clients and left for home at six o'clock. He parked his car, went inside and upstairs to his room, showered and changed and then went to look for his wife.

He found Cathy working at the kitchen table with her laptop, a puzzled frown on her face and so he asked her about the progress of her obesity report. She told him that she had mentioned the financial incentives concept to Dr Martin Armstrong and was annoyed that he had dismissed it out of hand.

"I told him straight, Damian, that he should give much more credence to my husband's innovative thinking but it was a hopeless task."

"Another idea bites the dust," he laughed. "Back to the obesity crisis".

"Oh no," she said. "I talked to one of my colleagues who works in the weight loss area and she could see its merits. Her comment was that one hundred pounds for losing a pound in weight seemed too much and she wondered about offering food vouchers."

They went into the lounge and sat down.

"They've been tried and they don't work, Cathy," continued Damian. "The whole idea is based on the need to overcome hunger pains and that needs money: plain and simple." He paused. "As we all know, it's a very powerful motivator."

Cathy nodded her head in agreement.

"That's interesting because my friend also had another thought. Many of our patients come from difficult backgrounds, single parents and the rest, and she wondered if the extra money might enable them to improve the diets of their families. In their situations it's inevitable that they rely on chips and cheap meats to feed the kids."

"I was surprised at the cost of the Greek mezze I bought us," he laughed.

Damian stood up and said that he thought he'd heard a noise and went into the kitchen to investigate. Cathy busied herself with the television remote control and tuned in to the evening news programme. She also sensed movement in the kitchen and began to stand up. A few moments later Damian came back into the lounge accompanied by Paul Marston who was holding a shotgun to his neck. He told Cathy to do exactly as Marston told her to do. Her hand went to her mouth and she dropped her cup.

"Sit over there," instructed the former police inspector, pointing to the settee where she went and sat down.

"What do you want, Paul?" she asked.

He pulled away from Damian and then lashed him across the face with his weapon resulting in the victim crashing to the floor. Cathy screamed and rushed to help him up and guide him to the settee. She wiped the blood away from his nose and held his hand.

"I'm sorry what I said to you, Paul," she pleaded.

"It's him I'm going to kill," he snarled.

"Why Paul, why ruin your life?"

"Do you think I fucked you for sex in the garden, Cathy?" He laughed. "It wasn't much cop, anyway." He wiped his mouth. "I fucked you to get back at him. Mr Wonderful, Mr Businessman. I watched the women flock to him at the party and found myself passed by." He spluttered as he felt his stomach cramp. "I never thought I'd father a baby. Your bloody fault, you bitch. You should have taken your pill."

Damian was recovering from the initial assault and was pulling himself back up.

"It's not your baby, you bastard," he spluttered. "I'm the father of Scarlett: we've had tests to prove it."

Marston stood up and glared down at Cathy.

"Bitch. You lied to me. You said it was my baby."

"You are Scarlett's father, Paul," said Cathy. She turned to her husband who was holding a handkerchief to his face. "I'm sorry Damian. I made it up about the DNA tests and I was amazed that you believed me. You can't just get a doctor to send samples off like that: there's a protocol to follow."

"You lied about it?" he yelled out as the blood trickled down his face.

"It was better for Scarlett once Paul's letters had been received and I thought it might help resolve the situation."

"You blatantly lied about who was the father of Scarlett?" he repeated.

"You two shut the fuck up," ordered Marston. "You seem to be treating me like a fucking afterthought."

"You need help, Paul, you're not well," said Cathy. "Are you on drugs because your pupils are dilating?"

"I'm catching a fucking plane to a new life," he said. "That's now a joint problem because I'm going to have to kill both of you." He laughed. "I had planned to finish just him but now you are dust."

It was totally cold bloodied as he raised the shotgun and pointed it towards Cathy. She ducked instinctively which pushed Damian to one side allowing him to bend his legs: he was not sure that he could reach the killer in time such was the distance between them. But Marston was feeling nauseous and suddenly there was a searing pain across his abdomen as the infected secretions from his stomach reached his raw flesh. As he dropped his guard, Damian leaped forwards as Marston fired the shotgun. The pellets shattered the ceiling as the two men collapsed to the floor and Damian made a grab for the shotgun. He prised it away from the attacker who collapsed onto the blood-stained carpet and dissolved into a gibbering wreck. He leaped on top of him and shouted for Cathy to telephone for the police.

She returned from doing so and suggested that Damian climb off the prostrate body of Paul Marston which she leant over and examined. She said that he was semi-conscious just as the siren announced the arrival of the police followed shortly afterwards by an ambulance.

The police stayed for nearly two hours, long after the killer was taken away to hospital for an emergency operation. They cordoned off the lounge as a crime scene and took statements from both Cathy and Damian. Before the police could object, Cathy telephoned Dr Martin Armstrong telling the officers that neither she nor Damian would be going to hospital. He arrived twenty minutes later and began by treating Damian's face and giving him the good news that his nose was not broken. He suggested that Cathy should go to bed and he administered a sedative to help her rest.

He found himself alone with Damian for whom he poured a whisky and soda. He asked about the evening's events and was told the full story. He expressed his concern for Cathy suggesting that he needed to watch her carefully over the next few days. "Keep her at home for as long as she wants," he said. They chatted on and discussed the recent bank raid.

Dr Armstrong frowned as he watched Damian sip his drink. "I hope that I did not cause any offence with my comments about your financial incentives idea," he said.

Damian smiled and reassured him that his comments were respected and that Cathy loved the interest he was taking in her dissertation. He thanked him for coming so quickly.

"All part of the service," he said. "I'm sure that you and Cathy have things to talk about but please let her rest tonight. I'll see myself out."

"Yes, we have," said Damian under his breath.

A little later he decided to walk into the garden and enjoy the Spring warmth. He was reflecting on the evening's events and the realisation that Paul Marston had come to kill him but another thought dominated his emotions. She had betrayed him. He'd been ready and willing to accept responsibility for many of their problems and he was becoming adjusted to her mother coming to live with them. But she had used the parentage of Scarlett like a rag doll. It was an act of unbelievable dishonesty and now he had to think about visiting his daughter to tell her that she was not his biological daughter. Cathy had crossed the Rubicon and there could be no tomorrow.

Damian realised what he was thinking and the implications for the future. He was now easing free of his marriage bonds and could commit to Marie for the rest of his life. He imagined being with her in the garden by the canal and holding her arm. He was rebuilding Hannon, Shannon and Smith, plus Mrs

Lydia Pennington FCA and Gerald Kimberly, and she was doing what she wanted the most: cleaning her patient's teeth, playing her piano and being with him.

"What a night, what a tomorrow," he thought to himself as he anticipated seeing Marie in the evening and telling her about their future together. He moved back indoors, tidied up and went upstairs to his own bedroom where he used the mirror to examine his damaged face.

+ + +

PART TWO

SUMMER

Whenever I'm alone with you
You make me feel like I am home again
Whenever I'm alone with you
You make me feel like I am whole again

'Lovesong'
(from 'Disintegration': the album by The Cure (1989)

CHAPTER TEN

Mrs Nettie Errington-Maxwell sighed with happiness as she spent the remaining time before the start of her bridge class in the gardens of the Cumberland Nursing Home. She had arrived six weeks earlier for a short-term stay and had, yesterday, negotiated a more permanent residency: the matron was absolutely delighted when she confided to her that she had found somewhere where she belonged. She explained that her late husband Henry (Harry to his friends) had loved life in the Isle of Wight and she had gone along with his wishes. He was now cremated and his ashes scattered across Luccombe Bay jointly by their grandchildren which had brought added happiness to their grandmother. She had expected Scarlett to make the journey to the funeral, but was, along with everyone else, staggered when, unannounced, into the church walked Arthur and his partner Faria. This was before he knew about his legacy payable at the age of twenty-five. Scarlett and Faria bonded within hours and an umbilical cord was established: the three of them met again to honour their pledge to say goodbye to their grandfather by standing in the waters of the Bay and dispensing his ashes over the gentle waves and within sight of the chine where Harry, over the years, had let his imagination run with the smugglers.

Nettie collected her possessions, moved inside to the converted country house reception which was now her home and climbed the Edwardian staircase to her first-floor apartment, closed the door and walked over to the windows so that she could see the Scots Pine trees. It was too ridiculous to take seriously but Edgar, on the floor above, was rather charming and he was an excellent bridge coach: she laughed and told Harry that she had every intention of behaving herself. She would spend the next hour mastering the card game, have her meal at six o'clock and await the arrival of her daughter.

Three hours later she was sitting in the communal lounge sipping a gin and tonic when in walked Damian Hannon. He strode over and asked his mother-in-law if she would mind if they went to her room to talk which she immediately agreed to although she was puzzled by his officious manner. He carried her glass for her and they soon settled into her abode.

"I'll come straight to the point, Nettie," he said, "and I wish I had better news for you but I've decided to defer the start of the building of your granny annex with us: if they can't extend your agreement here, I'll find you somewhere else. I hope you'll understand our situation but I have to consider everybody's position and it's not fair on Cathy for her to have the burden of so much extra work." He paused. "Do you have anything to drink?"

"Aren't you driving, Damian, surely that's not a good idea?"

"Don't you start, Nettie: everyone seems to want to run my life for me."

Nettie suggested that she make a cup of coffee which temporarily improved his attitude and which, once served, acted as a restraint, albeit briefly. She told Damian that she could not understand why Catherine was struggling with the extra burden to which he had referred as she was generally utterly competent. He ran his hand through his hair and sighed.

"She's not well, Nettie: she's getting tired and I realise that the surgery is busy but this is not like her: she's picking at her food."

"Is she sleeping properly, Damian?" she asked.

He responded by saying that he was not too sure and, when she expressed some bemusement, he admitted that they rarely slept together. He went on to admit that the additional problem was that Cathy refused to talk to him about her condition and a suggestion that they go to the doctor together had seriously backfired. He had resorted to asking Scarlett for help and she had visited at the weekend only for Cathy to be bright and bubbly.

"As soon as I'd taken Scarlett to the train station and got home, she'd reverted back to exactly as she had previously been."

"Is it me, Damian?" she asked.

"I cannot imagine why, Nettie. Cathy has always adored you and she talks about your new home as if it were her own."

"I have some news for you both," she announced. "I'll tell you exactly as it is because I don't want you to misunderstand what I have done." She made herself comfortable. "I was so grateful when you made your offer and, to be honest, I couldn't leave the Isle of Wight soon enough but, in my heart, I did not want to live with you both. I have friends who have made the same move and the problems that arise are not so apparent at the start. You and Catherine need your own space and I was going to propose that I buy a bungalow in the area because I want my own home. My health is good."

Damian was holding up his hands and trying to

emphasise that they both wanted her to come and live with them.

"No, you don't, Damian, please don't lie to me but before we go on, the matter is solved. I am staying here on a permanent basis: I am feeling happier after the sadness of losing Harry and I am wanted here: I love it: if I want company I go downstairs: if I want to go for a walk, I follow the pathways amongst the trees: if I want to go to town, they call a taxi for me."

"I assume you've not discussed this with Cathy?"

"You go and do that, please. I was wondering how to tell her."

Damian moved towards the door but was called back by Nettie. She put her hands up to his face.

"My eighty-five years on this earth tell me, Damian, that Catherine is not the only one with problems. Please take care of yourself."

He drove home carefully as he prepared to relate the last thirty minutes to his wife: he could not decide whether to cover his mother-in-law's news first or if it might be tactically better to read her the letter he had received in the morning's post.

Marie Cameron sold her property within four days and purchased a town house on Bryher Island in the Port Solent area overlooking the marina and close to the motorway giving her fast access to Portsmouth university. For her it was a non-stop life as she found that Professor's Warnock approach was predicated on unremitting hard work and preparation. She was initially shocked and then concerned that she knew so little compared to the full dental care syllabus and it took several weeks before she adjusted to an academic approach. There was also the distraction of the offers that came her way leading to days out on the sea waves. She now had her piano installed in the bay window of her home and introduced an hour's practice a day into her schedule.

Rebecca and her partner, Jeb, were frequent visitors which extended her circle further as she became acquainted with their friends. She joined an athletics club and decided to improve her time for the four hundred metres: the Olympics qualifying time was forty-five seconds which was eighteen seconds faster than her best time which was, in itself, pretty respectable.

Marie was uncertain about the status of her relationship with Damian: the level of affection was such that she was declining any suggestion of an approach from potential suitors but he had reacted badly to her news that she was moving to Portsmouth albeit his attitude was tempered by his respect for the level of achievement that it represented. He argued that she should have discussed the offer with him but floundered when asked to give a good reason as to why? She was now being tested because he was not in contact as regularly as before and he was making excuses about visiting her in Portsmouth which she thought he'd want to undertake. She told him about the colours she had used to decorate her bedroom but the attempted seduction seemed to fall on deaf ears.

She found that she needed to travel back to Bedfordshire to meet with her lawyers and she wanted to call in to the dental practice and see Mr and Mrs Choudhary. This took place early in July and in mid-afternoon, she and Damian met up and drove to the Chiltern Hills. As their time together passed it seemed to reignite their affection for each other but she was unable to draw out from Damian his exact stance on his marriage. She understood his anger over the misleading actions taken by his wife over the fatherhood of Scarlett but he still referred to his responsibilities as a result of his mother-in-law coming to live locally.

For Marie the bottom line was that she wanted to get back close to him but there had to be specific moves on his part and, as far as she was concerned, time was beginning to run out. She shared this with him and was even more perplexed when he said that it would be so simple if that was the only issue in his life.

On her way back to Portsmouth she relaxed back into the compartment of the train and thought through the correct message to send. As the carriages went noisily into a tunnel, she sent the following text:

Waiting, clock ticking, there's much we can achieve together. M x

The following day Damian was in his office early, reading and re-reading the letter that he had received. He used his computer to search for some information and then locked it away in his desk and wandered into the Board Room where his senior colleagues, with the exception of Rachel Smith, were waiting to go through Lydia's various proposals. He listened with interest because, and they were not to know, their direction of travel could fit in well with his plans.

Mrs Lydia Pennington FCA was maintaining her usual 'Giddy Liddy' impact delivery as a result of her hard work and preparation. The first item was the absence of their colleague which, with genuine regret, was explained by her fight with high blood pressure during her pregnancy and finally, the decision that she should go into hospital to be monitored. Lydia, without taking breath, suggested that it was unlikely that Rachel would return for some months. But, she explained, there was an immediate remedy from the practice's point of view because Gerald Kimberly was willing to defer his proposed retirement for several years and join as a partner. Damian realised afterwards that they never took a vote which was of no concern to him as the breaking news was music to his ears and Glen Shannon was nodding his agreement.

The next motion was one that he was expecting because she had discussed it with him prior to the meeting. A few minutes later Mrs Pennington was appointed a partner. There followed a discussion about the name of the firm: it was felt that Hannon, Shannon, Smith, Pennington and Kimberly was over the top and so Hannon and Partners was proposed. This was the moment when Damian changed the whole atmosphere as he made a short statement. They knew that he had experienced some concern about his appetite for continuing as an accountant and those doubts had recently resurfaced. Now that the firm was so much stronger and, in Lydia, had an ideal candidate for the senior partner position, he was proposing to resign in a month's time.

The strange thing was that there was virtually no discussion between his colleagues: perhaps so much had happened that there was an inevitability about this latest development. Damian said he was taking the rest of the day off and suggested they continue with their planning. As he was leaving, he handed Lydia a sheet of paper and said that he had set out his leaving terms. As the door closed, she scanned the page although she already knew, and had agreed, the details.

He went home, changed and joined Cathy in the garden expressing surprise that she was not at work. There was a table with a green salad, meats and fish prepared and ready for serving: they each selected their lunch and he opened a bottle of wine: they continued in relative silence with the occasional comment, once about the weather, finished eating together and then they both started talking at the same time. He held up his hand and laughed as he invited his wife to take the floor.

"I knew it could happen," she started, "but I never thought it would happen to me: I feel so ashamed of myself but I'm not able to fight it anymore."

Damian cleared the plates and brought the two chairs together and he placed the wine in the centre of the table so they could help themselves. He hurried inside and collected a sunhat which he placed on her head: he went back to the kitchen and filled a carafe with ice cubes and fresh cold water which he put down on the table. He blinked as he looked up into the sun.

"Something is troubling you, Cathy?"

"I'm going to give up nursing, Damian." She took off her sunhat, rubbed her eyes and put it back on. "I can't face anymore human bodies; I never thought that I'd talk in this way but with my responsibilities for weight control I have spent an increasing amount of my time with semi-naked people who are manifestly overweight and who are lying to themselves and lying to me." She paused as he handed over her glass of wine which she drank rather quickly.

"When I was nursing, I loved it because I could make a difference either by helping the patient or because I knew how to handle the relatives: there was real job satisfaction, not always, but enough to help me through the perplexing nature of illness. But now I spend much of my time playing games to satisfy the NHS masters who seem to live in a different world to me." She stood up and began to walk around the garden to be joined by her husband.

"They're getting fatter because they eat and drink too much. You know that idea you had about offering financial incentives to encourage people to lose weight, it was the only sensible solution I've heard in months. I told you that I mentioned it to Dr Armstrong who shot me down in flames saying amateurs should not involve themselves in medical matters."

"How long have you been feeling this way?" he asked as he took off his sweater.

"It's been growing for some time. I was asked to put in writing my ideas about weight loss strategies and, at first, that proved helpful but as I went on, my enthusiasm faded. Several weeks ago, a very large woman, whose only hope is bariatric surgery unless one of her illnesses gets her first, was brought into my clinic and I was told to take her through our weight loss programme. It was a farce as we went through the "I'm big boned' charade and she was just unpleasant. The next thing I knew was that she had put in a complaint against me: Dr Armstrong dealt with that and told me not to worry. I did worry because I realised that I was disgusted by her body, I let it show and I knew that I was in the wrong. I looked it up on the internet which talked about the insular cortex in the brain: it says 'it links sensory experience and emotional valence' which I found baffling."

Cathy went over to the garden chairs, sat down again and repeated her earlier announcement to Damian that she had reached a point where enough was enough and she proposed leaving nursing.

"Great idea," he said.

"How come?" she said. "I thought you'd object."

"Why?" he laughed. "First, we're discussing it and that's a step forward and you forget that I went through the keto diet. I learnt from doing the hard work that the reality of weight loss is beyond most people and, in fact, I've always admired the way you never seemed to lose your enthusiasm." He put his arms around her and delivered a sensitive hug. "You've served the NHS as well as anybody: time to change direction."

Cathy asked if he minded if she had a break and took a shower and wandered off while he checked the messages on his phone. She came back thirty minutes later with a pot of tea and scones. As he ladled the jam and cream on his pastries, he joked that it was perhaps a good thing she was no longer in charge of weight control.

"What did you imply when you said "time to change direction": what did you mean?" she asked.

"We'll come to that," he said, "we're still on item one."

"Are we?!" she exclaimed. "What is item one?"

"Your career in the NHS."

"I'll give them three months' notice that I'm going: I don't want to leave them short-staffed."

"Four weeks at the most," he said. Cathy looked at him

"You're right, four weeks it is." She laughed. "Item two?"

"Your mother, how did you find her this morning?"

"It's a miracle, Damian, she was radiant. They are lovely people and the matron is thrilled that she's staying with them. What an outcome!"

"I've cancelled the building work," he said.

"Can I suggest item three?" she asked.

"I think you're going to raise the matter of Scarlett and do we tell her? With the funeral and your mother's move we've not really had a chance to speak to her." He paused. "Matters became rather muddled but, at the point where she thought that Paul Marston was her father, she told us to get on with our lives."

"We have to tell her the truth," said Cathy.

"Yes, we do."

"As we are having a spring clean what's the news on Arthur?"

They discussed his appearance at the funeral, the re-appearance to scatter his grandfather's ashes, Scarlett's opinion of Faria and they decided that they would leave things as they appeared to be. They moved inside to enjoy the cooler atmosphere in their lounge and Damian began to discuss events at the firm telling Cathy that he was going to resign. She remained calm and suggested he tell her more before taking from him a copy of a letter which he handed to her asking that she read it carefully.

Former police Inspector Paul Marston lay quietly on his bunk bed on remand in the Northamptonshire prison cell. The weeks of hospital treatment and the reversal of his stomach operation had been painful but successful as the scars were now healing and the withdrawal of his prescriptions was allowing his body to regain some stability. His doctors wanted to know about his journey to the hospital in Estonia and what he had been told about the operation before paying for the procedure. One medic was interested in the actions of the private doctor who he had consulted and Marston was told that the matter had been referred to the London medical authorities. Arrangements were made for him to be placed on an alternative GP surgery list if, and when, he returned home.

His lawyers were preparing his defence which he thought should be based on the abuse he had received from nurse Hannon and her lies to her family about the paternity of Scarlett. At the time of the alleged assault, he was carrying a shotgun for protection and the fact it had never been fired would tell in his favour. He claimed that all he wanted to do on the night of his visit was to discuss with the Hannon parents, Scarlett's future and that the discharge into the ceiling was made in self-defence because Damian Hannon had attacked him. The defence lawyers had found two former police colleagues who were willing to testify about Marston's exemplary career and his personal bravery including the famed motorway rescue of an illegal immigrant.

He was using his time to plan his future as he expected, at worst, to receive a suspended sentence and possibly a complete discharge. He negotiated with his tenants to leave the house early for the payment of an incentive allowing Marston to move back home because all thoughts of travelling to Thailand were dismissed: he had other matters to consider. He had an uncompleted mission to fulfil because two people had damaged him badly and deserved to be punished.

During his time on remand, and with the exception of his lawyers, no other person came to visit him apart from the prison chaplain who was ejected without ceremony.

Nettie Errington-Maxwell was pleasantly surprised by

Edgar's suggestion that she should be his partner and, as she walked through the sunlit trees on the south side of the Cumberland Nursing Home, her memories drifted back to Luccombe Bay and the beauty of the Isle of Wight when she always had Harry by her side: in fact, apart from when he was in the army serving in the Falklands War and briefly in Northern Ireland, they had never been apart. She had relished her daughter's unexpected appearance in the late morning and even more her much improved morale which was explained by the news of Cathy's decision to retire from nursing. This required a fuller explanation which followed together with nods of agreement before they went on to discuss Edgar's proposition: Nettie was surprised by the encouragement Cathy gave her to consider it further, which she did, and which led to her confirming that she'd see him at four o'clock.

The tables were set out in the lounge area as nine groups of four players prepared for the weekly bridge competition. Edgar could not conceal his delight that Nettie had agreed to be his partner despite the reality that this would be her first ever competitive game. They had played a number of practice hands and now it was for real.

Their opponents were the married couple from the third floor who were, for Nettie, rather pushy in the sense that outside bridge, which was their passion, their only topic of conversation was the grandchildren, all nine of them and all of whom excelled in whatever they were doing. Edgar was whispering in her ear and succeeded in boosting her confidence, on the outside. Inwardly, Nettie was a nervous player.

The cards were dealt and it was Edgar who was to

make the opening bid which Nettie heard as "two clubs." She tried to remember what that was meant to tell her but she was rather perplexed because she held only one club but a strong hand of another suit. Her bid of three diamonds caused her partner to smile and finally it was he whose bid was the contract and Nettie, to her utter relief, was dummy. They won the hand and the next and then lost three in a row before it was time for dinner.

Later Nettie and Edgar sat together in the gardens and began to talk more about themselves and each other. Before receiving a peck on her cheek, she agreed that on the day after tomorrow they would catch a train south for a few miles and then go walking together in the Chiltern Hills.

Cathy Hannon lay back on her sun lounger and decided to live dangerously by allowing some of the strongest solar rays of the summer to hit her skin generating an unbelievable feeling of good health. She was still chuckling to herself as her mother's new partner, Edgar, was clearly following a path to companionship and, although she was yet to meet him, the vibes were encouraging if it meant that Nettie was discovering a new way of life ahead of her.

The day was adding up to an improved situation with the exception of the telephone call earlier in the day from Louisa at the reception desk of the accountancy business telling her the sad news that Rachel had lost her baby. She wrote a letter to her knowing that no words could overcome the pair's grief: she recalled meeting Matt on one occasion and thinking that Rachel was a lucky girl: she would visit her soon.

As she was leaving for the surgery to keep an

appointment with Dr Martin Armstrong her mobile rang and it was Scarlett returning her call from the previous evening. The banter was short-lived because Cathy wanted to get straight to the point which she did and delivered the news about Paul Marston and the truth about him being her father. She nearly fell over when Scarlett started laughing.

"You don't seriously think I was taken in by all that rubbish about DNA tests, do you Mum?" she said. "In truth, for a few moments I wanted to believe it but Joshua destroyed its credibility within minutes."

"Joshua?" asked Cathy.

"My soul mate, I've told you about him," she said "I don't understand why we went through that charade but, as I said at the time, let's get on with the rest of our lives, speaking of which, I met with Arthur and Faria at the weekend. Did you know that he's starting a university course?"

Cathy found that in the heat of the afternoon her eyes were closing as she relived the meeting with Martin Armstrong, her employer, who greeted her news with a beaming smile.

"Thank goodness," he exclaimed. "It's been obvious that you've been unhappy for some time and I get the feeling you've sorted things out."

Cathy stopped him at that point because she wanted to tell him the reason for her decision and her growing antipathy for the human body. He countered by telling his colleague that she was misunderstanding her condition.

"You're as good a nurse as you ever were, Cathy," he said. "We all experience what you are telling me. It's impossible to be welcoming to every patient and when I look at my list I think "oh no!" when I see a certain person due to come in. What I do is reverse psychology and I tell myself that the individual is the highlight of my day." He laughed. "I wish it worked more often." He frowned. "What makes it worse is that the difficult ones won't accept telephone consultations and in they come."

Cathy laughed and said that she'd work for another four weeks.

"Would you like to go now, Cathy?" he asked. She gasped and nodded her head.

"There are two conditions: first you come in on Friday for a party because I promise you that everyone of us will want to be with you for one final time."

"The other condition, Martin?"

"The paper you wrote about weight loss: I was far too hasty in my judgement. Any chance you can finish it and I want you to set out more fully the financial incentives idea: we'll pay you of course?"

"You won't pay me and I'll be delighted to do as you ask. It was Damian's idea by the way."

Dr Martin Armstrong stood up and walked towards Cathy.

"You are one of the finest nurses I've ever had the privilege of working with, Cathy, and I'm not sure that we would have got through Covid-19 without you: how many injections did you give?"

"I stopped counting, Martin." She smiled. "I won't miss that. I'll see you on Friday."

"And my paper on weight-loss?"

"Watch this space," she said.

The rays of the sun were beginning to redden her skin and so she turned over onto her stomach. There was, however, one final matter that she wanted to recall but decided to go into the kitchen and re-read the letter that Damian had asked her to consider. This was perhaps the fifth or sixth time she had done so and, as she looked at the heading and then the signature at the bottom of the single-page missive, she gasped.

"Why would anyone write in these terms?" she yet again asked herself.

She washed her face and ambled back to the lounger. This time she reverted to being face-up but pulled a towel over her exposed skin. As her eyes closed, she realised that she was becoming stimulated by the thought of her husband arriving home.

CHAPTER ELEVEN

Despite improving her running time for the four hundred metres by two seconds Marie was feeling well below par and was acutely aware of the two reasons for her mild depression. The workload imposed on her by professor Warnock at the Portsmouth School of Dentistry was unremitting and his latest list of her first-year lecture modules worried her: they included 'clinical concepts of dental hygiene', 'principles of evidence-based practice', 'foundations of general anatomy' and 'human disease application to dental care'. She was now studying on average over six hours a day and, even then, she suspected that she was falling behind her self-imposed timetable with the arrival of the students just a few weeks away.

It was the second influence on her that was more emotionally damaging and she was angry with her immature attitude but, put bluntly, the desire of Rebecca and Jeb to maintain an ostentatious, physical relationship was undermining her own stability. Only yesterday a group of them had sailed around the coast to Selsey Bill and, on landing, the two romantics had disappeared inland reappearing two hours later and asking where was the picnic? Marie had spent her time with two of Jeb's friends and his sister who was glued to her mobile phone for much of the time. The two sailors were decent and fun but made Marie more aware of her thirty-eight years.

She found a pool in the rocks where she settled

down and cooled her feet and ankles after splashing salt water over her face and removing most of her clothing. She knew that she was missing Damian and, as their messaging was becoming less frequent and more impersonal, she started to realise that, perhaps, she was near to making a clean break and transferring her life fully to the environment in which she now found herself. She remembered back to her own time at university and the intensity of the final year of study which left little time for other pursuits.

She climbed to her feet, covered up and climbed over the rocks towards the boat and the hilarity of Jeb's group which was evident. She was not yet ready to give up on Damian but she was not too far away.

Damian realised that he had an hour remaining before leaving his office to head for the surgery for Cathy's leaving party. He was still shaken by his earlier visit to the home of Rachel Smith who was utterly distraught by the loss of their baby as was Matt who was sitting at her side before offering to make some tea. Damian tried to discuss office matters and the impact being made by Lydia although he was going to withhold his own news until she was in a better condition. That strategy collapsed because Rachel already knew and expressed her concern that the auditing section would struggle without him. Matt returned with the refreshments and said that they were going to take a holiday before he started his university course. It was time for Damian to leave and he embraced his business partner as gently as he could. As he left the room, he heard Rachel say, "it was a little girl, Damian."

The atmosphere in the offices of Hannon, Shannon and Smith (to be renamed) was visibly positive as the triumvirate of Lydia, Glen and Gerald were uniting the whole business. Lydia had created a 'brain's trust' comprising six members of staff reflecting the whole team before she announced that every two months one member would leave and another join: she described it to Gerald as 'creative tension'. The four of them held an informal meeting and covered the key matters affecting the performance of the firm before Damian related his visit to Rachel earlier in the day. Lydia said that she was in regular touch but was discerning an increasing negative attitude: it was agreed to put the matter on hold. They reviewed the reaction of their clients to the news of the partnership changes and Glen Shannon applauded the work put in by Damian in contacting a number of important directors of their largest audit customers. They agreed to meet again at the same time in the following week. Damian left his car at the office and Louisa ran him in her own car to the surgery: she was genuine and generous when telling Damian that she was sorry he was leaving.

Cathy's leaving party was in full swing when he entered the decorated building: there were balloons and banners and the outside caterers were ensuring that the wine was flowing. The practice manager, perhaps on her second glass, made a grab for the new arrival and insisted that he promised he would stay in touch which he did if only to extract himself from another determined embrace. He did however respond with some emotion when he found himself being hugged by a stunningly turned-out Cathy whose visits to the hairdresser and the manicurist were paying off especially because he relished the occasions when his wife allowed her fair hair to lie naturally.

A bottle was tapped and Dr Martin Armstrong

promised to deliver a short speech which, to cheers and applause, is exactly what he did. His brevity was his secret because every word, all the phrases, the absence of jokes and his sincerity resulted in a delivery which was rather special. The room went silent as he recalled the coronavirus challenges and his amazement at the ability of every one of them to dig deeper than ever before. He recalled his medical school lecturer once saying that if you give a person a target way beyond their accepted abilities, time and again they will achieve it.

"I've never," he said, "ever contemplated giving Cathy a target because when you have a colleague who climbs mountains every day, why rock the boat?"

The toast was given, Cathy responded with some well-chosen and perhaps self-deprecating words, everybody cheered and the caterers opened some more bottles of wine.

A little later Damian found himself talking to Dr Armstrong who took the opportunity to comment on his "hale and hearty" mother-in-law who he had met at the Cumberland Nursing Home where he was the doctor on call. He then asked about his experience with the keto diet not only because of his visit to the practice but because of the reference to it in Cathy's paper on the issue of weight-loss. He said that he hoped Cathy would complete writing it only after she'd had a long rest.

Damian and Cathy decided to walk home together and, despite slowing a little after a mile or so, they talked about Paul Marston and the news that he would most likely be receiving a suspended sentence. They had agreed about their stance because they had to protect Scarlett: Cathy said that Marston had transferred to another practice in the town but she'd had the opportunity to see his medical notes before they were moved and his various operations had weakened him considerably. There was no fear for the future because they both believed that Paul Marston was in the past and they were able to concentrate on matters of a more personal nature. Cathy became aware that his arm was clinging to her with a renewed intensity.

They made it back to their home whereupon she went upstairs to change leaving open her bedroom door through which he charged with the intention of making the expense of her earlier visit to the hairdresser, a distant memory.

They later sat together in the garden revisiting the day's event: Rachel Smith's pain, Lydia's 'Brains Trust', Martin Armstrong's speech and her response which he described as breath-taking. Damian recounted his conversation with Martin Armstrong, his opinion of Nettie and the reference to the weight-loss paper.

"We'll see," she said, "and it's helpful that Martin is willing to wait for it because I'm going to have a long rest: I've brought home some travel brochures for us to read." She paused and kissed his cheek "But tomorrow, you and I have to discuss the letter: we cannot let it drift any further."

Damian stood up and looked down at Cathy.

"I assume that you've read it?" he said. "Do you have any thoughts on its contents?" he asked.

She stood up and put her arms around his neck.

"Mr Hannon," she said, "I most certainly do; we must talk about it."

At around three o'clock, in the middle of the night, she shook her husband, intending to wake him up and tell him that he must accept the offer made in the letter only to find that Damian was wide awake.

"I already have, Cathy," he replied. "I'm meeting Mr Heron on Tuesday." He squeezed her and asked that they go back to sleep.

The more senior of the two lawyers representing Paul Marston summed up for his client the situation as far as they could in view of certain developments. At first it seemed that the Crime Prosecution Service were intending to pursue an offence of the unlawful possession of a firearm with intent to commit an indictable offence which carried, if Marston was convicted, a maximum sentence of between seven to ten years in prison.

However, as matters progressed, their case began to unravel not least because Mr and Mrs Hannon were refusing to either make a complaint against Marston or give evidence against him. Their story was that he had appeared in their house and there was a misunderstanding which led to the shotgun being discharged. The damage to Damian's face came from when he tussled with Marston. The CPS realised that the real reason for their reluctance, in fact their refusal, to give evidence in a trial was because they did not want to talk about the parentage of their daughter Scarlett so avoiding the public disclosure of events at a party twenty-one years ago. The CPS wavered and were then hit by the possibility of a medical expert who was willing to give evidence suggesting that the combination of acute pain and poisoning in his stomach and the confusion with his prescriptions had rendered him temporarily insane.

The police in charge of the case were furious

especially as they were having problems getting a case together against the McMahon brothers who were sticking to their unlikely story that Marston had encouraged them to rob a bank. Finally, the McMahons were brought to justice and Paul Marston was charged with carrying an offensive weapon for which he would receive a suspended sentence. He was soon back at home with just one thing on his mind.

The meeting took place in a room at the back of a High Street charity shop in a Northamptonshire village ten miles from Damian's home. He was already intrigued by the letter which he had received in a 'strictly personal, private and confidential' envelope. The embossed heading stated 'Maydene Wealth Management Company' and little else: there was no address, telephone number, email or form of contact. He'd searched the register at Companies House but there was no record of any such company: he'd made a few telephone calls but no-one had heard of it. The writer, who signed himself as 'Mr Heron', invited Damian to meet with him at the address he had now entered and at the suggested time, 'to discuss a matter of national importance'. Below the signature, written using a fountain pen, was a mobile phone number and a request that he text his acceptance, which he eventually did.

The room had no windows although there was a fan cooling the summer air: on one dust covered wall was a faded landscape painting. Mr Heron sat opposite his visitor, the table and two chairs being the only furniture and poured them each a coffee from a flask. He straightened his striped tie and ensured that his suit jacket was tidy.

"All a bit John le Carre, Mr Hannon," he began, "and I understand that you are bursting to ask me your questions, but can you read this, please. He placed a sheet of paper, which had no heading but referred to their meeting, and which confirmed that Damian would never divulge anything which took place today to any other person.

"It has no legal basis but you are a professional man and I think I'm entitled to believe that you'll not sign it without intending to adhere to its strictures."

Damian signed it and sat back: the man opposite him was scary.

"My name is Mr Heron, which it isn't, but you will come to understand why anonymity is so important to the success of what I'm going to discuss with you. I can tell you that I work for a Government department and that's all I'm going to say about myself for the time being."

"If I recall," said Damian, "the heron waits in shallow water moving its head from side to side assessing the position of its intended prey."

"I do believe it does, Mr Hannon, although as you are still here and you've signed my piece of paper, I think we'll move on to Damian." He sipped his coffee. "I will be using the term 'we' and, by that, I am referring to Her Majesty's Revenue and Customs with whom you are very familiar: Hannon, Shannon and Smith are authorised to use a direct line into the Revenue which speaks well of your business."

"You're not an accountant," said Damian.

"But you are which is why we are here. Do you mind if I cover a few personal matters before we reach the point of this meeting? First of all, how is Mrs Pennington settling in?"

"Lydia?" he exclaimed. "What's she to do with all this subterfuge?"

"With all respect you don't seriously think an accountant with the stature of Mrs Pennington would want to work for a provincial firm? She agreed to help us by joining your firm so that we could make this approach to you." He smiled. "You rather helped the situation by announcing your resignation and from what I hear, Mrs Pennington is loving her new environment and has every intention of staying."

Damian sat back and reflected on this latest development: something had never been completely convincing about Mrs Lydia Pennington FCA and now it was beginning to fit into place.

"Is Mrs Hannon enjoying her retirement?" Mr Heron continued leaving Damian speechless. "I hope she was not too distressed by the Paul Marston attack?"

"How do you know about that?" he stuttered.

"It was always going to be difficult to convict him and we understood your reluctance to testify. The local police will be keeping an eye on him." He looked at his notes. "You have two children I believe. Scarlett is doing well at University and Arthur is soon to become a father. You will know that Faria, his partner, was born in Portugal but is now a British citizen: she is well thought of by her bank employer." He paused. "But I have to deal with, shall we say, a delicate matter: your relationship with Rosemary Cameron."

This was a bridge too far for Damian who stood up, shouted at his inquisitor and started to leave the room. Mr Heron looked up at him.

"Please sit down, Damian, because there are several things you need to know about her."

He held back, panicked and then did as he was asked.

"We know all about your relationship with Marie who, as you are aware, is now living on Bryher Island in Port Solent and working at the university. All that is in order. You probably know that she was born Rosemary Magellan Babikov: her mother still lives in London and Marie went with her step sister Khristina Babikov for a holiday in Egypt. Marie, who changed her name to Cameron, told you that she thinks her father, who is Russian, committed suicide because that is what her step sister told her. He is, in fact, still alive and met with Khristina in Cairo although we think that Marie knew nothing about that." He paused. "You should know that he has links to Moscow but we'll say no more on that matter."

A few moments passed while Damian sieved through this torrent of information and ran the back of his hand across his mouth.

"What right have you to tell me what to do in my private life?" he demanded.

"No right whatsoever, but when we go on to discuss the reason for this meeting, you'll understand that we must be certain of our ground. We simply suggest that it's in your best interest to sever all connection with Rosemary Cameron."

"Is that a condition?" he asked. "And it's Marie."

"It's a suggestion," replied Mr Heron. "Why don't we go and get some fresh air and then we can discuss what we have in mind for you, Damian?"

They walked out into the sunshine and Mr Heron bought his visitor an ice cream and a bottle of ice-cold water which Damian took with him as they re-entered the unwelcoming room at the back of the charity shop. There was a change in atmosphere as the Government official pulled out a file from his case and opened it.

"I will be leaving you with a summary of what we're now going to talk about," he said, "but, please, let me, as briefly as I can, explain the proposition I wish to make to you. You will know as well as anyone that the pandemic wrecked much of the British infrastructure. Whilst most of the focus has been on the National Health Service, which is battling to even catch-up with its basic responsibilities - social care, mental health and the rest - the Government and, in particular, both the Prime Minister and the Chancellor of the Exchequer, are concerned, in fact very concerned, about the state of play within HMRC. Putting it bluntly, millions, more likely billions of pounds are being lost in the non-payment of tax, fraud and crime." He paused to sip some water.

"Before Covid-19 hit us, the Revenue were increasingly efficient and effective in their role as a prosecuting authority. I am sure that some of your clients have received visits from the Inspectors and it can be an unpleasant experience even for the innocent.

There have been, however, two major problems which have enabled the real crooks to escape justice. The first is that we live in a democracy, which is great if you're a human rights lawyer but if, as happens time and time again, you are the Revenue and you are ninety-nine per cent certain about a massive fraud being perpetrated, the moment an action is commenced you're faced by an army of highly paid lawyers and advisers, many of whom are ex-Revenue employees and who know every trick in the book to fend off a successful prosecution." He paused and looked down at his notes.

"A decent barrister can delay virtually any court process by a minimum of two years and, if necessary, if they are fearful of losing a case, they'll invoke the oldest trick in the book: their client develops a serious illness and, surprise, surprise, a Harley Street 'expert' will persuade the judge that his client is too ill to stand trial." Mr Heron hesitated and wiped his brow. "All legal, all democratic and directly against the best interests of the genuine taxpayers who make up ninety-per-cent of the working population. What this all adds up to is cost because the Revenue is under enormous budget constraints and all too often the finance simply runs out and the case is lost." He stood up and took off his jacket.

"The second problem concerns the legal process itself. When it makes a criminal investigation, its aim is to secure a criminal conviction and here lies the next issue. The Revenue want to secure criminal convictions because they act as a deterrent to other potential fraudsters partly because they attract greater publicity. Criminal investigations are conducted under the powers within the Police and Criminal Evidence Act, which everyone calls PACE, which demand a draconian burden of proof. Time and again a case fails on a questionable point of law."

He hit the table with his fist. "It's so frustrating but the consequence is that the Revenue decide to fight cases on a civil basis which is often the aim of the advisers because they are small scale and may be the best option for the real villains. They are easier for the Revenue to win but have far less impact." He decided to take a small break before resuming.

"There is one other issue that the Revenue is coping with and that is because the whole structure is riddled with informers. Some take bribes, some are intimidated and some become resentful when they see others making so much money. We have managed to upgrade the internal management and there has been an improvement but not quickly enough for our political masters.

This is when a regional based senior manager came up with an idea which we are now implementing. We are creating an anonymous group of, we think, twelve investigators around the country who nobody will know about: in fact, I will be the only person who knows all the detail. It is to be referred to as the OF Group: obliterate fraud and no marks for creativity but as there will be no publicity it doesn't matter. If you join us, you'll be OF8."

"I was hoping I'd be OF7," laughed Damian.

"This is a bit more serious than misplaced James Bond jokes," reprimanded Mr Heron. He took out a mobile phone from inside his jacket pocket and handed it to Damian. He explained that he could use it day or night because it was programmed only to reach him or one of two other people who would never identify themselves.

"You'll be a consultant with Maydene Wealth Management Company which does not exist which does not matter because no-one will ever question it. If asked, you recruit investment clients for the company which outperforms most other similar companies and for which an individual must have a net worth of more than fifty million pounds. That should deter most of the people you are likely to meet. You'll be paid ten thousand pounds a month by Maydene direct into your bank account on which you'll pay no income tax: in fact, you'll never have to pay any personal tax again and you'll not hear again at any time from your local inspector of taxes on a personal basis.

You'll also receive a commission of three per cent of any unpaid corporation tax that you recover.

We'll meet from time to time at whichever charity shop you wish because we have made a substantial donation to the charity in return for the use of their back rooms: they all seem to have one."

Damian stared at Mr Heron and swallowed.

"What do you want me to do?" he asked.

"I want you to go home and think about what I have said and then I suggest we meet again in a week's time: assuming you're of a mind to join OF, we'll talk about the work ahead. The number at the bottom of my letter will no longer work so, if you want to contact me, use the mobile."

Damian stood up and walked around the table before asking Mr Heron three questions: can he trust him; can he talk to Cathy and why the imposition on his contact with Marie?

"You must make up your own mind on me," said Mr Heron, "as I'm doing on you. I understand that you'll need to talk to Mrs Hannon but can I suggest you leave out the James Bond stuff and describe it as being an associate of the Revenue and you'll be using your vast skills as an auditor of some major companies to recover unpaid taxes." He paused. "In respect of Rosemary Cameron, you cannot say anything to her and, if you do and we find out, you'll be excluded at once with no compensation." He hesitated. "I hope that what I've told you will deter you from seeing her again. You must see that you have so much to lose."

They shook hands and Damian reached his car feeling drained.

"OF8" he said to himself as he drove out of the town.

"I wonder if Giacinta Johnson is available as my assistant?" he said to himself, as visions of Halle Berry flooded into his mind.

+ + +

CHAPTER TWELVE

Marie was becoming frustrated as the complexity of Franz Liszt's 'La Campanella' etude tested her digital dexterity and resolve and she knew that, for once, she'd not complete the mandated hour's piano practice. She was frustrated that she'd only managed to improve her time for the four-hundred metres by two seconds and with her disagreement with Professor Warnock over the necessity for her to re-learn general anatomy which she knew but struggled to absorb again. Quite what 'imaginary planes' that intersect the body creating slices of inner body structures, had to do with dental hygiene, which she understood, perplexed her and, for the first time, the professor imposed a deadline for the submission of her next dissertation.

She was, however, honest enough with herself to know that the real reason for her destabilisation was the previous evening's put down. Jeb had introduced a rather affluent son of a local builder who managed to persuade her to accept a dinner invitation: the flourish with which the minder at the restaurant took his car keys with "Yes Mr Sinclair, certainly Mr Sinclair" told its own story.

Jonathan was pushy throughout the meal: he had charisma and looks but the flash point came when he told Marie that he had never dined a woman older than himself. She was able to cope with that but it was his next observation that ended their meal, when he asked her if her breasts had started to sag.

Her solution to the present introspective phase was to drive to the coast, strip down to bikini bottoms and a tee shirt and, barefooted, begin a long trek until she reached the headland where she drank a bottle of water and began the journey back to the car. Her sunhat shielded her from the fierce heat and if there were other holiday-makers on the beaches, she did not really see them. What she could visualise was Damian Hannon. On the outward section of her walk, she found herself unwinding with a mixture of thoughts and fears, not least the deterioration in her relationship with Professor Warnock. She planned a response which was to submit to him her best-ever paper, on time and so attempt to regain the initiative. The running target was tough but achievable and Jonathan Sinclair had made a fair point: she was getting older and just a year away from her fortieth birthday so perhaps she'd adjust from running for speed to rounding the track for pleasure. As for Mr Liszt and his piano complexity, she'd transfer her allegiance to Jamie Cullum, which resulted in her applauding herself.

She was walking through the edge of the gentle waves and occasionally splashing seawater over her legs and face. There he was again, in her thoughts, the man whom she thought at one time represented her future. It was not over and Damian had texted her the previous evening telling her he had some news and was planning that they should meet but gave no details. What did she really think? As she reached her destination, she acknowledged that she did not really know.

When she returned back home, she had one outstanding task and that was to reply to an email from her step-sister, Khristina Babikov, who was suggesting that they meet up and she was happy to come down to Portsmouth.

If there was one aspect of Cathy's personality which caused her husband to feel occasionally uncertain it was her unpredictability. This was a regular in many a stag night speech: "I told my wife that she'd cooked a lovely meal and she replied by asking weren't all her meals lovely?" However, the characteristic which Damian had never really mastered was her change of direction, mood swing and speed of travel. He was now experiencing exactly that: Cathy had, two days earlier, dismissed his description of the meeting with Mr Heron and told him to take the job, she showed no reaction to her mother's installation at the Cumberland Nursing Home, she flipped over her call with Scarlett and could not remember saying she was going to take a long rest with the additional mystery that the travel brochures had disappeared.

They were sitting in the garden awaiting the arrival of her friend when she said, "I'm far too young to be put out to grass, Damian, and I expect you to support me. You've been treating me like an inpatient in a geriatric ward."

He could have dealt with all that but was completely foxed by her next announcement which was that she had decided to concentrate on the completion of her paper on weight-loss for Dr Armstrong. She told him that she felt she could make a real contribution because the obesity crisis was becoming acutely more serious. She then read out to him an extract from the morning's paper which highlighted the growing concern over child obesity rates as revealed in the latest 'Child Measurement Programme' which showed that 32.3%

of four and five-year-olds in Northern England measured as overweight or obese.

He was desperately trying not to stir her ire despite the completely irrational nature of her commentary on a national medical tragedy and was unprepared for the next development which concerned the imminent arrival of her friend, Anisha Khan.

"As you know I worked with Anisha for several years until she left to join the hospital paediatric unit but we have stayed in touch and we recently had afternoon tea together when I told her about my paper and your idea about using financial incentives to encourage people to lose weight. Anisha thought it was a crack-pot idea and so she'll be here shortly for you to sell the idea to her."

"Why do I want to do that Cathy? It was a half-hearted plan which I thought up to help you."

"It makes sense to me, Damian, but what today will tell us is if you can convince a medical professional. Anisha is highly thought of at the hospital and tells me about the overweight children who they are seeing more regularly."

She paused and went inside the house reappearing with a nurse in uniform which was explained by her rushing over to see them after her shift had been extended. Cathy made the introductions although they each remembered meeting at the surgery a number of years ago. A pot of tea and cakes was produced, the conversation drifted towards Cathy's paper on weight loss and Damian responded to her request to introduce his thinking on the use of financial incentives.

Anisha Khan sat back and considered carefully the information that Damian had delivered. She helped herself to a second cake and began to analyse his concept.

"I always find it difficult," she said, "accepting non-medical people who are trying to infiltrate my world. You're an accountant Damian and I've no doubt you're good at what you do. However, you talk about the issue of obesity as though you were adding up a column of figures. We're talking about human beings who need all the help we can give them."

"So, what's your answer to the problem of overweight patients?" he asked.

"I nurse them, Damian, and there's a massive effort within the NHS to combat the problem. I'm sure that Cathy has told you about the lengths we are going to and I suggest that throwing tax-payers money around will attract every chancer there is out there."

"No, it won't," snapped Damian, "because the process starts with the doctor who selects patients needing to lose weight to join the scheme. The whole process is controlled by the nurse who weighs the individual on a regular basis and if there is a loss of weight, the patient receives a sum of money in their bank account: that's the incentive and it's a real one. Two hundred pounds for losing two pounds in weight is a helpful sum of money."

"They go home laughing all over their face and put the weight straight back on," accused Anisha.

"In which case they receive no further funds. It's possible that the money might be used to help mothers feed their families more healthily."

"Oh! You're now a dietician, are you?" she said. "A man of many parts." The nurse stood up and said that she needed to get home. Damian noticed that it took her a little time to lift herself up from the chair. She embraced Cathy and made her way back to her car.

Damian started to tidy up when Cathy returned.

"I think a dead mackerel could have made a greater impact," she said. "Why didn't you make an effort to impress her?" she snapped.

"It's rather difficult to discuss anything with a bigoted woman who came here intending to wreck my idea," he said. "Perhaps the fact she's overweight herself did not help my cause."

"What right have you to comment on another person's physical condition?" she yelled.

"I thought that you gave up your career because you couldn't face patients' bodies anymore?"

"What gave you that idea? You heard Martin Armstrong say at my party that I climbed mountains for the NHS."

"He also said you should take a rest. I second that, Cathy."

Damian had driven quickly to his office and now stared at Lydia wondering how much did she actually know about Mr Heron and OF? He realised that he was unable to ask her any questions because if she didn't know about the events which had taken place at the charity shop in a Bedfordshire village, she would not understand what he was talking about and, if she did, he was breaching Mr Heron's sanctions.

The meeting proceeded with the usual enthusiasm and discipline that Mrs Pennington seemed to engender. At one point, Glen Shannon took the floor and summarised a recent edict from the HMRC concerning a growing trend whereby directors of companies were increasingly unwilling to declare their earnings for the payment of personal tax liabilities and sought to generate profits that were hidden.

One that was increasingly popular was where a company either set up its own car dealership or linked with another business where the owners were prepared to indulge in sharp practice. A director of the first company purchased a vehicle from the second-hand car market and, by offering cash, waited until a really competitive transaction was available.

"Two months later," said Glen, "the vehicle is sold to the dealership at an inflated price, the director returns the original cash to the company and pockets the profit. On a thirty-thousand pounds transaction, the director can make perhaps three to four thousand pounds and if that is repeated five or six times a year, he is pocketing around twenty to twenty-four thousand pounds annually." He paused.

"Even if the Revenue catch on, they have to prove a link between the director and the car dealership and it's generally not serious enough to be worth their while. But just think about it. Assuming the director is paying a tax rate of forty-five per cent, it means they are generating extra income of perhaps forty thousand pounds a year on top of every other perk they fiddle."

"What's the actual offence?" pondered Gerald. "I suppose it's misusing company funds to avoid paying tax and the only way to spot it is by examining the cash ledger and we don't always do that as thoroughly as perhaps we should."

"Surely the director commits a second offence when he or she signs their annual tax return?" said Lydia.

"Of course," said Glen, "but it's too small to attract the Revenue's interest though, as Damian has always said, any director who knowingly breaks the rules, cannot be trusted."

"You'll miss all this Damian, in a week's time when you leave us," said Lydia.

"I'll manage to tear myself away," he grinned.

A few days later, Damian met Mr Heron at the charity shop in a Bedfordshire village. He drove carefully to the rendezvous as he pondered the sudden deterioration in his relationship with Cathy stemming from the ludicrous row about his failure to back her up on the writing of the weight-loss paper. She seemed to be lost in a meaningless project which went against all they had talked about. She deserved a rest from nursing and a holiday was certainly on the cards. Yet, on one night the bedroom door was open and the next it was slammed shut in his face. He decided to lose himself in the world of OF8.

Initially there was a certain amount of confusion because it was two weeks since their first meeting and due to Mr Heron insisting on referring to him by his code, OF8, as Damian explained that there was much for him to consider and the use of OF8 made him nervous. But he was here and surely that was enough for his inquisitor?

"I'll accept that you have needed two weeks, OF8, and we'll assume we can now proceed," continued Mr Heron, "but I want to show you something that I hope will ensure that you'll never again question the agreement we have."

He removed from a buff envelope in front of him three black and white photographs showing what was once a human being lying in a peat bog. The eyes were no longer in their sockets, one hand had been cut off and the left leg protruded away from the torso at a strange angle. Damian's stomach turned and that was before Mr Heron told him that the body was a woman.

"Obliterate Fraud is a second incarnation of a project thought up by the Revenue," he said, "and being amateurs, they made every mistake possible including thinking that a twenty-seven-year-old employee could manage to infiltrate a company where the tax schemes being used were losing up to two hundred million pounds a year for HMRC." He paused and took out of the package another picture showing an attractive brunette with a seductive smile on her face. "This shows the woman before the directors decided to send the Revenue a message."

He was holding on to his sanity at this point helped by the awareness of his opposite number who sat quietly before offering additional information. He took out his handkerchief and mopped his brow.

"It reached my desk at the same time that, as we discussed before, the powers that be were getting militant about lost fiscal income and so my department devised OF and started work recruiting agents about six months ago."

"How much success have you had?" Damian asked.

"I'm asking the questions OF8," he said. "Your payments have already started as your bank account will attest to and so I think it's time to give you your first assignment. Are we in agreement OF8?"

Damian nodded as he pushed the photographs away from him.

"In the next four weeks you will receive on your mobile phone, which I see you have with you, a message giving a grid reference which will be in the countryside. You should look for a pink pebble behind which will be a package containing the information on a company we wish you to investigate. You should complete your initial research and then we'll meet to enable me to approve your strategy for exposing the fraudsters." He paused. "You can go now, OF8."

Damian sat still and then stood up, moved towards the exit and then turned back.

"Mr Heron," he said, "is this for real?"

"Brilliant," shouted Mr Heron. "Sit down OF8."

His elation seemed genuine as he explained to Damian that lying beneath his approach was a psychological programme which he had to pass. Today saw the final three stages which were the taking of two weeks to meet again, his controlled reaction to the photographs of the dead body of the Revenue operative and there being no reference to the financial arrangements.

"I told you that your payments had started and, of course, you already knew that but what you did not mention was the commission arrangements on recovered tax income. That told us what we wanted to know."

Damian stared at Mr Heron.

"Your first letter made reference to being of importance to my country or something like that."

"Yes OF8," he replied. "And that is exactly what this is about."

"Serving my country," he said to himself as he left the charity shop.

Paul Marston threw himself into renovating his home: he was feeling much healthier and had already seen his new doctor who was not particularly friendly. He had three different prescriptions to take and was controlling the daily routine more seriously as he would need to return to hospital for a day in out-patients. This was to ensure that his stomach was healing properly and the surrounding damage had been rectified. He used the time available to read the diet sheets given to him by the hospital staff and was cooking fresh vegetables for the first time. The one blemish in his life was the weekly visits to the police station which were part of the terms of his release and would last for a year. He despised the sniggers and the looks which he himself had been guilty of during his own career: coppers detest bent coppers: end of story.

Marston had reached two decisions: he wanted a woman which he anticipated would not pose any real challenges because his reduced weight and improved physique, together with a new wardrobe, should make the nightly visits to the local pubs, rewarding. He was financially solvent; his ex-wife's lawyers had gone away and he would find a side-line before too long to pay for his foreign holidays. Life for Paul Marston was on the up.

There remained the outstanding mission on which he was now decided and it made him smile as he worked out that the police were going to help him. He relived all the events which had led to his downfall starting with Cathy's frantic desire for sex in the garden, her lying about Scarlett, her taunt in the surgery that with his small dick he couldn't fuck a watermelon and the brazen way she had talked about things when he had confronted them in their house.

He drank deeply on his glass of whisky and raised it in the air. He toasted his decision that Cathy Hannon was going to die and the murder would take place when he was reporting in to the local police station. There was, of course, his recent meeting with the third McMahon brother who had not been involved in the bank robbery: he had blinked at the fee suggested but a deal was done.

Cathy Hannon was going to die and it would be the best day in the life of Paul Marston.

Two significant events now occurred in the life of Marie Cameron and even reverting back to the smoothing music of Chopin and running the four-hundred metres without a stopwatch did little to relieve her inner tensions.

The first was unexpected and unfair. Professor Warnock criticised her dissertation on dental anatomy with an exaggerated and impersonal style which made her feel like a first-year student. It was at this point in time that Rebecca told her that there were rumours circulating suggesting that the professor had exceeded his departmental budget and was looking to make cost savings. Marie realised that she had not received from him a signed copy of her contract.

The second event involved the arrival in Portsmouth of her step-sister, Khristina Babikov, who stayed the weekend and proved to be stimulating company with her range of interests despite her reluctance to talk about her own work in London. It was on the Sunday morning that the real reason for her visit became apparent. She apologised for misleading Marie but she revealed that their Father, Fyodor Babikov, was alive and she'd met him in Cairo at the conclusion of their trip to see the Pyramids.

"He's an old man, Marie, and he's dying of something: he'd not tell me what. But he had a request to make and I agreed to pass it on to you. He wants to meet you: you're his daughter and he wants to apologise for not being a good father: he says he can make it to London."

Marie allowed several days to pass while she considered her options: she had no wish to contact her mother and wasn't too certain that she wanted to meet her father who was an irrelevance to her life. She warmed to Khristina, enjoyed her company and wanted to maintain the association and for that reason alone she agreed to meet her father. A week later she received a text message giving a Saturday, two weeks ahead, a time and a restaurant in Covent Garden, London. She booked a hotel in Bloomsbury for two nights and began to look forward to the event.

Two days later Damian contacted her and asked that they have a telephone conversation which took place on a local beach as she paddled gently in the waves. She was stunned by the passionate way in which he talked and said that he was proposing to come down to Portsmouth to see her. When she managed to turn the conversation to her news, he expressed great concern about the attitude being displayed by Professor Warwick and said he'd make some enquiries as to the financial position of the university. Marie went on to reveal her coming meeting with her father and tried to answer his questions as Damian attempted to make sense of these events.

"Marie," he said, "did you say you'd booked a hotel room in London?" he asked.

She confirmed the details and responded positively to a suggestion that he join her on the Friday evening: he emphasised that he could stay the night. She then had another thought and asked Damian if he could come down on the Saturday instead and join them for the meal at the restaurant.

"Are you suggesting that I meet your father?" he

said.

"You can ask him if you can marry me," she teased.

+ + +

CHAPTER THIRTEEN

Mr Heron was clearly becoming flustered as the two men on the other side of the table seemed increasingly dubious about the answers which they were hearing.

"You've selected a provincial accountant who has never served in the armed forces and who has had no track record of undercover work" said the older of the two, "meaning you have no indication on whether he can fulfil the task you are setting him?"

Mr Heron shuffled from side to side in his uncomfortable chair as the noise from the Piccadilly traffic could be detected through the armour-plated glass windows. He had given up smoking but dearly wanted an E-cigarette at that moment. He began to repeat his earlier explanation of the recruitment programme which had been followed by his team and detailed again his two meetings with Damian Hannon. The second of the interrogation duo echoed his boss's concerns and said that he could not understand how Hannon had accepted everything that had been said to him. Heron was not going to fall into the trap that was being set of trying to take the credit for his success in setting up OF8.

"No-one will deny the risks involved, Sir, but Hannon responded exactly as we had been led to believe which suggests that he is a sound choice, not that we had many other candidates. He reacted all the way through in a way that we hoped for: he's not money driven and resented the brief excursion into his private territory in a manner that the psychologists wanted to monitor."

"And he hasn't sussed that you're listening in to his mobile phone?"

"Definitely not, Sir. There has been no change in his manner on the calls he makes and receives and he and his wife seem to be irritating each other." Mr Heron swallowed before continuing. "Please remember he's an accountant and from all that Mrs Pennington has told us, a very good accountant. His success has been his ability to work with directors of companies and gain their confidence."

"But it still leaves us with the key question and that is, will he make the move we desperately need him to make?"

"I can't answer that, Sir, but I believe he will."

"For your sake I hope that you're right," said the senior of the two men.

Two days later Damian Hannon's mobile phone was recorded giving the content that Mr Heron desperately wanted to hear. He was left with a few days to prepare for the next move which would determine the success or otherwise of this particular assignment. In tidying up his file, and noting down the meeting in Mayfair, he came across the graphic photographs which he had shown to OF8 at their meeting in a charity shop in a village in Bedfordshire, and shuddered. He had been taught never to reflect on past events and he didn't except on this occasion. The victim had been so excited about joining his team and it should never have ended the way it did.

"Tibet!"

Damian was sitting under the sunshade in the

tranquillity of his garden having spent the morning and early afternoon cutting lawns, tidying borders, trimming hedges and feeling rather pleased with the results. His feel good state of mind lasted less than ten minutes as a result of an announcement from Mrs Hannon that she was going on a three-week holiday to Tibet.

"Before I tell you all about it, Damian," she ordered, "I want to inform you about my mother's situation."

"She's become an international bridge player," he suggested.

"Her relationship with Edgar Valentine has developed at rather a pace: apparently he's loaded and they've decided to buy a bungalow together, locally, so there'll be no added pressure on you."

"He's well named," said Damian.

"I had tea with the two of them yesterday at the Cumberland Nursing Home and he's so courteous: a bit of a charmer, if I'm honest."

"Do you know how he made his money?" asked Damian.

"They were full of the visit last weekend which they received from Arthur and Faria: it was a great success, so mother says."

"And they didn't come here?" he exclaimed.

"Mother is giving them fifty thousand pounds."

"She's what!?"

"Faria is doing really well in her job at the bank and if they can raise a deposit of one hundred thousand pounds, she will qualify for an employee mortgage: they've found a two-bedroomed flat in Maida Vale which will allow them to get on to the property ladder."

"Where does the other fifty-thousand come from?"

"Arthur has saved five thousand pounds and Faria

has the rest in her savings account."

Damian stood up, went indoors, poured himself a large scotch and soda, rubbed his face with the kitchen towel and re-joined his wife.

"Arthur has saved five thousand pounds?" he continued.

"Apparently Edgar was impressed by his commitment to his studies," she said. "Scarlett has visited them again. Isn't it wonderful to see our family prospering?" She paused. "Arthur has sent you a message. He says that if you want to meet up in London, he'll try to find the time."

"Do you think you might contact our son and suggest that he has a responsibility to come and see me?"

"Why would I do that, Damian?" she asked. "Now, my trip to Tibet. I leave in early September and I calculate I should be back for the birth of the baby."

Damian finished his glass of whisky and sighed before waiting to hear the background to her decision to visit the Far East. It had started with a meeting of her book club at the church and someone suggesting they read 'Wild Swans: three daughters of China' by Jung Chang. For some it was a re-read as this was an international best-seller published over thirty years ago and telling of three generations of China: grandmother, mother and the author.

With the start of the pandemic in Wuhan the previous year and the change of American presidency leading to an improved international relationship with China, Cathy had started taking a greater interest in the country and was captivated by Jung Chang's masterpiece. She had researched the potential for travel and settled for a company offering the 'High Road to

Tibet' journey starting at Kathmandu, reaching Lhasa, seeing the Dalai Lama's Summer Palace before returning to where they started.

"We'll be eating Nepalese momos, which are traditional dumplings," she laughed. "Not allowed on a keto diet, I would think."

He resisted telling her that she was not going to see much of China whose treatment of the Tibetan people was an international outrage and he was not on the keto diet anymore. He asked why she was choosing to go on holiday on her own? Cathy reasoned that they had been married for twenty-three years, he would soon be fifty and the longevity tables were predicting that he should live until he was at least eighty-two and a brief time apart could revitalise their marriage.

"Leaving aside the reality," she added, "that you can't take your attention away from your mobile phone so I think it safe to say that we're hoping for a call from one's girlfriend."

There was no way that he could explain that he was waiting for a grid reference from Mr Heron.

The enigmatic Cathy Hannon looked stunning as the taxi collected them from their home and took them to the town's main hotel where a crowd of over eighty staff and clients were waiting to bid farewell to the founding partner of Hannon, Shannon and Smith (to be renamed). Lydia had delegated the arrangement to two junior members of her team and they had come up trumps including the pianist and guitarist playing away in a corner of the room.

It was an evening of surprises trumped by the appearance of Rachel and Matt Smith who seemed rejuvenated partly because the hospital had confirmed that all was well for them to try again for a baby. Matt and Damian lamented England's failure to win the Rugby Six Nations championships managing to lose to Wales at Twickenham. Matt liked Damian's suggestion that the selectors should have picked him. His attention was diverted as he spotted his daughter coming towards them, man in tow. Scarlett kissed her father and introduced Joshua.

Cathy was circulating at a rapid rate of knots and was relishing meeting again some of the senior members of staff who she had known in the early days of the partnership. She gave Glen Shannon a genuine hug but somehow never met Lydia.

It was Glen who called for silence and delivered a remarkably empathetic speech combining humour with respect and his admiration for the way Damian almost single-handed, had masterminded the breakaway from the previous partnership and created today's success. This was followed by Kingsley Wilkinson, owner of the town's largest estate agents, who claimed that Damian had been over-charging him for years and unless he reduced his tax payments, he'd have to find another accountant.

"The only problem with that threat," he continued, "is that there will never be another Damian Hannon. You, Damian, have been a credit to your profession, to your business and to yourself and I can only think the best way to celebrate your retirement is to drink the champagne that you're paying for!"

Damian said a few words in response emphasising his gratitude to his now thirty-eight ex-colleagues who, collectively, were the business. He grabbed a brief chat with Lydia and agreed to call in to see her during the following week. Louisa drove them home and, after sharing coffee and their individual thoughts, they both went to bed. Cathy's bedroom door remained half open.

Marie spent an isolated weekend reflecting on her coming meeting with her father. She remained on edge about her relationship with Professor Warnock, who was now on two weeks holiday, and had written him a personal letter in which she displayed humility and commitment but acknowledged that she was finding the breadth of the course syllabus rather demanding. She proposed that they meet on his return and have an honest conversation about her future. She concluded by repeating her sense of privilege being a member of his university team and she'd hoped that she could have the opportunity to assuage any concerns he might have.

She spent Sunday afternoon on the beach, alone, having turned down an offer to go sailing with Rebecca and Jeb. She slept for part of the time and then wandered out to the edge of the seawater, bathed her face and thought about Damian. In six days, she would be with him in a hotel room before a dinner in Covent Garden. She was elated that he'd agreed to her suggestion that they should meet and the availability of privacy for a night was tantalising. Did she use the opportunity to extract a greater commitment which she felt that she deserved or should she let matters drift a little further? He said he had some news for her which suggested that a 'wait and see' approach was appropriate plus, of course, she wanted to enjoy herself.

As she walked back to the car park, she thought about Khristina Babikov: their holiday together to see the Pyramids had been a success and whilst she found her a little mysterious, they had fun together. In her own mind she still did not understand how her father was reported to have committed suicide and now he was alive. He must be in his sixties or early seventies and yet her step-sister had described him as being an old man who was dying of something. And what exactly was the relationship between Khristina and him: they were meeting but how often? She could not consult with her own mother who had remarried and with whom she did not relate apart from the occasional letter. She splashed around for a final time before moving off the beach to her car. "A weekend of discovery" she said to herself and decided to give the piano keyboard a real hammering with some jazz classics. Jonathan Sinclair had invited her to dinner and, briefly, she wondered whether to accept. She was confident about her anatomical structure but less certain that she wanted to cheat on Damian.

By the middle of the week Damian was becoming increasingly unsettled as he found himself glued to his OF8 mobile phone awaiting the signal that his first assignment could begin. He knew that Mr Heron had said it might be four weeks before he would hear from him but time was slipping and he was keen to begin his new life as a government agent. He spent much of his free time envisaging how he would approach the investigation of a business unknown to him and coping with the conundrum that the best people to unearth a fraud were the present auditors of the company accounts. This was the aspect of the whole charade which caused him uncertainty. In recent times auditing standards had been under the spotlight following a series of corporate collapses often at great expense to the taxpayer who was left holding the responsibility for the bailout funds. As a consequence, accounting standards were enhanced and the regulation of the accounting profession improved with a series of sanctions and fines levied against the partners of several household names.

But that was not the real change which was more subtle. The furore over auditing standards enabled the firms to raise their charges by very considerable amounts to pay for the many more auditing hours needed to implement the additional checks and questioning of the directors and the latter had no choice but to pay the higher amounts, if they wanted their accounts signed off. Damian knew this all too well as clients initially resisted the increase in costs.

On Tuesday afternoon he messaged Mr Heron and asked that they meet which happened the next day, mid-morning at the charity shop in a Bedfordshire town. He came straight to the point and expressed his surprise that he'd not heard from his mentor.

"Impressive, OF8," said the government official. "You really are keen to contribute to the national interest."

"If you like," said Damian. "I'm keen to prove to myself, if you like, that I can deliver the goods and, until I can experience a live case, I'm in a foggy cloud of uncertainty."

"Next week, OF8. We'll be contacting you and it's a major investigation for you to undertake. I don't need to remind you of the photographs which I showed you."

"She was a young woman. I'm an experienced accountant," he said.

"Yes, fair point," he said. He stood up. "Off you go,

OF8 and prepare for the challenges ahead."

Damian thanked Mr Heron and left the charity shop for a slow drive home and an afternoon in the garden: Cathy was visiting her mother and looking at several bungalows which Edgar had selected for he and Nettie to view.

Mr Heron waited for Damian to clear the building and then made a call to a Mayfair number.

"Heron here, Sir. I've meet with OF8 and he's stable but a bit impatient to get going." He paused and wiped his brow. "But, as I said at our last meeting, we are only going to have one chance."

He listened to the voice at the other end and replied carefully.

"Yes, I think it will be the best opportunity that we'll get, Sir."

Paul Marston was clear on the objective he had set himself and the reasons for it. She had abused him, insulted him and belittled him and she was going to die. Her execution would take place on a Wednesday afternoon at around three o'clock when he would be reporting to the local police station as per the conditions of his release from the Northampton prison. His priority was to complete the contract for which he needed the McMahon brother and therein lay a problem. Marston did not like him or trust him but he knew that the imprisonment of his two brothers for a long time had damaged their reputation and this was a chance to restore it in the dark world that they occupied. And it was quick, easy money.

Their meeting the previous evening was a shambles from the start and following evasive chitchat, the youngest McMahon brother demanded more money and somewhat above the agreed fee. Former police inspector Paul Marston knew exactly how these people thought and acted and slammed down on the 'try-on' followed by a reminder that he knew of other felons who would be only too pleased to take the contract. They parted having reached a final agreement except that Marston could not tie down McMahon on an exact date.

He reached home, took some pills and poured himself a large drink before picking up the letter from the hospital and re-reading their request that he make an appointment for them to carry out some further tests. They did not say that it was urgent, which made him feel better, unlike the blood in the toilet bowl which scared the living daylights out of him.

He pondered his options: he could still call it a day and fly out to Thailand and start a new life which, in one way, was attractive especially as his evenings in the pubs and clubs seeking companionship were proving frustrating; it was almost as though someone had put out a caution about him. He knew that he was ageing and the series of operations were taking their toll over and above the years of abusing his body.

He, however, remained driven to fulfil his objective: to kill Cathy Hannon. He decided that McMahon would deliver and then he could settle down as he would be entirely innocent of the crime. McMahon, if caught, would never talk: that kind had a code to follow. And it would work in his favour as any reputational implication from the first incident in the Hannon's home would be overtaken by his clear innocence when she did finally die. She would: of that he was certain.

Cathy Hannon raised not an eyebrow on being told that Damian would be away on Saturday night as he was attending a meeting of his new employer and was invited to an informal dinner in the evening so he was going to book a hotel when he arrived in Bloomsbury: he'd be back for Sunday lunch. She showed no interest whatsoever and, unlike in the past, offered no assistance with his packing. She told him that the church service on Sunday was to be followed by a barbecue for the children of local people and she'd leave him something in the kitchen. He went to the car cleaning service on the by-pass and had his vehicle valeted while he chatted away with his Estonian friend before generously giving him twenty pounds. As he drove away, he was sensing a growing anticipation of meeting with Marie: he could not explain it, even to himself, but it was as if the weeks of indecision were finally to come to an end.

Marie was torn as to what to wear on Saturday evening: the summer sunshine shouted out for a colourful loose-fitting dress and she had a choice of three unless she went shopping. She dismissed any lingering thoughts about meeting her father and was reassured by an email she had received from her step-sister confirming the evening arrangements and a message of thanks that she was honouring her father's wishes. She made a visit to the athletics track and pounded round and round the four hundred metre circuit until she was physically exhausted but emotionally elated.

Damian drove down the M1 towards London with Bernstein's 'West Side Story' loaded on his CD player. Traffic was light and he reached the North Circular

Road before turning off for Highgate and Central London. He reached the Bloomsbury area and parked his car before striding to the hotel where he knew that Marie was staying: he hoped and believed that she'd be near to the entrance waiting for him.

She had arrived on the Friday evening and, after booking in at her hotel, went straight to bed. The next morning, she put on a matching light blue pair of shorts and top after luxuriating in the shower. She skipped breakfast, choosing instead to have coffee and a croissant in the park watched by a scruffy pigeon. She laughed at it and threw some pastry which rather sealed their friendship. She looked at her watch and realised that there was less than an hour before Damian was due to arrive. She loved the fact he had messaged her to say that he had left home and was approaching the motorway. She stood up, waved to her friend and strolled around the central fountain which sprayed its waters over the square. Marie Magellan Cameron was feeling supremely confident and sensed that this was going to be a weekend that she would remember. She walked slowly towards the hotel entrance and waited for him to appear.

+ + +

CHAPTER FOURTEEN

For many Londoners and global visitors to the capital, Russell Square is the centre of one of the most loved cities in the world. Its location in Bloomsbury radiates history with its architecture and from which every direction leads to places of interest. East takes the tourist to the High Courts of Justice and onwards to the financial centre including the Bank of England and the London Stock Exchange. Go north for Lord's cricket ground and a little to the left for Wembley football stadium. Walk to the west past the British Museum into the best shopping parade available, Oxford Street, and, dropping down a bit, the road will take you to Downing Street, the Houses of Parliament and to Buckingham Palace.

Dominating Russell Square, a grade 11 listed area, is the Hotel Russell where Marie had booked her room. The magnificent Victorian building, (finished in 1898), with its marbled staircase, has links to a shipping disaster. The designer of the RMS Titanic also completed the internal decoration of the hotel and some of the wood in the dining room is said to have been from the same source as the fated liner.

For Damian and Marie there were to be no icebergs in their way as each glimpsed their first sight of the other, gathered speed and, as he dropped his case on to the pavement, threw themselves into each other's arms. As Damian sensed her fragrance and she, his ownership of her body, they finally released their grips, rescued his case, climbed the steps up to the hotel, reached the lifts, ascended to the fifth floor, arrived at her room, inserted the electronic key, entered the room, left his case on the floor, faced one another, took off their clothes, entered the shower, adjusted the hot water and soaped each other's bodies, dried off using the warm bath towels, went back into the room, rushed over to the bed, disappeared underneath the covers and re-emerged two hours later.

"That's my friend," she said waving her hand.

They were sitting in the recreational area of Russell Square drinking coffee and munching sandwiches when he realised that Marie was referring to a pigeon.

"We spent the morning together," she said.

"Has he a name?" asked Damian.

"Noddy," she said.

"It's breaking news time," he said, "so we need to decide who goes first."

"I've given this much consideration," said Marie, "and, after a vote, I'll go first," and they hugged each other. She started by recounting her concerns over her relationship with Professor Warnock but, when he heard the contents of the letter which she had written him, suggested that she'd done exactly the right thing. He felt that the only way ahead was to draw out the university on the whole situation. Marie said that she was enjoying the work, albeit the syllabus was demanding, and it was better than looking into people's mouths and waiting to be seduced by randy male patients. This outburst led to a threat from Damian to put her over his knee and administer corrective punishment, the problem being that the sight of her tight blue shorts and seductive bottom nearly led to a return to the hotel.

She regained her poise and fetched some more drinks and cakes which she started to eat. She talked about her home, her music and her times for running the four-hundred metres. Marie managed to recount trips on the water with Rebecca, Jeb and friends without mentioning Jonathan Sinclair. The conversation then drifted towards an attempt to rationalise tonight's dinner.

"In one way," said Marie, "I know so little about Khristina despite spending a holiday with her in Egypt. She can be chatty and fun but then she's a closed shop and during her recent trip to Portsmouth she seemed, at times, distracted. As for my father, all I know is that he's a diplomat from Russia, or was, because I don't understand whether he's still working. He divorced my mother and married a French woman in Paris who gave birth to Khristina. She says that she sees her father from time to time and he recently contacted her to say that he's not well and he wanted to meet with me because he needs to apologise for being a poor father. We are all meeting tonight: I've booked a restaurant in Covent Garden and I've managed to secure a confidential corner table for us."

"Who do they think I am?" asked Damian.

"I wish I knew," chuckled Marie. "They have been told that you are a man who means a lot to me and I've disclosed that you're married. Funny, but Khristina showed real interest in that piece of information and asked how it worked for me."

They decided to walk round the Square avoiding the group of alcoholics gathered together in the far corner. After some discussion it was agreed to return to the hotel, shower and secrete themselves in the lounge when Marie would hear Damian's news. She expressed interest in his departure from the accountancy firm and absorbed his brief summary of working as a tax investigator and he left it at that, which seemed to satisfy her. Her real interest was to understand where Mrs Hannon fitted into all of this. Damian said that he felt a responsibility to try to make the marriage work but he was finding his wife was becoming more distant, a point he emphasised by telling her about the Tibetan holiday.

Marie sipped her cocktail and turned to face her companion. She gave him a mesmeric smile that turned him to jelly.

"Are you ready to commit to me, Damian?" she asked.

He looked her fully in her face and kissed her cheek.

"I'm very near, Marie, very, very near."

"Promise me, Damian, nothing can stop us from being together?"

"We're an express train," he said, "on the rails together and hurtling toward paradise station."

"No ticket collector to derail us?"

"Nothing will stop us now, Marie," he said.

They returned to the fifth-floor hotel room knowing that they had two hours remaining before it would be time to leave for the restaurant.

She had selected the plainest of her three dresses featuring flowers on a pastel colouring and belted at the waist with a white cardigan thrown back over her shoulders. To her surprise Damian was wearing a light grey suit with an open neck shirt which she loved. They sauntered out of the hotel passing the re-opened British Museum and into the outskirts of Covent

Garden which was back to life after nearly two years of lockdowns and economic recession as the Government battled the pandemic. The tourists were returning and the theatres were, at long last, playing to full audiences.

Her hand was through his arm and they spoke few words as they ambled along simply relishing being together. Their lives were falling into place and neither, at this stage, needed any further reassurances. He had sent a message to his wife confirming his arrival but, so far, had not received an acknowledgement, and, almost for the first time in their relationship, he did not care.

They reached the restaurant, which was near to the Royal Opera House, made their presence known to the receptionist who asked a waiter to guide them to their table where, to their surprise, they found that Fyodor and Khristina Babikov were awaiting their arrival. The two sisters embraced and Damian stared at the Russian diplomat fully in his face only to receive a smile and a vigorous hand-shake. Marie went round to her father and kissed him on his two cheeks leading into an embrace. She then took the lead by returning to her seat and asking Fyodor about his health.

"I'm flying back to Moscow shortly for an operation which will lead to me losing one of my internal organs. The prognosis is positive but I must face the reality that I might not make it. What is certain is that I'll never travel abroad again as I have retired and this will be my only chance to meet my first daughter."

The waiter arrived with a tray containing four glasses and a liquid which each guest received. Fyodor stood and held up his glass waiting for his three companions to also stand.

"Nostrovia" he toasted and then burst out laughing. "We Russians say nothing of the sort but, as you all watch Netflix, it'll do. Waiter," he shouted out," bring the bottle."

Damian found the burning sensation of the vodka hitting the back of his throat rather exciting but was relieved when Marie managed to return them to normal service with the waiter bringing bottles of wine and menus. He looked again at the Russian visitor.

"Your English is near perfect," he said.

"I was here in London for five years and I also speak good French and German."

"Your career was in the diplomatic service?" asked Damian.

"Yes, although I've been in Moscow for the last fifteen years."

The orders were placed and the anti-pasti served allowing Fyodor to focus on Marie and enabling Damian to try to get know Khristina which he found was not easy although Marie had prepared him for this situation. She wanted to know all about him and his daughter. Damian was keeping half an eye on Marie who had absorbed herself in her father. The plates were cleared and after perhaps ten minutes their main courses arrived with Marie maintaining her attention on her father. He and Marie managed to disagree about the British political system although she liked David Beckham.

After another thirty minutes, Damian decided that he could not drink any more alcohol, and he noticed that the restaurant seemed to be emptying. Marie announced her surprise for them and asked the waiter to serve the Medovik, better known as Russian honey cake, and the inevitable round of vodkas at which point

Khristina stood up and gave a little speech which was as beautiful as it was brief: Marie wiped away the tears from her eyes. Her step-sister said that it was a tradition that she always gave her father a small present and she handed him a package which he put into his pocket. Despite the urging of Marie, he said that he never opened her gifts until he was on the plane home.

Damian left the table to use the facilities and found himself asking the receptionist if they were outstaying their welcome in view of the empty tables. She smiled and said that they were most welcome for another thirty minutes and so he returned to the table, went behind Marie, and put his hands on her shoulders.

"Fyodor," he said, "I wish we could have met in happier circumstances but we hope that your operation is successful and perhaps you might one day come back to see us."

"I have met my daughter and now I know what a wonderful person she is and I have conversed with you Damian and, whatever happens between the two of you, I wish you great happiness, hopefully together."

At which point in time there was a major commotion as through the windows of the restaurant came the pulsating blue lights associated with the authorities and, suddenly, there were three officers facing them.

"We are armed police! Do exactly as you're told and stand still."

They parted and through the opening came someone clearly of some seniority.

"I am Detective Chief Superintendent Marcus Redding of the Metropolitan police: please sit down," which Damian and Marie did. The officer looked at the Russian pair. "Mr Babikov," he commanded, "sit down." At this point a second civilian joined the group causing Damian to leap up in the air.

"Mr Heron," he exclaimed, "What the fucking hell are you doing here?"

"Please sit down, Mr Hannon, will you: all will be explained."

"My name is OF8, that is the fucking nonsense you filled my head with, you shit."

Marie became distressed and a female police officer came to sit with her talking firmly into her ear.

"Are you arresting me?" shouted the Russian.

"No, Mr Babikov, we're not arresting you," said DCS Redding. "What we are doing is taking you to your hotel room, which we have cleared out in the last hour, we'll collect your cases and then you'll be taken to Heathrow airport: your flight for Moscow leaves at three-twenty tomorrow morning and I suspect there will be certain officials waiting to meet you on your arrival. You will never return to the United Kingdom."

"Then please release my daughter to accompany me to the airport," he said.

"I think not," said the DCS. "Khristina Babikov, I am arresting you for breaches of the Official Secrets Act and specifically for the offence of passing Government papers to a foreign power." He followed up with the necessary caution never talking his eyes off the defiant traitor.

Khristina stood up and spat at the police officer.

"Fuck you," she said. "I'm proud of what I've achieved." She turned to Marie. "Sorry, Marie, but you and I are very different people." As she passed one of the armed police officers, she kicked him on the shin.

"Before we go, Mr Babikov, may I please have the package that your daughter passed to you during the evening," asked DCS Redding.

Fyodor Babikov knew that there was no point in protesting and handed over her gift which the officer showed to Mr Heron.

"I think, Mr Heron, that is what we have come for," he said.

The police took their prisoners away and Mr Heron invited Damian and Marie to sit down at the table where cups of coffee were served. He explained that they'd arranged with the restaurant owner for them to have thirty minutes together. He asked them to allow him to explain everything in one go except that Marie needed to use the washroom and disappeared.

"While we are waiting can we have our phone back please, Damian."

Marie returned and Mr Heron said that he worked for the government security services. In recent times there had been a major breach of security and they had become aware that Moscow was far too well informed about current British links with the Americans and that they were reading confidential papers. The leak was traced to the Foreign Office and, specifically, the Russian desk where suspicion fell on a senior clerk, one Khristina Babikov, who spoke fluent Russian. As the investigation furthered, it was found that the clerk was the mistress of a junior Government minister who worked in the office of the Foreign Secretary. She was copying material from his laptop and handing over all the information on a memory stick to her father which is why they were meeting.

"It's ironic," he said, "that in this day and age of espionage techniques, eaves-drops, telephone taps and cyberspace, the worst breach we have had in recent years is a clerk sleeping with a Government minister and downloading the hard drive from his laptop." He paused. "DCS Redding will open Khristina's gift to her father and find a computer memory stick containing the Government's secret papers which will condemn her to prison for a very long time."

"But a clever defence barrister will question the validity of the evidence," said Damian. "Khristina will say that she knew nothing about it and claim that the evidence was planted."

"Which is why we have filmed your table for the whole evening," responded Mr Heron. "We have everything we need including the moment she passed the package to her father."

Marie stood up, her eyes ablaze with anger.

"You've filmed me having a private dinner with my family," she shouted. "This is a breach of my human rights and I'll make sure that you never show that film in a court of law."

"Please sit down, Ms Cameron," instructed Mr Heron. "When it comes to national security, we can do what we like." He paused. "There are times when I shudder at the measures we have to take and I deeply regret the hurt that you are feeling. I hope that in time you will come to understand the vital role you have played in defending your country." He again hesitated. "These incidents always have far reaching consequences. I think you'll read in your Sunday newspapers that an MP has decided to resign his post and spend more time with his family," he said.

Damian put his arm around Marie, said that he wanted a fuller explanation for their involvement and warned Mr Heron "or whatever your fucking name is" that he was getting ready to belt the living daylights out of him.

"I understand that but please hear me out," he answered. "The leaks have been getting very serious and we could find no way of incriminating Khristina Babikov. At one point we were following three suspects although she was always number one. Then we came across her relationship with you, Marie, and although we quickly eliminated you, we overheard you talking to Damian. We struck up a plan to try to get you to trip up your sister-in-law but all the advice we had was that you'd not co-operate, purely because it was too far- fetched. Then we thought of involving you, Damian, asking you to work with Marie. Lots of 'ifs' and 'buts' I grant you but we were under ever increasing pressure from Downing Street. The OF8 charade was designed to give us a chance to test you out Damian and you were superb. However, we then heard you agree to meet in Covent Garden with Khristina and her father: we were given special powers to go ahead and we have pulled off a massive result tonight."

"I'll talk to you separately about OF8 and all that fucking nonsense" said Damian, "but did you have to involve Marie and myself in your spy games?"

"We had to see Khristina pass the information to her father without which we'd never have made the case stick."

"The photographs you showed me, the girl in the peat bog, is that the way you treat human beings?" he asked.

"Let's meet at the charity shop next Tuesday, eleven o'clock, and tidy things up."

"You've taken my phone" said Damian.

"You'll be there," said Mr Heron.

As Damian wrapped his arms around Marie and started to leave the restaurant, Mr Heron called out to him.

"One more thing," he said. "The Home Secretary will want to meet with you to express the Government's appreciation for your service to the country."

"How is she at mending damaged relationships?" he asked.

They walked back to the hotel in silence. When they reached Russell Square Marie asked that they sit down on a park bench underneath a lamppost.

"I'm not going to talk to you tonight, Damian: you're going back to the room to collect your case and then you are to go away. You will not contact me: don't try because it'll be a waste of your time."

"I can explain everything," he pleaded.

"I need to work out how I have managed to find myself a pawn in other people's games without any respect for me. Mr Heron, or whatever you call him, never even acknowledged the abuse of my position. Just go away, Damian."

He did as he was instructed, collected his possessions from her room, left the hotel, collected his car and drove to the Scratchwood motorway services where he spent the night. By seven o'clock on Sunday morning he'd had enough and drove back home where he found Cathy having breakfast in the kitchen. He said that the event had gone well except that he selected the wrong hotel and had left early. She let him unpack his case and after he'd showered and changed, he found that she'd left for church. He spent an hour in his study writing up notes covering the events of yesterday and then sent a text to Marie wishing her a safe journey back to Portsmouth only to receive an immediate reply:

You should have stayed: we could be talking now. M.

After an hour weeding in the garden, he poured himself a drink and went to lie down on the sun-lounger. He found himself struggling to cope with yesterday's happenings and wondering whether he could have reacted faster when the police arrived. Had he left Marie to fend for herself?

Cathy came home in the late afternoon and wanted to tell him about the success of the children's church party. They then drove about two miles to view the bungalow that Nettie and Edgar had decided to buy.

Later that evening, Damian received a message from Marie:

I'm struggling. Mx

"I want you to reassure me that everything that Marie and I have been through was necessary."

It was the same table, same chairs, same room, same charity shop, same lukewarm coffee and the same people. The main difference was that OF8 was a thing of the past.

"The exposure of Khristina Babikov as a Soviet spy is one of the biggest successes we have had in recent years, Damian, and sets the Russian machine back a long way. You will have read that we are expelling a number of their diplomats which is the accepted way of sending a warning. As you will hear from the Home Secretary when you meet her, without you and Ms Cameron we could never have solved what has been a major problem."

"You have no regrets that you have used me and Marie?"

"Damian, I take you back to our first meeting: you could have said "no"."

"Don't you start," he smiled to himself.

"Pardon? You do accept that you had free choice?"

"Can I just clarify the situation. There is no Maydene Wealth Management Company, we'll never meet again and I'm free to resume my life."

"Yes, but we will be honouring the contract you agreed. For the next three years you will receive ten thousand pounds a month and you'll never hear again from the tax inspectors because you'll never again pay UK personal tax."

"Mrs Pennington? I want to clarify her situation."

"It's exactly as I told you, Damian. She agreed to help us but has found life here in Bedfordshire to her and her husband's liking and enjoys being a partner in the accounting firm, so she's staying."

"Does she know what has happened?"

"Yes, she does."

"Marie Cameron?" he hesitated. "What about her?"

"We all deeply regret that she felt so damaged but, in all honesty, there is nothing more we can do. She was not involved in any way in the espionage, her file is clean, and, if I may say, she is a rather impressive woman."

Damian stood up and began to leave.

"So OF8 never existed?" he smiled.

"I have no idea what you are referring to," said Mr Heron.

Damian turned back to address his audience.

"There have been twenty-four James Bond films and, until I met you, guess which was my favourite?"

"I've no idea, Damian."

"'From Russia With Love'," he said.

Paul Marston was struggling rather badly. His meeting with the McMahon brother had produced more fireworks as they could not agree on the final fee required to ensure the killing of Mrs Hannon and then there were disagreements over the date as the Irish killer seemed unable to understand the important of the need to coincide with Marston's weekly visit to the police station.

He had started again to confuse his prescriptions and was late for his hospital appointment. When, finally, they came to examine him, it was discovered that his trousers were soaked in blood, he was immediately admitted and underwent emergency surgery. Eight days later Paul Marston died of septicaemia.

The hospital sent his records to the wrong doctor's surgery and they ended up on the desk of Dr Martin Armstrong who telephoned Cathy Hannon to tell her the news.

Damian walked along the tow path and passed the bottom of Marie's garden although the new owners had transformed the inlet wherein a new motor boat was berthed. He relived their times together and checked his phone to re-read her message:

There's so much we can achieve together Mx

More than anything he wanted to hold her in his arms. But he was honest enough to know that this time there could be no equivocation.

The time had come for Damian Hannon to make a final decision.

+ + +

PART THREE

AUTUMN

CHAPTER FIFTEEN

The August sunshine enveloped the beach as Damian and Marie lay together in the comfort zone that they had negotiated for themselves. She had met with Professor Warnock who dismissed her concerns albeit there was half an apology when he disclosed that the funding for his department had now been agreed. She now had a starting date when the students would arrive and he suggested that she took some holiday to prepare for the task ahead. Her time for the four hundred metres was not improving and she could not care less.

In a series of text messages, telephone conversations and this, the second of two visits, they had relived every moment of the evening in the Covent Garden restaurant and Damian had explained his final meeting with Mr Heron. He had declined to meet with the Home Secretary: there were a series of newspaper reports about the arrest and coming trial of Khristina Babikov and, to their relief, no mention of her sister-in-law. Damian had no wish to visit the accounting practice and was deciding what he might undertake next although the monthly financial payment into his account, tax free, made his life somewhat easier.

They succeeded in recapturing the emotion of their time together during the Saturday spent in the Russell Hotel and around the Square and they reached an agreement that when Cathy Hannon returned from her holiday to Tibet, he would leave home and come to live with her. This led to some tension because Marie wanted him to stay on now but she could see he wanted to use Cathy's time away to plan everything including seeing Scarlett and Arthur and his mother-in-law although it was now Nettie and Edgar.

They discussed Marie's career at the university and her three-year contract (which she had now received) and her wish to see it through although she then added that she'd like to start a family. Damian was relaxed on these issues because he was quietly spending more time in the marina and reading biographies of round-the-world sailors. The time came for him to return to Bedfordshire and, as he was getting into his car, he realised that Marie was handing him a present: they agreed that he should open it immediately.

He looked at his copy of (Dame) Ellen MacArthur's book 'Taking on the World' and her story of achieving, in 2005, the then fastest solo circumnavigation of the globe. He beamed and hugged (again) his partner.

"You want me out on the ocean waves, do you?" he jested.

"Yes, I do," said Marie.

"Surely you'll miss me?"

"Of course, but I'll also know you cannot get mixed up with MI5 agents in the middle of the Pacific!"

He drove home thinking that although he was nearly fifty years of age, he was feeling nearer to thirty years old. He garaged the car, went inside and found Cathy in the lounge reading a book. They exchanged small talk and then Damian said that he was going to bed.

"Something I should tell you," she said in a way that put him on edge.

"I've cancelled my holiday to Tibet."

Damian came back and faced her, sensing the need

for caution.

"That's a surprise," he said. "I had the impression you were looking forward to what sounded like a unique opportunity."

"How would you know," she said. "You've shown no interest in it. Anyway, it's nothing to do with you. While we are catching up, Paul Marston is dead. He succumbed to blood poisoning in hospital."

"How do you know that?" he asked.

"Martin Armstrong telephoned me."

Damian was now walking round the lounge when his attitude wavered.

"Just a minute, Cathy," he challenged. "Were you going to a foreign land because of being scared Marston might make another attempt to attack us?"

"Don't be ridiculous, Damian, and stop treating me in such a patronising way," she snapped.

"Why aren't you going?" he asked.

"I'm just not going, end of story." She paused. "Sorry if it messes up your plans to see your girlfriend."

"Shall we book a holiday together?" he suggested.

"I didn't say I haven't made other plans," she said. She stalked out of the room and went to bed.

He poured himself a drink, put on some jazz music and settled down into the lounge, bewildered by this latest turn of events. He decided to drive out to the Chiltern Hills in the morning and use the space and fresh air to reach a final decision although, in truth, he already knew what he was going to do. He had a strong instinct that his wife of twenty-one years couldn't care a damn.

That was that: he'd tried and if she had met him half way perhaps they might have sorted matters out. He recalled the moment he had hugged Marie outside the

Russell Hotel. Was he being honest about events? What was one of the first things Marie had said to him? "You could have said "no"." But, equally, perhaps he was entitled to have expected Cathy to say "yes" when he was trying to repair their relationship.

He started to climb the stairs.

"It's a bit bloody difficult to say "yes" from behind a closed bedroom door," he thought to himself.

The following morning, he arrived in the kitchen to find that his breakfast comprised fresh scrambled eggs on granary toast served with cups of freshly ground coffee. There was background music playing which reminded him of the English Chamber Orchestra and all of this was overseen by a bright, almost ebullient, Cathy, who was wearing freshly pressed jeans, a white blouse and a blue casual jacket. The build-up became quickly apparent as she sat down and smiled at her husband.

"I'm going into hospital next Tuesday," she said, "and I'll need your help because I'll not be able to drive my car for two weeks." She wiped her hand across her forehead. "Please don't ask me too many questions, Damian. Let's just call it female engineering." She paused again. "Then I want you to look after things here because I'll be going to London for a week to help with the arrival of Faria's baby." Again, she paused but purely to sip her cup of coffee. "Then we'll put the house up for sale because I'm buying a new home for myself in Milton Keynes." She hesitated because she wanted to ensure that he was listening to her.

"Once there I'll be starting my new job as deputy head of nursing at a recently opened private hospital: my boss will be Anisha Khan who was here recently and to whom you were rude. I calculate that everything will be settled in perhaps three months." Again, she paused as if trying to remember the script. "We will go to the lawyers and tell them what to do: we split our assets straight down the middle, no arguments."

Yet another pause. "I know who Marie Cameron is because I had to have a filling and the dentist told me all about her: she's a bit of a pin-up girl in view of her success in becoming an assistant professor at Portsmouth University. I was told that she's rather attractive which came as no surprise." A final hesitation. "Do we have a deal? Work with me over the next three months and possibly, just before Christmas, you can sail off into the sunset and wrap yourself around Ms Cameron. If she has anything about her, I'm sure she'll be prepared to wait for perhaps twelve to fourteen weeks."

The breakfast plates were cleared away and Cathy placed a fresh pot of coffee on the table pouring cups for each of them.

"Is this a discussion?" asked Damian.

"What is there to discuss?" she smiled. "I've thought it through from your point of view which is more than you did for me. You're free of the accounting practice, you have your job with that Mr Heron, I'm looking after Arthur and Faria who will be moving into their flat very soon, Scarlett and Joshua are in the Antarctic and my mother and Edgar are preparing to move into their bungalow."

"The job with Mr Heron has not worked out," he said," but they are paying me ten thousand pounds a month for three years."

"Why would they do that?" She paused. "I'll add that to the financial calculations. And, on that subject, we'll be receiving a small amount of money back from that crazy property investment you made."

"I want to ask one question: this operation, is that the reason you've been closing the bedroom door?"

"It's a private matter and not for discussion," she said.

Damian was playing around with his cup and saucer.

"The job, how did that happen?" he asked.

"I contacted Anisha about the weight-loss paper I was writing for Martin Armstrong and she became quite interested in it. Then, out of the blue, she asked me to meet her in Milton Keynes and introduced me to the owners of the new hospital and it all fell into place. After Covid-19 it's inevitable that private medicine will play an increasing part in the nation's health. Talk to Dr Armstrong and he's passionate about the NHS and he's right: we achieved so much at the surgery. But waiting times for even basic surgery are spiralling out of control. The waiting time for a basic hip replacement operation is now between nine and twelve months. Have you seen the pain a patient with a damaged hip is going through?"

Damian pondered this further information and then he asked why they needed twelve weeks to sort out her plans which produced a sharp retort including a reminder that it might take fourteen weeks. The next four weeks would be taken up with her operation and the birth of Faria's baby, the lawyers will need perhaps four weeks to sort out their agreement and the sale of the house will take several weeks even though the market was buoyant.

"Where will you live?" he asked.

"In my new home," she smiled. "I've already

bought it, overlooking the lake. You haven't asked about my new salary."

"Silly me," said Damian.

"We'll also be paid a commission based on the profits of the hospital," she added.

"You surely aren't part of turning medicine into a commercial venture?" he accused. "That's against all the principles of the founders of the NHS!"

"And this from someone who thinks obese patients should be paid tax-payers money to lose weight," she sneered. Cathy stood in front of her husband. "Right, Mr Hannon. We have settled everything and it's one of those situations where everybody is a winner. I'll need you here from Monday onwards so why don't you go and have a nice time at the seaside with Miss Wonderful. She laughed. "I'm sure that Ms Cameron will be elated when she hears that in twelve to fourteen weeks, she can have you to herself for the rest of your lives together."

Damian left the house, drove to the Chiltern Hills and walked over the downs trying to work out how to present this latest Cathy landmine in such a way as to prevent an explosion of frustration and perhaps disbelief from his future life partner.

They were settled into the marina picking their way through an ice cream Everest and watching the arrivals berth their boats, dive into the nearest bar and try to book a table for their evening meal. Damian and Marie were beginning their third serious conversation since his arrival and were reaching a point where the tensions were surfacing. As she consumed the last of her glazed cherries, Marie launched the offensive which he was fearing.

"Stop pissing around, Damian," she began, before building up to the bombardment. "She's stringing you along and this is not for the first time." She paused." No, Damian, it's my turn so please don't interrupt me because this is about my future." The last of the ice cream was eaten. "As you have said on a number of occasions, this latest salvo has been launched without any discussion. I don't care that she had made an effort with her appearance: at her age she needs all the help she can contrive. She laid the law down without any equivocation. You will look after her when she has had her operation, you will house-sit while she goes off to help Faria have her baby, you and she will see the lawyers when, I promise you, she'll screw you all the way and you were mad to tell her about the OF8 payments. Meanwhile you'll do all the selling of the house while she moves into her new home. Game, set and fucking match to Catherine Hannon."

Damian secured a time-out by disappearing to use the public facilities. It briefly interrupted her salvo but the additional fuel enabled a re-launch.

"She's laughing all the way to her future with you, generous Damian, paying for everything. Yes, I accept the operation is a serious matter, whatever is wrong with her, but why can't her mother come and look after her? She seemed, from what you tell me, to have been re-energised by the Bridge-playing Albert."

"Edgar."

"She can sell the house and she can move herself to Milton Keynes and what about all her friends at the church? Then, of course, you silly billy, she'll play her trump card."

"Which is what?"

"Towards the end of the twelve weeks she'll

discover another reason why you can't leave her."

"Like what, Marie?" snapped Damian.

"What she's doing is to make sure that I never manage to get you. She's a bitter woman and they are dangerous. I've no idea if she has any feelings for you but I can guarantee you that her prime motivation is to stop you and I getting together."

"But there's a simple way out of this," he pleaded. "I'll go back home, the gloves are off anyway, and tell her that I'll give her ten weeks and, at the end of that, I'm leaving her for good."

"You're not listening, Damian, you've made that commitment several times before and she'll manipulate you again." She stood up and straightened her clothes. "Several questions that need answering: how sure are you about this operation? Why can't she tell you what it's for? Have you noticed any additional prescription bottles in the bathroom?"

"Are you suggesting she might be exaggerating her condition?"

"No, I'm suggesting that she's lying to you," said Marie.

"Cathy wouldn't do that."

"She lied about who was the father of Scarlett."

"That was different, Marie. She was trying to deal with the Paul Marston issue."

"If she's told one untruth, how do you know she won't tell another?"

They decided to stroll along the beach in what remained of the early evening sunshine. There was some respite from the turmoil that each was feeling. They watched the surfers trying to generate some momentum in the dying waves and stepped aside as several horse riders passed them. The gulls were feeding at the water's edge and making a lot of noise about it. It was Marie who broke the stalemate. She was frowning as she began her latest offering.

"There's no point in agreeing deadlines because we never keep to them so I have a proposition for you, Damian." He stopped and turned to face her. "Professor Warnock suggested I take some holiday before term begins and so what I'm going to do is get on a plane and fly to somewhere in the Mediterranean and lie on a beach. I'm actually quite happy with my own company. Then, in two weeks I'm asking you to come back here with your decision made. In other words, you'll stay this time and for good."

"Last chance saloon?" suggested Damian.

"No, I wouldn't see it that way. You have got to see through Cathy. I really do understand the years of marriage, children, careers and the rest but you have to make the decision or we don't stand a chance." She put her arms around his neck. "The bed will lose its attraction after a time and then we'll find out whether, when we wake up each morning and look at one another, that's the person we want to be with for the rest of our lives."

Damian perked up immediately because he was seemingly surviving the latest crisis in their relationship.

"How long will the bed retain its attraction?" he asked.

"Oh, about twenty years, would be my estimate," she smiled. "I suggest that the matter needs some investigation, so why don't we hurry home and turn on the shower?" She grinned. "I've invested in a bottle of vintage Happy Bunny Shower Gel: cost a bit."

"Surely my chemist's men's gel will achieve the

same result."

"Gosh, no. Never."

"How can you be so sure?"

"Because my bottle of vintage Happy Bunny Shower Gel has added glitter."

The drive back to Bedfordshire was one which Damian now knew well and yet it was not long enough for him to sort out the conflicts he was facing. They therefore ended up in Port Solent enjoying a passionate and compelling time together and an apparently rejuvenated Marie talked continuously about her plans for when he joined her, including an extension to the main bedroom and the building of a study for him. He lost a brownie point for not having started reading his gift, 'Taking on the World' but recovered the position when he let slip that he'd already had the house valued and the estate agents had buyers lined up for it.

As he neared home, his thoughts turned towards Cathy and her hospital visit tomorrow. He could not rationalise Marie's thoughts that she might be misleading him but there were certain anomalies to be explained. She'd had a hysterectomy eight years ago and that had proved to be a successful operation from which she'd made a complete recovery. Marie asked a good question when referring to any additional prescriptions or medicines in the bathroom which he could not remember seeing.

The evening was strange in that Cathy and Damian acted like two ships that passed in the night. There was a forced atmosphere and she made it clear that she was not up to answering any of his questions: she went to bed early without saying anything.

On Tuesday morning the complexities of her

situation continued when she insisted on being left at the hospital entrance and did not want Damian to come in with her. She made the point that she was a qualified nurse and she'd deal with the procedures in her own way, she did not want him to visit her and she'd keep him informed by text messaging. He was not to bother the harassed staff with telephone calls. She'd made the same arrangement with her mother and Arthur and she'd no idea where Scarlett was but she'd left her a message.

On his way back home, he stopped at the Cumberland Nursing Home to speak to his mother-in-law who initially seemed rather harassed but calmed down when Edgar joined them. The only conversation concerned their move into their bungalow in two days but they did not need any assistance as one of Edgar's sons was coming up from London to help out. Damian left them to their labours puzzled that Nettie seemed unaware that her daughter was in hospital awaiting an operation.

He spent the rest of the day catching up on paperwork before he put a ready meal into the microwave. Marie sent two messages and he replied reassuring her that he'd soon be on his way to Portsmouth on a permanent basis and could she order some more of the special shower gel. Cathy sent a brief confirmation that she'd settled in and would contact him tomorrow. He spent a restless night unable to gain any degree of confidence that he understood what was actually happening. Cathy had given him a piece of paper with a phone number written on it in case of an emergency.

In the morning, following a restless night, he decided he wanted to know more and so he phoned the number she had given him: it was unobtainable. He immediately drove to the hospital, parked his car and went into the front where he began a conversation with a helpful, youngish, receptionist who was rather keen to answer his questions. She sensed that he was becoming a little agitated and tried harder and harder to provide him with the information that he required.

There was just one problem. The hospital computer system contained no record whatsoever of a patient named Catherine Hannon.

+ + +

CHAPTER SIXTEEN

It is said by some romantic historians that the British Empire was built on the custom of drinking tea. The American author, Henry James, when living in London, said, 'There are few hours more agreeable than the hour dedicated to the ceremony known as afternoon tea'.

Damian was sitting in his kitchen pouring himself a cup of Earl Grey and writing out a list of possible suspects who might know where was Cathy Hannon. He had stayed at the hospital for a further thirty minutes until the receptionist called for her supervisor and, together, they convinced him that they had no knowledge of her whereabouts. He asked that they watch the CCTV for the morning of her arrival at which point the atmosphere changed and he was told they would have to take more serious action unless he stopped harassing them.

He drove home bemused and with Marie's words echoing in his ears. She was now lying on a Costa Brava beach improving her suntan and he decided to message her later in the day when he had found out where his wife had disappeared to, assuming he could find her. He consumed a second cup of tea, went upstairs, showered, changed into a suit and tie and prepared to visit the first of the suspects. He was polite and firm and still the receptionist at the doctor's practice refused to breach patient confidentiality. Damian remained focused and, finally, Dr Martin Armstrong came out and invited him into his room where he told him, in quite strong terms, that nobody at the practice would talk to him about the whereabouts of his wife. His suggestion that he'd be willing to pass on to her a letter from him left Damian singularly unimpressed.

He drove to the Cumberland Nursing Home and found Nettie Errington-Maxwell in a state of geriatric panic as she attempted to pack her belongings into the removal van but help was on hand in that Edgar understood his dilemma and manged to obtain from Cathy's mother a statement that she had no idea where her daughter was and surely her husband should know that?

His next visit was, illogically, to the dentist where Cathy had heard all about Marie and where he found a Berlin Wall of obstruction and the suggestion that he was due an appointment with the hygienist caused him to storm out. He drove on to the offices of Hannon, Shannon and Smith (still to be renamed) because he believed that Louisa had remained in touch with Cathy which she had but unfortunately had not spoken to her for several weeks. He ran into Lydia who managed to capture him and imprison him in the Board Room while she ran through a series of questions which were of no interest to the increasingly desperate Damian Hannon. From here he went to the church which Cathy attended to find that there was an afternoon prayer meeting and one of the leaders came out to ask him where was Cathy?

He went home, put on his shorts, sat in the garden and continued his analysis of the situation. He telephoned the hospital again but that was unproductive, he rang Cathy's number which was on answerphone, he tried the number she had given him which was still disconnected, he phoned Arthur who said he'd not spoken to his mother for several days and he was in the middle of his studies.

He tried to contact Scarlett and managed to just hear her voice which sounded as though she was in the middle of a snow blizzard which she was and which was the last contact he managed to achieve. He had a thought, dressed and went round to a number of the neighbours all of whom, those that were in, were friendly and helpful but offered him no comfort apart from Ingrid from three doors away who was Swedish and who tried to drag him into the garden where she had her hot tub in use.

He retired, defeated, and returned home where he connected with Marie who did his morale no good at all by revealing that she was having dinner with a man she'd met at the Spanish poolside. She listened to his situation and, while asking some questions, made no significant comment on the disappearance of his wife. Damian spent the evening drinking too much alcohol, crawled up to bed and missed three messages on his mobile:

'I hate it when you're hurting. Mx'

This was followed twenty-two minutes later by the following:

'I am fine. Cathy'

The last of the messages read as follows:

'There's so much that we can achieve together. Mx'

The following morning, Damian decided to take a different approach to the situation that he was facing by driving into the hills and walking a total of perhaps twenty miles drinking his bottle of water and eating energy bars. He avoided speaking to anyone and, for long periods of time, did not check his messages. He drove home feeling better and decided that he would use the following day to break the riddle of where was his wife and, if necessary, speak to the police. He talked at length to Marie who said that she'd never again accept an invitation from a Spaniard but who did not mention Cathy.

Damian woke up feeling equally determined and was preparing to make his action list when there was a knock at the front door. He opened it to find his wife fumbling with her handbag.

"Sorry, Damian, but I can't find my keys," she said. "Can you pay the taxi please."

She pushed past and left him to settle up with the driver and to bring in her case which he left at the foot of the stairs only to find she was making herself a pot of tea. They sat down together.

"Yes, I know you have questions," she said, "but I'm feeling rather sore and I've had very little sleep thanks to the woman with adenoids." She finished her drink and stood up.

"You must tell me where you have been?" he demanded.

"I don't ask questions when you've been with your girlfriend, do I?" she snapped.

"You're my wife. I have a right to know what's been happening," he said, raising his voice.

"You have no rights left, Mr Hannon," she said. "But if you really want to know what I've been doing, the answer is simple. I've been saving someone's life."

His attempts to further their conversation ground to a halt as she stood up, asked him to take her case upstairs: she climbed the steps, went into her bedroom and closed the door, firmly shut.

He returned to the kitchen and realised that she'd left her handbag on the table. He opened it and looked for some evidence which he found. There was a patient card prepared by the Alexandra Private Hospital in Milton Keynes and under the heading it said, 'Renal Unit: Mrs Catherine Hannon.'

He went into the lounge and put his head in his hands.

*

Dr Martin Armstrong accepted the proffered cup of coffee and sat down at the kitchen table.

"You were absolutely right to contact me, Damian. I'm surprised they discharged her so soon: I'd have preferred she'd have stayed in for five days, which is more normal, but I suspect we might find that Cathy discharged herself. She's fine. I've given her a full examination and a sedative and I've checked all her prescriptions she's brought back from the hospital. She now needs complete rest for the next few days and she's told me that she has to go back next Monday for a full check-up."

"You knew all about this?" he asked.

"This is where it gets a bit tricky. My surgery is under strict instructions from Cathy that we are not to discuss anything about the matter with you. It was absolutely right to call us in but I think you may have to wait a day or so and then she can tell you the whole story: quite amazing, what she's done."

Cathy slept for the rest of the day and, intermittently, during the following twenty-four hours and then re-appeared looking fresh and healthy. She said that she was sore but ready to talk and that they should sit in the garden together but it was 'no alcohol' for the next week. They settled down and she told Damian her story.

It began when several months ago she was visiting her friend Anisha Khan at the Alexandra Private Hospital in Milton Keynes and the subject of a job offer arose and led quite quickly to a meeting with one of the two doctors who had founded the medical centre. At one point they were interrupted by Dr Haydon taking an urgent phone call at the end of which he seemed to be deflated. He explained that his wife had health problems and was waiting for a kidney transplant. The call was to tell him that a potential donor had failed the blood test. Cathy admitted to Damian that even now she was not certain that she was serious but she said that she had two kidneys so why didn't they test her blood. Dr Haydon immediately declined her offer but Cathy persisted and she was eventually introduced to a Living Donor Coordinator who she found to be empathic and professional. She also talked to Dr Martin Armstrong. She laid down two conditions: nobody was to talk to her husband and she did not want to meet Dr Haydon's wife. The next step was for her to be assessed by a psychologist and, following a positive report, she was put through an exhausting series of tests including urine, blood, x-rays and scans. She was told that she'd be in hospital for between three and five days and the recovery period was between four and twelve weeks. Cathy paused, stood up and looked around her before finishing her story.

"That's when things started to become complicated because Mrs Haydon's condition required urgent attention and I was the solution. I hoped that my mother might look after me but she's totally absorbed by her new relationship: I spoke to Scarlett but she's stuck in the Antarctic and Arthur is due to become a father. You are itching to go off with Marie and so I devised my twelve-week plan to keep you here. I accept I might have handled things better but I've had a text message from Anisha saying Mrs Haydon is recovering after the transplant."

"Why didn't you talk to me," angered Damian.

"You've been trying to go off with Marie ever since you first met her." She laughed. "There are regular articles in women's magazines: 'five ways to tell if your husband is having an affair'. I didn't need one. I think I knew almost from when you first met her, that you were on your way. You're a decent man and I think you've tried to be fair to me. But what was it that Princess Diana said in her interview with Martin Bashir? 'There are three of us in this marriage so it is a bit crowded.'" She hesitated and drank some water. "I've probably got that wrong but it's how I started to feel."

"Can I just…"

"No, Damian. You can't. There has been enough talking and indecision and now, at last, my future is settled. As soon as I'm back to good health, which will be no more than two weeks, I want you to leave, for good. I have my new home in Milton Keynes and this house will sell quickly according to the estate agents and I have my new job. If I'm honest the thought of a fresh start is invigorating: I'm not yet forty-five and I'm going to be a granny."

Damian stood up and looked around his garden before turning back to face Cathy.

"Why did you agree to give your kidney to this Mrs Haydon who you don't know?" he asked.

She looked up and he thought that there might be a tear in her eye.

"I take full responsibility for everything that has happened and this Marie did not get you, I let you go and I must live with that. But all that happened has shattered my self-confidence and you may remember the incident at the surgery with the overweight woman. That was not me and I knew I had to pull myself together. When Anisha first mentioned the possibility of the nursing role at the Alexandra Hospital I was immediately interested and then came along the meeting with Dr Haydon and the look on his face when he was told about the aborted kidney donor. I saw a chance to be me, to give something back instead of losing everything. When I woke up from the operation, I knew that I had succeeded in being me and I must tell you, it's a great feeling." She hesitated. "Give me two weeks please Damian and then go. It's best for both of us."

He walked away, reached his car, drove to the canal, walked along the tow path and reached the bottom of the garden where he and Marie shared their early times together. The motor boat was out on the canal and he began to think about Ellen MacArthur's story, 'Taking on the World' which he had finished reading. While lost in admiration for her unique achievements, he found her rather singular and self-contained, which she was. In a similar way he discovered during Cathy's telling of her story and her remarkable selflessness in donating a kidney, a similar person to whom he'd been married for nearly twenty-two years and who was now someone he did not recognise. He'd do all he could to ensure that she made a full recovery and then he'd leave, as she wanted.

That evening, from the seclusion of his study, and after ensuring that Cathy was comfortable in her room, he spoke to Marie for over an hour and told her the whole story. She made little comment on the medical details and said that once she was back in Portsmouth, she'd be starting her university work and so the extra free week before he arrived could be put to good use. About thirty minutes later he received a text message:

'Details matter, it's worth waiting to get it right.' Steve Jobs. Mxx

The two weeks that were agreed with Cathy passed without further difficulty as each showed consideration to the other and avoided any reference to the past. Cathy recovered steadily from her time at the Alexandra Hospital, attended on the Monday for a positive post-operation check-up and saw Dr Martin Armstrong at the surgery. The house was put up for sale and sold within a week to a cash purchaser who initially tried to reduce the asking price but quickly changed his mind after one meeting with a resolute Cathy. They each attended meetings with their lawyers and, although there was to be some negotiating over the details, the settlement followed the mutually agreed basis. There was common agreement on a wish to start the divorce procedure. Damian drove her everywhere including her mother's bungalow, to church meetings, to the hairdresser and to Milton Keynes to meet with Anisha Khan to discuss the starting date for her new role as deputy head of nursing at Alexandra Private Hospital. They spoke to Scarlett who was heading back to University with Joshua and to Arthur who said that the hospital thought the baby was two weeks away but that you could never be certain on these matters.

Damian had another meeting with Lydia Pennington and was delighted to speak to Rachel Smith who was back at work: Glen Shannon was out visiting clients. Louisa was friendly and cheerful but as he left Hannon, Shannon and Smith (still to be renamed), he sensed he was parting from a different world.

His future lay ahead on the south coast, on the waters of the English Channel, within the new freedom now available to him, with ample financial resources, with many years ahead of him and with the companionship of a rather special person. He returned home to complete the packing of a van he had hired to take his possessions to the Port Solent and to pay the driver who was to take it to Bryher Island.

The time came for him to leave his home of the last twelve years and he managed to undertake this by pecking Cathy on her cheek and driving straight off towards the motorway. Four hours later he arrived at Marie's home and noticed that building work had started on the extension which would deliver him a study, a base and a centre of privacy as he planned their lives together.

They had dinner at the marina and then walked along the beach both wearing jackets as the autumnal winds were starting to blow. She wanted to talk about the start of the university term and a rather demanding workload although Professor Warnock seemed to be taking more of an interest in the details of her syllabus. They reached back home and Marie played the piano for him. They finished the evening in the lounge watching the ten o'clock news which included the expulsion of a number of Russian embassy officials from Washington as American foreign policy hardened against the duplicity of the Kremlin. It is probable that they both thought back to Khristina Babikov although nothing was said. They went to bed, together.

*

Angelina Haydon was finding it difficult to hold back the tears as she faced the donor of her life-saving kidney.Suddenly, there was a mutual release of tensions and she and Cathy embraced sharing a rather special moment, together. They were joined by her husband who also gave Cathy a hug.

"Thank you for joining us," said Russell Haydon, "I hope the taxi collected you on time?"

"That was thoughtful of you, Dr Haydon," said Cathy.

"It's Russell and Angelina," he said. "We only need to be formal when we are working in the hospital, speaking of which Anisha Khan tells me that we've agreed a starting date which is good news. Obviously, you need the all-clear from the consultant but I gather that is likely. What an occasion this is!"

"I'd be happier if we talk about Angelina's health," said Cathy.

"No, Cathy," said Angelina, "we're talking about getting my life back and we'll never be able to thank you enough. You'll meet our children in due course but they all want to hug you."

"Now the bad news," laughed Russell. "Angelina has a little way to go and so I've cooked dinner: my paella will be memorable."

As they moved into the dining room Angelina took Cathy's hand and reassured her that her husband was a tolerably decent chef which proved to be the case. The conversation initially centred on their journey to Milton Keynes via New Zealand where she was born, to Leeds when they met at the General Hospital where he was an A & E doctor and she was an administrator, followed by a meeting with an entrepreneurial medical colleague and the decision to move to Milton Keynes and build the Alexandra Private Hospital.

"Joseph Rubenstein, my business partner, is more business than medicine whereas I'm the other way which has resulted in a constructive partnership," said Russell. "Covid-19 changed the outlook for patient care and the reality that GPs now offer a different service and private medicine is playing a much greater role. It used to be the playground of the rich but now the general public are much more willing to pay for their health. The politicians have always tried to adhere to the general principle of free health care for all which is a great idea but is no longer feasible. The Alexandra is part of the new wave and Joseph wants to build ten hospitals."

"What did an administrator do at Leeds General Hospital?" asked Cathy.

"Panic, for most of the time," laughed Angelina. "The NHS never catches up because we were always chasing beds, nurses, doctors, ambulances, supplies and the most important people of all."

"You've mentioned me," laughed Russell.

"The maintenance crews," she said. "The buildings were in a poor condition and the answer was to start again but the patients refused, en masse, to stop being ill for two years." "She paused a little thoughtfully. "I was at the Leeds General for six years and I cannot recall one single day on which all the lifts were working."

After coffee it was announced that Angelina was going to bed which resulted in another embrace between the two women. Russell suggested they put the taxi back an hour and invited Cathy to share a liqueur with him. They settled down together in the lounge.

"It might be easier if I explain my personal situation," she began and, seeing the nod of her host's head, summarised her background, discussed her children and the expectation of becoming a grandmother, her own reborn romantic mother which caused some mirth and, finally, the decision of her husband to leave home for a younger woman."

"I'm afraid us men can let ourselves down, at times," he said.

"No, Damian remains a good man. I let him go and must accept my degree of responsibility. But I'm sitting here with my new boss, my home looking over the lake is nearly ready, I've a sound financial position and looking forward to a job I'm going to relish." She stared at Dr Haydon. 'I'll not let you down, Russell," she said, "and I'm confident Anisha and I can deliver you a top-class nursing team. You'll be medically pleased and Joseph can make lots of money!"

A second glass each of Bailey's Irish Cream preceded the next question from Russell who asked Cathy to tell him about her work in the surgery: he mentioned that he'd met Dr Martin Armstrong on one occasion. She took him through the main demands and her specialisation as a weight-loss nurse.

"I'm interested in that, Cathy because Anisha mentioned the paper you've written for the surgery on losing weight."

"It's not yet finished but I will complete it. It's a private submission for Dr Armstrong on ways to help patients lose weight. I don't need to talk about the obesity issue."

"You don't, Cathy. Last week we had a caesarean section which nearly went wrong due to the amount of subcutaneous fat that the surgeon had to cut through and it was too close for comfort."

"It's complex and frustrating because I feel I can write something helpful for Dr Armstrong but I need a run at it."

"Have you come across the keto diet?" he asked.

Cathy explained that she had first-hand experience of the diet due to her soon to be ex-husband putting himself on it and she detailed the consequences for herself."

"But it works?" he asked.

"Yes, it works, but at a cost." She outlined the basic principles and how the adherent achieves a state of ketosis."

"You make it sound like a religious cult," said Dr Haydon.

Cathy pondered his interjection and nodded her head saying that, in some ways, that's how it came across to her.

"The individual must purify their body free of carbohydrates and proteins and live on fats. "It's much more complicated than that but it worked for Damian and he became obsessed with cooking his own food. I reacted badly because I felt he was invading my kitchen."

"Joseph, my partner, has been studying it in some depth and thinks it could become a money spinner."

"It's global with practitioners all over the United States and Europe," she said.

Russell suggested that it was getting late and that she should be on her way home: he phoned the taxi company and asked that her vehicle came as soon as possible. He repeated his interest in her work on weight-loss and said that Anisha had mentioned something about financial incentives.

"She had a rather confrontational discussion with Damian about it," she said. "He was just trying to help me write my paper and he came up with the idea of paying people to lose weight."

"How does that work?" he asked.

Cathy said that she was feeling a little weary and why didn't she ask Dr Armstrong if he could let him have a copy of her dissertation when it was completed, an idea that was accepted with some enthusiasm.

They made their farewells and, within forty minutes, Cathy was back home for nearly the last time as she would be moving into her lakeside residence within a week. The house was no longer home for her because it was cold and lonely and contained too many recent memories that she would consign to the scrapheap. She was feeling elated because she had cemented herself into a new, vibrant environment, she had a future on which to rebuild her life and now she was determined to complete the writing of her paper on weight-loss.

Early in the following week she telephoned the

surgery and spoke to Dr Armstrong who, initially, was resistant to the idea that his paper should be shared but Cathy persisted and, in the end, obtained his agreement to the suggestion on the proviso that he read it first and then he would give his sanction for her to release it. This struck Cathy as both a sensible idea and a check that the copy of the dissertation that would eventually go to her new boss had been vetted. She also wondered about Dr Joseph Rubenstein and looked forward to meeting him. Her initial reaction to his idea that the keto diet could have financial implications did not appeal to her but she was willing to be adaptable.

As she sank beneath the covers of her bed and closed her eyes Cathy began to feel more relaxed than she had for many months and she was going to be grandmother. She was nearly forty-five years of age and was beginning to feel like a spring chicken although she was still a little sore. That would pass and the future would develop as memories of Damian Hannon evaporated into the past.

PART FOUR

WINTER

CHAPTER SEVENTEEN

Marie and Damian adapted into their adventure together like newly-weds.

Within days, he was unpacked, settled, organised and relishing the walks around the executive environment of Bryher Island while congratulating her on the choice of residence where the extension was being completed. They usually ended up at the marina and adopted what was to become their favourite restaurant. Within two weeks Damian had purchased a single sail boat and was taking professional lessons on how to sail safely. His tutor was decidedly careful but it was not too long before, on a calm day but with enough wind, they left the marina, sailed into Paulsgrove Lake, through the dockyard and into the Solent sighting the Isle of Wight and, although they did not know it, tacking past Luccombe Bay where Harry used to walk and imagine the smugglers unloading their contraband in the chine.

Marie was determined not to be left out and the three of them trained together on the lake until the day came when Damian made his first solo trip before rushing back to the house, collecting Marie, and taking her with him. They were exhilarated by the experience especially when the afternoon thermals increased the winds. On their return they walked around the marina and began to discuss a more adventurous nautical investment but decided to wait for the springtime.

Marie was uncompromising about her study

schedule and banned him from reading her paperwork. He circumnavigated this problem by sneaking downstairs during the night and looking ahead at her next set of revision notes. The following day he asked if she could explain to him the meaning of periodontal therapy and the management of soft tissue which impressed her so much so that she started to talk to him more often and then, as the students arrived, she chatted about their varying personalities. Professor Warnock and his partner joined them one evening in the marina for a meal together. Marie paid little attention to Joss although it took Damian a little time to feel comfortable especially when they started to talk about their wedding plans.

Later Marie explained to her partner that she had to work hard to understand the world that her students inhabited which she exampled by their wish, in many cases, to be 'woke' and care about social and racial justice. The bigger issue was that trends come and go and she needed to keep up to retain her credibility. Sometimes in the evening she played the piano for him. She mentioned that she'd spoken to Rebecca about Professor Warnock being gay and was told that everybody at the university knew and why was it such a big issue? She felt she had been put down a little by her friend.

Marie sensed that he was becoming restless and when she left for the university on a Monday morning he would return indoors, tidy up, talk to the builders, answer emails and text messages and drink coffee. Cathy was reliable in keeping him informed on the sale of the house and the lawyers eventually sent him a separation statement. His lawyers wrote saying they could obtain a better settlement for him but were asked to complete the process as had been agreed. He spoke to Scarlett who was hesitant and rang off whereas Arthur wanted to talk about his studies and the new arrival, a girl, who had been named Genevieve Summer Hannon. Cathy sent him several photographs.

Their first stumble resulted from an invitation from a couple five doors away who were having a bonfire party on Friday, the sixth of November, and said they were asking a few friends round for dinner. When they arrived, they realised that no expense had been spared and the professional display of fireworks was memorable. The eight guests returned to the table where cheese and port was being served to the now separated parties, at the hosts request. Damian found himself talking to a brunette who explained that she was divorced and currently in a 'hating men' phase: she was head teacher at a local school as well as being bitter and damaged: her other topic of conversation was sailing on the Solent which she described as her passion: he played down his own interest in an attempt at self-preservation as he sensed she was working up to inviting him to join her.

That, however, was not the cause of the tension between himself and Marie. She was sitting opposite him and his teacher companion, with the host who was slowly wrapping himself around her. In fairness, she was looking rather stunning in a low-cut dress and not too much else. His jealousy simmered as his own companion asked if she was talking too much and what were his interests? At this point Damian noticed that various other couples were seemingly becoming more engrossed with each other and then he saw that the host had put his hand on Marie's cleavage.

He thanked the school teacher, who was telling him

how interesting she was finding his company and would he like to go sailing with her, excused himself, went round to Marie, lifted her out of her chair while telling their hosts that they had to make an early start in the morning and many thanks for an enjoyable evening. His tactic of complete surprise worked in that everyone was caught on the hop and within minutes they were walking home. His problem was that Marie was angry and their row gathered pace as she took exception to being treated like a teenager.

"Where was that going to lead to," he snapped, "and where was Mr Wandering Hands heading towards?"

"He had his other hand on my thigh," she giggled. "It was totally harmless and they are our neighbours."

They were heading for a disagreement and so Damian suggested that he sleep on the sofa and they'd talk it through in the morning. Marie disappeared upstairs and he heard her in the shower. He followed her up, undressed and joined her under the water.

"Oh good," she chuckled, "I've bought a new gel,"

"Does it contain glitter?" asked Damian.

"Does it matter?" she laughed as she welcomed him in.

Cathy was learning the walks open to her around Walton Lake which was part of the Ouzel Valley waterways. The flood plain grassland was home to the Reed Warbler, little over thirteen centimetres long, and with its short, rasping call as it searched for insects. Above Cathy spotted a kestrel circling and preying on the fauna beneath it. The grass snakes had now retreated into safer vegetation having used the summer sun to hunt for frogs and toads.

She was still experiencing slight soreness in her abdomen but was elated by the 'all-clear' from the consultant the previous afternoon and the agreement with Anisha that she'd visit the hospital next Tuesday for a familiarisation afternoon before starting half day shifts the week after and then full-time thereafter. She was interested to receive an email from Dr Joseph Rosenberg who was looking forward to meeting her.

Earlier that morning she'd completed the final task of moving into her new home by deciding which photographs to put on display and where they were to be positioned. In the lounge her granddaughter Genevieve, Mum Faria and Arthur managed to dominate the displays although fresh-in shots of Scarlett and Joshua standing on an iceberg added interest. In the dining room there were a number of photographs of her leaving party at the surgery and of her mother and Edgar outside their new home. In her bedroom there were several pictures of her father, Harry, taken in Luccombe Bay and of her early years up to medical school. She was using the third upstairs bedroom as a study and was already organised.

She had been stimulated by the meeting with Dr Haydon and his comments on her dissertation being written for Dr Martin Armstrong on weight-loss. She had revised her initial document and mapped out the structure of the final paper. She decided to develop the chapter on dieting and include an analysis of the state of ketosis. The conversation with her new employer and his references to the financial implications of private medicine were occupying her thinking and had been stimulated by a general email she had received from a health insurance company offering quotations depending on age for medical care. The advantages were set out in stark terms: 'skip NHS waiting lists', 'high quality treatment', recover in your own private en-suite room, and 'benefit from independent and impartial research'.

Cathy reflected on her career and relived those many times in the surgery where they worked as a team to cope with patient demand: she was often dazzled by the dedication of the doctors, nurses and administration staff and recalled the day a group of gypsies came in with an injured child and the care they were all given including clearing up several skin problems. Her whole approach was predicated on the National Health Service although the coronavirus turned everything up-side-down and reorganised the surgery into distance consultations which worked well and left physical attendances to those who needed direct contact with the doctor.

Covid-19 left one huge problem behind it, not that it was ever likely to disappear off the radar, and that was the waiting times for general surgery. It was inevitable as whole hospitals were adapted to trying to help the thousands struck down with the various strains of the virus. There were more doctors being trained for the NHS but that took time. For Dr Armstrong and many of his colleagues their world was universal medicine and they accepted the role of private medicine but it was not for them. Cathy was about to cross the Rubicon and join the other side and the reality of her position was becoming clearer. Was it right to allow financial means to determine access to medical care?

She took comfort from the words spoken at her leaving party and decided to commit herself to providing the best nursing care possible to the patients in Alexandra Private Hospital. As a final contribution to the NHS, she'd complete the writing of her dissertation on weight-loss before beginning her new journey: and she was still well under fifty years of age.

She was wondering whether to walk another mile by veering off the main path and circling round a secondary smaller lake spurred on by the reading off her bathroom scales earlier in the morning which suggested she had put on three pounds over her ideal weight and, in truth, she knew it. She was finding it more difficult to shed the pounds because, although she'd discipline herself to eat sensibly and she did enjoy the Mediterranean recipes, it was the early evening when she was alone and nobody was coming through the front door that temptation took over with the vodka and tonics and the snacks. Cathy stopped and looked across at a duck that was hunting for its lunch.

The truth was that she was not adapting to being on her own as well as she tried to show the outside world. She sat down on the slightly damp grass and vowed that this was the moment when she'd banish any resemblance of self-pity. She'd do something about it: she'd take in a lodger.

The November winds did not stop Damian from wearing shorts but he did decide to pull his new sweater, a present from Marie, over his head and then wander down to the marina for coffee and a read of the newspaper. He was, at last, at liberty to build up a new life and, thanks to Mr Heron, free of financial constraints. He and Marie would decide over the winter months which boat to buy in the spring and, in the meantime, he'd potter around the coastal waters in his sailing boat. He was finding that for the first time in many years he had time on his hands and he was starting to feel ambitious. He'd always been a man driven by achievement and his horizons were clear. He had no reason to believe that the separation from Cathy would not proceed to completion and the dinner party incident had led to he and Marie having a candid re-assessment of their feelings for each other which concluded with a need to replace the shower gel.

He was reflecting on what were his skill sets. He most certainly was determined to avoid any project involving accountancy although his knowledge of finance might prove helpful. He was leaning to a complete change of direction but, for the time being, was failing to identify where to go. He was nearing fifty years of age and had plenty of gas left in the tank. Marie was talking about starting a family and that could take its course without affecting his freedom, due to her flexible working hours at the university.

The man had been staring in his direction for some time, stood up and came over to speak to him.

"Can I join you?" he asked.

Damian looked up and saw a middle-aged seafarer, tanned and friendly if his smile was to be believed. He indicated that he should sit down and looked for a waitress who was on her way over to them to take an order for two coffees and a selection of biscuits.

"Name's John," he said. "I've seen you with that beauty who follows you around."

Damian made a note to ensure that Marie never heard that description and encouraged John to keep talking, which he did.

"I have a boatyard on the north side of the marina: repairs and all that and I manage to run a few errands, getting holiday-makers to their yachts and the odd trip round the coast."

"Interesting," said Damian. "Why are you telling me all this?"

"I'm looking for someone to take a share in the business."

"I'm not in that market," he said. "Try your local business advisory groups because my guess is that the banks are not helpful."

"You look successful," said John.

He knew that he was being irrational but Damian decided to ask his new acquaintance to show him his yard and, after John insisted in paying for their refreshments, they wandered around the walkways, with their rows of luxury boats, before arriving at a surprisingly impressive separate group of small workshops leading down into the water. There were five boats of various designs and three men and a woman working on the individual vessels. John allowed his guest to walk around the yard before inviting him into his office where a young assistant seemed to be holding the fort. "Phone Mrs Withers," she prompted as she left the premises. "Be back in thirty," she said.

Damian accepted an invitation to sit down and looked at his new companion.

"We were ok and then along came the virus, lockdowns and the rest and though the government has helped we're struggling."

"Bank?" asked Damien.

"Fifty thousand overdraft, up to our limit."

"Taxes paid?"

"Yes."

"Do you owe much?"

"Creditors? Generally, fairly comfortable. Most give

sixty days."

"People paying their bills?"

"Yep. Susie who you just met is a rottweiler. She's an apprentice on a Government Scheme."

"New business?"

"Picking up. The whole area is much more buoyant and my only problem is that while I'm trading in surplus, I'm carrying baggage and that's holding us back."

"Are you from this area, John?"

"Peterborough. Keen sailor, berthed here twenty-two years ago, never wanted to leave. Wife didn't see it that way so she buggered off back home. Bought into this in two thousand and twelve and bought my partner out five years ago. Love the way of life and I'll never leave: it's just the last two years have been testing."

"Have you asked anyone else for money?"

"Investment, you mean. Two possibilities."

"And what's happened?" asked Damian.

"They're still possibilities."

"Why me?"

"A hunch. Spotted you when you first started wandering around the marina but, truthfully, noticed the woman. She's so content. You looked like someone I might trust."

"How much are you looking for?"

"Fifty thousand. Free of debt I'll make much better progress."

"What share are you offering?"

"Thirty per cent."

"Have you your accounts?"

He reached into a drawer and took out a document telling Damian the accountant would be willing to answer any questions.

It was time to leave and so he thanked John for a most interesting morning and that he'd come back in the next week."

"We're not going anywhere," he said.

That evening he told Marie all about John, his boatyard and his need for investment but was dismayed that her dental students seemed to be occupying her attention. He retreated into his study and read the accounts which were to his approval although he needed to speak to the accountant who had prepared them. He thought about the conversation with the boatyard owner and came up with an idea which he spent the following twenty-four hours refining.

The following day he returned to the yard and called in to meet with John who appeared to be going through a pile of invoices with Susie. She left in response to a request for two coffees.

"Didn't expect to see you so soon," said John.

"I have an idea on how to raise fifty thousand pounds," said Damian.

"Highjack an oil tanker on the high seas," he said.

"Eight times ten thousand pounds," said Damian.

"That's eighty thousand pounds: thanks. Why would anyone put in ten thousand pounds, just like that?" he asked.

"Because for their investment they get five per cent interest and a free boat. They do it by way of a loan over five years so you retain ownership of your business."

John looked at Damian with a look of incredulity and suggested that the sea air must be affecting him.

"I'm new to all this nautical stuff," he said, "but I do know that owning a boat is a bit of a status symbol:

think of the harbour at Monte Carlo: most of the craft never move." He paused and drank the coffee now brought in by the apprentice. "I've been surprised at how cheap smaller boats are and so, if you offer one costing around three thousand pounds, you still keep seven thousand pounds which is fifty-six thousand pounds less six thousand pounds for legal costs: you are left with fifty thousand and eight new customers who will use you to repair their boats." He paused. "I've written you a summary."

John scanned the paper handed to him and became lost in thought before uttering his first reaction which was that he'd be able to source quite decent craft for that amount of money.

"How do I find eight investors each of whom have ten thousand pounds?" he asked.

"You find one and let the grapevine do the rest. Ten thousand pounds is not a lot of money, especially in a marina, and once you have one taker, they will talk, perhaps boast, and others will follow."

"What do I pay you?" asked John.

"Nothing. I'm relishing the voyage of discovery." He hesitated. "There is something you can do," he said. "I'd love to go out into the channel in a motor boat."

"Boarding is tomorrow at ten," advised an elated boatyard owner.

*

Cathy shook her head in total bemusement as she reflected on the notion of taking in a lodger: she gave herself a reality check and looked into the bedroom mirror, again, to confirm that her appearance met the high standards she would be setting at the Alexandra

Private Hospital. She was preparing to make her way into Milton Keynes for her 'familiarisation' afternoon as a prelude to undertaking the first of her half-day shifts the following week. She had started to drive her car and at the weekend would be travelling down to Maida Vale to see her granddaughter. She checked her jacket and brushed away an imaginary crease.

Anisha had arranged a parking space for her and as she entered the main reception area, the memories came back of her recent stay in the renal ward. She was taking a little more notice of the surroundings and felt as though she was booking into a four-star hotel which was certainly the impression one of the three receptionists seemed keen to convey. She attached her visitor's badge to her lapel grimacing at the photograph which was now part of her security identity. She was asked to take a lift to the second floor where Senior Nurse Khan was waiting to meet her. Cathy smiled at the recollection of the comment made by Angelina Haydon as she saw that all the four lifts were in working order. She stepped out of the compartment and into the path of her new working colleague who ushered her to a work-station where there were six other medical staff mostly staring at computer screens.

"There are no operations today," explained Anisha, "which is why I suggested you to come in as we can visit all the wards and meet the teams. This is what happened as Cathy absorbed what was, for her, an almost surreal atmosphere with organised patient care, calm and unhurried medical personnel and space: there was room for everyone and everything. Her time in the kitchens was an eye-opener and the conversation was dominated by menu selection which was driven by the objective on ensuring that every patient remembered

277

their stay at the Alexandra Private Hospital, favourably.

"Because," explained Anisha, "the objective is that they recommend us to their friends."

As Cathy was digesting something she had never experienced when working in the NHS, where most patients' ambitions were to leave either the surgery or hospital ward as fast as possible assuming they had received the attention their condition necessitated, she found herself being introduced to Dr Joseph Rosenberg who, she was to discover, rarely, if ever, smiled. As she was taking the chair which was offered to her in his executive office , he launched into a summary of the philosophy underlying the growth of the private hospital group that he and Dr Russell Haydon were building.

"We're the future," he said. "The key is customer satisfaction. Forget all those silly television series that glorify doctors and nurses and have a life-saving drama every episode: the reality is that most medicine is routine. Take your recent kidney transplant: I checked your file and it's excellent. Every single part of the process was followed, all the safeguards were actioned, your recovery was textbook and the Alexandra met its own self-imposed standards."

"And what about me, the patient, Dr Rosenberg?" queried Cathy. "You make it sound as though I was incidental to the operation."

"You were," he said. "We can't govern how the patient reacts: what we do is to ensure that the treatment delivered is to the highest clinical standards: can you think of a better away to achieve patient satisfaction?"

"Are you suggesting that the Covid-19 crisis and the dedication of the NHS staff was a myth?" she asked.

"The pandemic was a totally different experience and, for most of us, was a one-off experience. I'll make two points for you to consider: A & E and ICU are different branches of medicine and ones that we are not part of: we offer routine care. All our patients come here by prior appointment. The second matter I would ask you to understand is that during Covid-19 Dr Haydon and myself returned to the frontline working in London hospitals. Later we turned the Alexandra, which was not fully opened, into a vaccination centre. Russell and I personally vaccinated thousands of the elderly as fast as we could, but those days have passed and we have returned to our project."

Cathy reflected on the disclosure but was still struggling to feel comfortable with the nature of private medicine.

"Dr Rosenberg, I appreciate all that you are saying but please understand that my background was about the concept that everyone matters. Here we discriminate between those with the financial means to come here and the majority who can't afford us."

"A large percentage of our patients come here through private health insurance schemes. They are the people who have prudently provided for their needs and I cannot understand the argument that they should not benefit from their own prudence. We also offer a range of finance plans so access to our services is within the range of many more people than you might imagine. I think when you come here full time, you'll see the vital role that we play within the whole spectrum of medical care."

"I look forward to it," she said and stood up to leave.

"I understand from Anisha that you have some

experience of the keto diet?" Dr Rosenberg asked.

"It's a bit more than that: I'm writing a paper on weight-loss which was my speciality and keto is within that."

"Next week I'll ask Anisha to release you for an hour so we can talk about it," he said. "Welcome to the Alexandra. I think you'll fit in well."

Cathy drove her car back to her home feeling a little weary and with much to ponder: the Alexandra Private Hospital was going to prove to be a different world from her years in general practice.

+ + +

CHAPTER EIGHTEEN

Marie called it correctly, insisting that he was properly attired for his nautical adventure and gave him a special hug before she left for the university. He arrived at the boatyard with about ten minutes to go to the departure time. John was busy with one of his workmen but was soon at his side ensuring that he was fitting his lifejacket correctly and reassuring him that the waters were relatively calm. He pointed out the boat that they would be boarding and introduced a friendly sailor-type who was called Cyrus and who, he was told, ran trips around Portsmouth Harbour and the Solent for holiday-makers.

Before long they were out on the waters as Cyrus described his RIB or rigid inflatable boat as he explained the term for Damian. The three men were soon out into the Solent, past the historic forts and the Mary Rose and turning to starboard to circle, anti-clockwise, round the Isle of Wight, powered by the one hundred and ten horsepower engines and travelling at around thirty knots which John translated into thirty-four miles per hour.

Damian was exhilarated by the experience and the hour spent on the seawaters was a seminal moment in his growing love for the southern coast, the Solent, the English Channel and beyond. Cyrus invited him over to see his base whenever he wanted.

He and John went back to the office where Susie announced that she was off for her lunch. They discussed Damian's finance proposal and John was keen to understand the implications of taking on, prospectively, eight loans of ten thousand pounds each. He immediately understood that, assuming all the loans were taken up, the annual interest cost at five per cent was four thousand pounds which was offset by the savings in bank charges on the overdraft and would be deductible against corporation tax, which pleased John. The loans were for five years which meant that the business would need to reserve sixteen thousand pounds a year from profits, to build up for repayments of the loans. Damian pointed out that some lenders might agree to renew their loans. John wanted to also understand the legal procedures and said that he'd arrange to meet with his lawyer and would Damian come with him? They sat back, agreed to go for lunch together and headed off for the centre of the marina.

After their orders were taken by a rather bubbly waitress, Damian lifted his glass and said that all that needed to be done now was to find eight people who were willing to lend the business ten thousand pounds each.

"Seven," smiled John.

"No," said Damian. "It's eight times ten thousand."

"We already have one taker," said John.

Damian could not contain his curiosity which was satisfied when it was explained that Susie had taken a copy of his proposal home to her parents who thought about it overnight and then told their daughter to put them down for one of the loans.

"It was the free boat that did it," said John. "Apparently her father thought it was a fantastic offer and is coming over to tell me what he wants." John raised his glass. "You are an amazing man," he said.

They agreed to meet again when the time and date of the meeting with the lawyer was known. Damian could not wait to tell his partner about his seafaring achievement.

Marie looked across the kitchen table and grinned.

"So, you are an amazing man," she said.

"Was it ever in doubt?" smiled Damian, having told her about the whole day including the memorable boat trip. Marie seemed lost in her thoughts.

"I'm beginning to wonder if we are overlooking your real talents," she said. "The free boat is a brilliant idea and it will not surprise me to hear that all eight loans are taken up." She sipped her cup of green tea. "Do you recall that idea you gave to Cathy about using financial incentives to encourage people to lose weight. You seem to have this ability to think outside the box."

"I didn't think outside the box when you seduced me," he said.

"I didn't seduce you," she laughed. "I made you an offer which you accepted." She stood up. "Let's go for a walk."

They took the well-trodden route to the marina and watched the remaining boats with crews aboard preparing to lockdown. She mentioned that she'd heard from the police about her step-sister, Khristina Babikov, who was going to plead guilty to the charges levied against her and they would not require any further involvement from Marie. Damian asked if she'd heard from her father but had forgotten that there never had been any contact although she admitted that she was pleased that she had met him.

She suggested that Professor Warnock was having rows with his partner judging by his short-tempered attitude to the students, that she seemed to be the flavour of the month and that Rebecca had split from Jeb. She completed the 'Marie News Bulletin', as described by her partner, by saying that Mr and Mrs Choudhary had invited them up to Bedfordshire before Christmas.

They returned home and he asked her to play Bernstein's "West Side Story' which Marie undertook without any sheet music. He sat at her side, having invested in a new double piano stool, and marvelled at her keyboard skills. As she caught the brilliance of 'I Feel Pretty', 'Maria', 'Somewhere' and his favourite, 'Tonight', he watched her from the side and simply could not believe that he had found someone almost beyond description.

They returned to the lounge, talked some more and went to bed.

Cathy was a little frustrated when she discovered that there were no parking spaces available in front of the Alexandra Private Hospital which necessitated her going to the nearby multi-storey carpark where she had to drive up to the seventh floor before finding a vacant space. When she reached the hospital reception, although she was immediately recognised, she was required to complete the security procedure, including photograph, albeit that if she completed the requisite form and had it signed by a director, they'd obtain a permanent pass for her. When she approached the lifts, two were at the upper floors, one was out of action and the fourth was being used to take a stretcher to the orthopaedic floor. She hurried to the stairs and reached the second floor where Senior Nurse Anisha Khan was looking at her watch.

She was required to spend much of the afternoon sitting with a lady who was recovering from a varicose vein operation on her legs and who was unhappy with the pain she was experiencing despite the medication she had been given. She had four grandchildren and it was not long before Cathy knew their individual personalities down to their eating habits. After two hours she went to speak to Anisha only to find that the use of her Christian name was considered to be too familiar and she should be referred to as Senior Nurse Khan. They agreed that Cathy should go and find a signatory for her security pass form to ensure that she was not late on future occasions.

The executive offices were on the top floor and, somewhat to her disappointment, she was told that Dr Haydon was at a medical conference in Manchester but Dr Rubenstein was available. After a wait she was shown into his office where he was sitting on a sofa reading a book. He signed her form and asked her to stay for a few moments as he explained that he was reading up on the keto diet.

"It's extraordinary," he said. "There's a world-wide ketosis movement and we know nothing about it: the claims this book makes are staggering and I've trawled the net: it's unbelievable the global support it now has. You were telling me that your husband tried it out and I want to understand how he approached it."

"He's my ex-husband," said Cathy, "and it would have helped our relationship if he'd told me about it at the start. At its simplest level ketosis is when the body has a therapeutic level of ketones circulating in the bloodstream and the claim is that it is a natural state resulting from eliminating carbohydrates from your diet which then means the body exhausts its store of glucose: the body then needs energy and that is provided by a careful diet of natural fats. It requires a scientific approach and is based entirely on the control of food and drink consumption."

"One article says that it reproduces what happened to primitive man who hunted for his only source of food which was meat," interrupted the doctor.

"The one thing that I learned from Damian was that there must be a total commitment to the diet. Whereas with the standard, eat less fats diet, the individual can break it without too much damage being done, with keto, it has to be total."

"Your husband, sorry, ex-husband, lost weight?"

"Yes, and at one point he became almost emaciated. What you need to know is that it changed him: he spent hours in my kitchen preparing his meals: it was as though he'd joined a religious sect."

"We're thinking of setting up a specialist keto diet unit," he said. "They'll pay a fortune to lose weight and I'm not a fan of bariatric surgery: far too many risks and, frankly, if a patient has a BMI over 36, which is the accepted guideline, they are beyond help, in many cases."

"But that's strictly against NHS beliefs," snapped Cathy. "Everyone has the right to our total commitment: we never, ever give up on anyone."

"Quite right, Cathy," said Dr Rubenstein, "but my role is to make this hospital profitable which we'll do by refining our procedures to eliminate risk and achieve a level of efficiency that the NHS can only dream about. Once the Alexandra is making money, we'll commission another hospital and help more patients to experience risk-free surgery. By the way, the NHS is completely broke and the taxpayer is not being told the true level of the Government subsidy."

Cathy wiped her brow and ran her hand though her hair.

"The obese patient needing bariatric surgery: what happens to them?" she asked. "We cannot surely desert them?"

"They should have joined our keto diet unit," he laughed. "It's a money maker!" he added.

She tried to find Senior Nurse Anisha Khan but to no avail and so she left the hospital, found her car, drove home and slumped into her favourite chair in the lounge helped by a generous measure of vodka and tonic. She turned on the news but was distracted by the post being delivered unusually late through her letterbox and which she read: she did not want to release equity from her home, the electricity bill could wait and then she came to a hand-written envelope which she immediately recognised but could not recall the last time her son had written to her.

She felt a sense of relief because she had been uncertain that her visit at the weekend to see her granddaughter had been a success. Faria had seemed distracted but Cathy put that down to a lack of sleep. She knew she had been wrong to suggest that the baby's milk was not sufficiently warmed up.

Cathy read Arthur's hurriedly written missive with utter horror: on a single page, with several crossings-out, he said that Faria did not want her to visit them again, at least for a year. She was smothering Genevieve and did not understand modern child-raising techniques. Arthur was sure that she would understand.

Damian liked Nelson Smith from the moment he and John entered his office in the centre of Portsmouth. It did not take much time to establish that the solicitor had been born in East London, his father worked on the railways, his mother was a waitress and he had no idea why he had been christened with an historic, nautical name. He had represented John Middleton for many years, he had read Damian's fund-raising suggestion and he had several questions. What became almost immediately clear was that Nelson knew the corporate requirements for the issuing of legal loan documents and quoted a fee of four thousand pounds for completing the proposal and a further one thousand pounds for acting as the receiver of the funds raised and dealing with money laundering regulations. He estimated it could take around six weeks to complete the transaction but he did have one concern.

"As your proposal states, Damian," he said, "In five years' time the business must repay £80,000 and your suggestion is that John must put away sixteen thousand pounds a year to build up the reserves. I've looked over the last five years' accounts and on only two occasions has there been sufficient profitability for that to happen and yes, this is a clever idea to give away eight boats which will bring in more revenue but it's a risk. I would like to suggest we reduce the risk."

"How do we do that, Nelson?" asked John.

"We issue four loans over a five-year term at 4% interest, two over six years at 5% and two over seven years at 6%."

"Smart," said Damian.

"It will be a matter of first come, first served and your receptionist's father can have his choice. It'll be interesting to see which loan he selects."

"Only seven to go," said John. "It seems a long way."

"But closer than you might think," said Nelson. "My partner is interested: this giving away a boat is a tantalising idea. Kathleen has all the boating she wants as her husband is rather successful but she's going to give the boat to her son."

"Six to go," said an elated boatyard owner.

"She's yet to commit but she seems interested," smiled Nelson.

Farewells were said and Damian and John went back to the marina and settled outside the restaurant for coffees and a further chat. They talked about plans to extend the boatyard and to introduce a staff scheme so that they shared in the profits. John asked if his companion liked fishing? It transpired that Damian's interest was lukewarm but his enthusiasm was increased by an invitation to join him and two other pals on an evening cod catching trip.

"We hire a boat called 'Trent': it's an eleven metre, purpose-built catamaran with Suzuki engines: it glides through the water. The owner takes us out and we're planning to leave around three o'clock. We get a cheaper rate because he'll have come back in with his main group of holiday-makers. We'll go out about a mile, anchor and use rods to catch the cod."

Damian asked when the trip was happening. immediately accepted and on being told that he was a guest, said that he'd bring the refreshments. This was to fire up Marie's interest and she said that she'd prepare a feast for them all.

Cathy decided to occupy Friday by visiting her former friends, calling in to see Louisa at the accounting practice, where she was also able to catch up with Rachel Smith, and then on to see Nettie and Edgar who she found in the lounge of their new home preparing for afternoon tea for which she was invited to join them.

The conversation was about their news, the regular bridge evenings, their holiday plans for the coming year, a small operation which Nettie needed, which was to be done privately, and their joy when Arthur and Faria came to see them. They brought out pictures of Genevieve and commented on what a wonderful mother Faria was and how proud they were at Arthur's dedication to his studies.

Cathy brought up the topic of Christmas and said that she hoped they'd be able to join her. Nettie was gushing in her thanks but said that they had already committed to travelling to Bristol to spend a few days with Edgar's elder daughter. Cathy suggested that they usually discussed these matters and was surprised by her mother's reaction as she said that Cathy must appreciate that she was now sharing her life with Edgar. Cathy reassured her that she understood and perhaps they could meet up at the New Year. She kissed her mother, waved at Edgar and drove home. She decided that she would apply herself during the evening to finishing off her paper on weight-loss and send it to Dr Martin Armstrong, except that she was simply not satisfied with the contents.

Her recommendations for improving weight-loss success at the surgery were weak and, in truth, no more than a rehash of several NHS projects which had little success. She was nervous about promoting the keto diet, if Dr Rubenstein's commercial aspirations were to be an outcome, and Damian's financial incentives concept, while innovative, had so many pitfalls she was reluctant to place too much emphasis on that section. It was a weak report and she was aware of the flaws in her conclusions. It was clear that she was going to have some spare time over the Christmas period and so she put it away in a drawer and promised herself that she'd bring it out, for a final time, on Boxing Day.

Dr Russell Haydon, Dr Joseph Rubenstein and Senior Nurse Anisha Khan were together on the executive floor sharing an end of week review together. The policy at the Alexandra Private Hospital was to try to empty beds as far as possible keeping costs down as a skeleton weekend staff was more than adequate to ensure those patients left with them were fully cared for: there were always two doctors on call, if required.

Dr Rubenstein was talking about his research on the keto diet and expressing a concern that he'd found his discussion with the new nurse less than helpful. He said that he wanted to discuss the effectiveness of ketosis and he found her defending the National Health Service.

"That's her background," explained Anisha. "She's a wonderful nurse and it'll take time for her to adapt to the world of private medicine."

"I get that," he responded, "but I sensed a pushing back if you like. It was as though I was being asked to defend our approach to patient care."

"I'll talk to her: she's in next Tuesday for half a day and then full-time after the Christmas break."

Dr Haydon stood up and reminded his colleagues that their taxis would be arriving in thirty minutes. He mentioned that he would be forever in Cathy's debt for donating her kidney to Angelica.

+ + +

CHAPTER NINETEEN

There was enough daylight at three o'clock on a bright, cloudless December day for the party boarding the 'Trent' to expect good visibility in the English Channel. The skipper Dan, who introduced his son Zach, was keen to leave the harbour and, after checking everyone's lifejackets, hurried John, Damian and the two others, aboard: Damian was carrying a hamper provided by the vivacious Marie who was soon waving them on their way.

Dan explained that they'd head out for about two miles off-shore into the Channel to where he suspected some submerged rocks might prove a fertile fishing ground. This proved to be a correct assessment and the two friends of John, who were obviously intent on making the trip productive, were soon attaching squid and lugworm to the hooks at the end of their lines before casting off in their hunt for cod. Almost immediately, there was a bite and the first of many fish was landed.

Time was passing and the light was fading so Damian opened up the hamper and distributed sandwiches, pies and beers to the others. He was relishing the open, if not chilly, air to be found out at sea and the limited conversation was fine with him: they'd no doubt talk afterwards as they'd be back into the harbour by six-thirty. This was a new life for him and John was proving to be a good companion.

It was Zach who first thought that he could hear

shouting on the port side and soon they were trying to see from the beam of Dan's torch what was out there. The answer became apparent as a small rowing boat came into view: it seemed to be holding up to three people one of whom was waving and shouting.

"It can't be immigrants this far west," said John.

The vessel was soon at their side and they co-operated in hauling the castaways aboard, one by one. They were rather similar in that they were perhaps eastern Europeans, none spoke English, and one was in a serious condition and was lying on the boards, groaning. Dan was on his radio speaking to the coastguard when the mayhem started. Two of the immigrants produced hideous weapons, one a serrated knife and the other a machete from under his shirt and lunged at Zach getting within six feet of his head. He was impeded by the arrival of a body between the skipper's son and the weapon which landed on Damian's shoulder. He screamed out in pain but tried to regain his stance only to face the second attacker who plunged his knife into Damian's upper thigh. One of the two fishermen had found an oar which he unleashed at the head of the knife carrier who was laid out cold. Zach was holding an arm of the machete wielder and John landed on him at a rush. He stayed in that position for the remainder of the time they were out to sea. Dan had now alerted the authorities to the attack and, before long, a helicopter appeared overhead and lit up the scene with its searchlights. The focus was now on Damian who was bleeding badly from his leg wound.

Dan advised coastal command that their best option was to power ahead for Portsmouth harbour rather than attempt to hoist Damian up to the helicopter. One of the fishermen was cradling Damian's shoulders and shaking his own head in bewilderment as he tried to come to terms with the assault which had come from nowhere. The skipper, who was powering his vessel at full speed, was speaking into his radio the whole time.

As they neared the harbour a lifeboat came out to meet them and the area was lit by pulsating blue lights. They docked and within minutes Damian was stretched off into a waiting ambulance and rushed by a police escort to the main hospital. The immigrants were secured by the police and taken away for a full medical assessment as part of the processing procedure: no other person on board the 'Trent' was injured.

Prompted by John, the police traced Marie and took her to the hospital. The incident was already being followed by the media and, an hour later, a Downing Street spokesperson was quoted as saying that the Home Secretary was dedicated to stopping illegal immigrants reaching our shores. Marie arrived in A & E and was immediately taken into a side ward and told that Damian was in the operating theatre. Half an hour later Professor Warnock arrived and said he had talked his way in: he sat still and held Marie's hand. Two hours later a consultant came in with another doctor who asked Professor Warnock to give them some space. They then faced their patient's partner.

Marie listened as they explained that the operation had been as successful as they could hope for but the news was concerning. The knife wound in the thigh was the easier damage to repair although the loss of blood was worrying. The real challenge was the machete blow into the shoulder which had caused massive trauma, nerve damage and internal bleeding. They asked Marie if she would like to see him.

Although trained in nursing and dental hygiene, Marie discovered that seeing your own in an Intensive Care Unit was something altogether different. He was lying there with the monitor bleeping away, several tubes providing medical inputs and a hoist holding up his leg. Marie sat down, found his hand, and held on. A nurse came in and explained that it was a change of shift and she'd be here for the night. She looked at Damian.

"Is this the Channel hero," she said. "He saved their lives."

Cathy was to recriminate with herself for the rest of her afternoon shift at the Alexandra Private Hospital after arriving fifteen minutes late following a lorry and car colliding in the road leading to the hospital. Senior Nurse Anisha Khan left her in no doubt as to her annoyance and an offer to stay on for an extra hour fell on stony ground. She was told to make her way to the orthopaedic ward where she began by serving afternoon tea to the eight ladies who were in the process of having parts of their bodies replaced: there were two recovering from hip replacement operations, one receiving a new elbow, another a replacement knee and Mrs Swinton from Marlborough who, on the advice of her doctor, was having her ankles cleaned out.

Cathy mentioned to her that in all her years in general practice she had never come across such a procedure only to be told that Mrs Swinton always went to a private doctor and had mentioned to him that occasionally her feet felt tired and a little sweaty and his advice was that debris can build up in the ankle joints as a result of wear and tear and it's a straight forward process for the surgeon to open the base of the lower leg and essentially hoover it out. Mrs Swinton also expressed her annoyance that the cucumber sandwiches were made with day-old bread. Cathy managed to look into her file and discovered that the operation was costing just under five thousand pounds and Mrs Swinton did not seem to need health insurance cover.

As the afternoon progressed another issue arose which resulted from Cathy challenging a patient, a fifty-two-year-old woman who was nearing discharge after having her shoulder manipulated, who was insisting that she be given pain killers. The nurse explained that this prescription needed careful administration as too many analgesics could, in time, damage the lining of the stomach. The patient flared and insisted that a more senior member of staff was called which led to the arrival of a young doctor who immediately dispensed the required pills. As they walked away from the bed Cathy politely suggested that she was surprised at the ease with which the pain killers were dispensed. The doctor laughed and said that "in this hospital the patient gets whatever they want."

Towards the end of her allotted shift Cathy received a message saying that Senior Nurse Khan would like to see her. They met and went into a private office where concern was expressed about her attitude to several of the patients. Cathy managed to inflame the situation by suggesting that several of the patients would benefit from seeing what the real world was like and perhaps they'd like to wait in a queue in A & E for four hours while waiting for a broken arm to be put in plaster.

Anisha said that perhaps they should talk matters over with Dr Haydon, who was in the operating theatre, and so she'd make an appointment for her to see him when she next came in.

Cathy drove her car home, changed and ended up in the kitchen where she poured herself a vodka and tonic. She was angry with herself because she understood the basis of private medicine and its role in the modern health care community and if someone wants to have their ankles surgically cleaned out, fair enough, it was their money that they were spending. She refilled her glass and read a message on her phone from Scarlett thanking her for the invite to Christmas Day lunch but she and Joshua were penniless and were working in a hotel over the whole of the festive period to earn some cash.

Cathy stood up from the kitchen chair, stumbled and knocked over her glass. She went into the lounge, turned on the news channel and watched a report from Portsmouth about a clash between fishermen and an immigrant boat leading to an incident where a local man was said to have saved the life of the son of the skipper. She gasped as pictures were shown of an ambulance arriving at the hospital with a critically wounded man who they named.

Damian's heroics in the English Channel did not remain national headline news for long due to the decision taken by the General Secretary of the Party and Chairman of the State Affairs Commission, Kim Jong-un, to fire an Inter-Continental Ballistic Missile which landed on the Mariana Islands and more specifically, on the Pacific Island of Guam which was an American protectorate. The United States of

America was, at long last, reunited as Republicans and Democrats came together to protest at the violation of their territory inflicted by the North Koreans and threaten retaliation which caused panic in the European Union.

Damian remained unconscious in intensive care with Marie sitting by his side. She had been given a room with her own bed but nothing was going to move her, apart from the regular checks by members of the ICU team. She did not ask any questions because she knew that he was receiving the best care the medical world could provide and she was not interested in the local news frenzy which was being fuelled by endless interviews with Dan, the skipper of 'Trent' and his description of the moment that Damian dived between his son Zach and the machete wielding attacker.

"Right, Damian," said Marie, "this morning I'm going to tell you about the work of the dental hygienist and the vital role we play in ensuring the health of our patients. It is a demanding responsibility because one experiences such close contact with the individual in the chair but we are taught to be disinterested so that we concentrate on the work we undertake."

She realised that it was time for him to be assessed and went outside to gasp in some fresh air. Thirty minutes later the consultant approached her and said that there was no change in his condition and that it was a matter of waiting. When she asked what they were waiting for, the consultant looked at her and said, "God."

She returned to her place by his bed and resumed her conversation after kissing his forehead.

"As I was saying, Damian," she continued, "we play a vital role in the dental care of our patients but it's important that we always keep our distance." She paused and looked at his closed eyes. "Except in your case, Damian Hannon, in which case the hygienist is permitted to fall hopelessly in love with the patient."

Despite her best efforts the tears began to fall and, for the first time, she began to wonder if she was strong enough to survive this ordeal.

"For fuck's sake, Damian, open your bloody eyes, please."

Marie began to lose her sense of time and, although there were medical staff around her, she lapsed into a meditational state of mind as she repeated her mantra of pointless chatter directed to her unconscious partner. She occasionally drank from her bottle of water and ate some grapes from the bedside bowl of fruit. She used a flannel to wipe his forehead and almost continuously held his hand learning to guard against a sudden muscle spasm in his arm making her think he was regaining consciousness.

The following day, after she had spent some restless hours in her room, she confronted the doctors and demanded to know what they were doing to help Damian. The ICU consultant came to see her in the afternoon and said they were continually monitoring his condition but that there was no change. He suggested she went into the gardens for some fresh air but that lasted ten minutes before she rushed back to his bedside and took hold of his hand.

The rest of the day passed without further incident and at around nine o'clock in the evening one of the nurses guided her to her room and put her to bed. She lapsed into a deep sleep which was punctuated by a dream wherein she was on a boat with her arm being pulled as someone wanted to tip her into the water.

She opened her eyes to see a nurse rubbing her arm and a doctor who had a look on his face which told her all she needed to know. She dressed and followed them into the room where they stood back as she approached the bed. His eyes were open. Marie sensed a moment of sheer exhilaration as she realised that she had him back.

"You forgot to pack the mustard," he said.

"What mustard!" she exclaimed.

"No-one puts pork pies in a hamper without including the mustard," he said.

"I remembered the pickle," she smiled.

The medics left the room: Damian and Marie were united and ready for their future together despite the long road to a full recovery.

Cathy achieved something on Christmas Day which was a little unusual: she wrote a letter of resignation to Dr Russell Haydon at the Alexandra Private Hospital. She had started the day alone by making an effort to be positive. She had telephoned the hospital in Portsmouth and, after about ten minutes of medical red tape, managed to convince them that she was Mrs Catherine Hannon and she wanted to know about her husband and then thanked them for giving her the latest, more positive, up-date. She telephoned her mother who was on answerphone, then Arthur, who was rather abrupt, saying he was feeding Genevieve because Faria was so tired, before he rang off and then she tried Scarlett who was at the hotel and said she could not talk.

Cathy had decided to go to her old church because she always enjoyed the Christmas Day service but half way there, she turned back home because she realised that it was a retrograde step and she must concentrate on the future. She was sitting on her favourite stool in the kitchen and, because it was a national holiday, allowed herself a pre-lunch vodka and tonic. As the bottle was nearly empty, she fetched another from the back of her car.

She pulled her laptop towards her and re-read the draft of her letter. This was about her fifth attempt because she did not want to say that what was on her mind was that she thought they were all greedy bastards who were milking the growing numbers of rich people by providing medical services which, in many cases, were an absolute waste of urgently needed resources. In her second draft she referred to the statistic that it costs the Government about seven years and six hundred thousand pounds to train a doctor and the outcome was that medics such as Doctors Haydon and Rubenstein go off and milk the system in order to make personal fortunes.

Cathy poured herself another drink and printed off the final copy of her letter which simply asked Dr Haydon to forgive her but she felt she was not suited to the world of private medicine and thanked him for giving her the opportunity and she hoped that Angelina would continue to enjoy good health. She went outside and walked, perhaps stumbled, to the post box and posted her letter. She experienced a moment of exultation as she returned home and poured herself the last drink of the day: that she promised herself. She raised her glass and giggled. She proposed a toast to Dr Joseph Rubenstein and hoped that he choked himself on the keto diet.

Half an hour later Cathy was fast asleep on the sofa.

+ + +

CHAPTER TWENTY

Marie now had an established routine and entered his hospital room carrying a parcel. Damian was slumbering and seemed much more organised being in a side room off a men's ward. His leg was still held in traction, there was a tube attached to his shoulder, there were get-well cards everywhere together with flowers, bottles of wine and several magazines. One well-wisher had sent him a huge, personalised, rainbow teddy bear with 'hero' embroidered on its jumper. He had completed an interview with the local press and his picture appeared everywhere as his bravery captured the popular imagination. The story gained an added dimension in that the boat carrying the immigrants was towed back into harbour by the lifeboat and its ownership was traced back to a group of haulage contractors based in Essex.

She kissed him and held his hand tightly as she wiped his face with a flannel which she had brought in with her and tidied his sheets while he smiled at her.

"Why did you do it?" she asked while continuing to straighten-up the room.

"Do what?" he asked.

"Throw yourself in front of the crazed machete wielder?"

"I didn't," he said. "It wasn't me: it was an apparition pretending to be me. If I'd had a moment to think about it, I'd have dived overboard and swum away: did you see his photograph? He was gruesome."

"Perhaps he was scared because when you read about what these people are fleeing from you can understand why they are desperate to avoid capture." She smiled. "I've bought you a present," she said. "It's about a woman."

"Are there any pictures?" he laughed.

"There are," she triumphed as she handed him a copy of Ellen MacArthur's autobiography 'Full Circle'. "The cover notes make interesting reading," she added. He said "thanks" and then asked her to come and sit with him. She sensed that Damian was wanting to express himself.

"When I was in the ambulance going to the hospital, I was semi-conscious and listening to the paramedics assessing my condition and they did not rate my chances too highly. It's not something that happens to you all too often in your general life. We all know that we're going to die but, at our stage in life, it's not something that you believe will happen for a long time. This was different because I thought that I was not going to make it."

"You nearly didn't," said Marie.

"I know that but the point I'm making is that the shock of knowing your time is up makes you concentrate on the priorities. I'm on lots of drugs and I'm probably gabling away but I know what I want to say to you."

They stopped their conversation to allow her to wipe some spittle away from his mouth and to give him a drink of water.

"The one thing that I could see was you, standing on the marina and looking like the most beautiful woman in the world, which you are, Marie, and I panicked because I was scared that I would never hold you again. It frightened me like I have never been scared before."

He lay back, already tired, but he continued to stare at her.

"I've always thought that everything in life has a purpose," she said. "I don't believe in predestination because my life would be pointless otherwise: I must have free choice. Do you recall that I told you my long-term partner hit me, actually rather a lot, but what I didn't explain was that he developed some strange habits when we were in the bedroom? Initially I went along with his fetishes but it became personally unpleasant and sometimes hurt so I tried to discuss matters with him but he blanked me. Then I said "no" which resulted in him lashing out and so I threw him out of the house but the strange thing was he went without a whimper." She stood up and walked round the room.

"I decided that I'd take a year off from all relationships. As you know I'm comfortable with my own company and my interests and then you came into my life. Even now I can't explain what I did, but when I was leaning over you something happened: the rest is history. But the point I'm trying to make is if I'd not had that showdown with my previous partner, I'm not sure I'd have been so certain about approaching you."

Damian lay back and reflected on the weeks of lying and indecision as he battled with the conundrum he had faced. He pulled himself up to be nearer to her wincing as he moved his injured leg.

"You're lucky in one way, Marie, because from the start you were secure about what you wanted. I also knew pretty early on but each time I managed to be certain an event would happen and I'd be derailed."

"But that helped me, Damian, because when you did finally commit, I was left in no doubt about the certainty of our future. When I was sitting with you in the ICU, I pleaded for you to open your eyes because it was something that I desperately wanted to happen: I had to have you back with me."

For the time being their conversation ended at that moment in time as each pondered the period of reflection that they had just shared. Marie held his hand and squeezed hard.

There were weeks ahead of recuperation and painful physiotherapy to enable him to walk again but there were to be many years of being together, perhaps in Portsmouth, maybe elsewhere: it did not really matter although, one day, they would need to plan the schooling for their two children.

Cathy decided to double the dose of aspirin as she attempted to clear her headache. Her Boxing Day had started with an attempted run around Walton Lake which proved an error in judgement as she felt her muscles tighten and she completed her self-imposed course by limping home and diving into a hot shower which had marginal benefit. She looked at the clock and the bottle of vodka and wondered whether eleven o'clock was too early to resort to the hair of the dog. She knew that she was fighting self-pity and, once more, went over the decision to resign her job. She accepted that her mother and Scarlett were elsewhere and she hoped to restore her relationship with Arthur and Faria because she wanted to see Genevieve.

She reasoned that she was still in her prime and she'd find a way of creating a future for herself but, even as she thought about it, she sensed her morale sinking and she began to become swamped with self-pity: her life was in turmoil.

She moved her hand towards the bottle of vodka and stared at the mobile phone which she knew had been ringing but she was not available to anyone today. She picked it up and saw that a text message had arrived:

Please phone me: Dr Martin Armstrong.

She pushed the bottle away and made the call.

"Cathy, I'm so appreciative that you've phoned me," he said. "I do hope that I'm not disturbing your Boxing Day?"

"No, Martin," she replied. "I'm always available to you. If it's about my weight-loss paper?"

"Let me get right to the point of this call," he said. "I'm hearing that the job at the Alexandra Hospital isn't, perhaps, shaping up as you hoped."

"How do you know that?" she asked.

"I know that because one of my patients was in the orthopaedic ward and overhead your discussion with a certain lady. She knew you from sometime back."

"If you want to know, Martin, I've resigned," said Cathy. "Private medicine is not for me."

"Nor me, Cathy. What great news!"

"For whom?" she asked.

"There has been much change at the surgery. The demands on us have broadened out of all perspective and I need more staff."

"Are you asking me to come back as a nurse?"

"No, I'm not."

Cathy sank back down in the chair.

"I want you to come back as head of our nursing division. We've landed a special NHS grant and we're going to recruit two more nurses making four in total.

I and my colleagues want you to come back and head the unit."

"When?"

"Tomorrow morning at eight o'clock. Don't be late," he laughed.

"There's a condition," she said.

"Ok. What?"

"We forget the weight-loss paper."

"It'll never be mentioned again," he said. "Do I hear a "yes"?"

"Yes, you do."

"Best Christmas present I've ever had," he said. "Bye Cathy, and thanks."

She put the phone down and thought carefully about the call from Dr Armstrong. She picked up the bottle of vodka and poured it down the sink. She went upstairs and changed into an old tracksuit. She went out to her car and drove to a local carwash where she had it valeted inside and out returning home and reversing it into the drive so that it faced outwards for a fast start in the morning. She went back inside and cleaned her house from top to bottom managing two loads of washing at the same time. She threw herself into the shower and came out pristine clean. She went to her wardrobe and took out her nurse's blue Smart Scrub Tunic which the surgery had given her as a leaving present. She put it on trying to look as professional as she could. She stood in front of the mirror and imagined herself back in an environment where she belonged.

"Now ladies," she said, "let's get down to losing some weight, shall we?!"

She changed and went downstairs before going back to her study and taking out a package from one of the storage boxes. She went back to the lounge and placed on the mantlepiece a photograph of Damian, Scarlett, Arthur and herself on their last holiday together.

Cathy Hannon had a past and now she had a future.

+ + +

NEW YEAR'S DAY

"There's so much that we can achieve together"

Marie Magellan Cameron

THE END

ABOUT THE AUTHOR

Tony Drury is a Fellow of the Chartered Institute of Bankers. He built a London-based corporate finance

house and has travelled globally, chairing companies in Hong Kong, China, Japan and in the UK.

He is one of the six founders of Earn Your Health Community Interest Company which is dedicated to helping those people who are overweight and obese (www.earnyourhealth.org).

He has written six DCI Sarah Rudd City thrillers drawing on his career as a London financier to expose the underworld of dark practices and shadowy characters. He has written five titles in the *Novella Nostalgia* series.

He lives in Bedford with his wife, Judy, and values his visits to Watford to be with grandson Henry.

Email: tonydrury39@btinternet.com
Website: www.tonydrury.com
Twitter: @mrtonydrury
LinkedIn: uk.linkedin.com/tonydrury